Rebecca Harding Davis

Doctor Warrick's Daughters

Rebecca Harding Davis

Doctor Warrick's Daughters

ISBN/EAN: 9783743367319

Manufactured in Europe, USA, Canada, Australia, Japa

Cover: Foto ©Andreas Hilbeck / pixelio.de

Manufactured and distributed by brebook publishing software (www.brebook.com)

Rebecca Harding Davis

Doctor Warrick's Daughters

DOCTOR WARRICK'S DAUGHTERS

A Novel

BY

REBECCA HARDING DAVIS

ILLUSTRATED

NEW YORK
HARPER & BROTHERS PUBLISHERS
1896

TO

C. B. D.

ILLUSTRATIONS

DOCTOR WARRICK'S DAUGHTERS

CHAPTER I

Doctor Samuel Warrick was a surgeon in a Federal regiment from the beginning to the end of the Civil War. His wife, in the meantime, lived with her children in the old Warrick homestead near Luxborough in eastern Pennsylvania.

Even as early as '65, Luxborough was called a city by the contractors who had recently pushed in and built mills. They elected themselves mayors and councilmen : their dwellings rose around the new Park near the Works with Greek porticos in front and Ottoman minarets at the back, and within, much plenishing of gilt and plush and vases of alabaster.

The old settlers, who lived in crooked, shady lanes on the hill, ignored these people and their city. They always talked of "our little burgh" with proud humility : as the great Louis was known to his people only as " Monsieur," because there could be but one gentleman in France. Of course they knew that there were other towns in the country, but they thought of them vaguely, as one does of affairs in the Antarctic circle. Luxborough was the final result of the creation. For it Columbus had sailed, and Washington fought, and the Bible been written. They delighted to tell each other that "with our resources and water power we could easily have surpassed Philadelphia at any time. But our people, sir, have had higher pursuits than trade." A small college gave a scholastic flavor to the pursuits of some citizens; others were army and navy officers on half pay; still others derived their support from the meagre dividends of the venerable Luxborough Bank. But a meagre income did not interfere with the self-respect of any Luxboroughan. He wrapped his poverty about him as a royal garment and smiled down patronage on the world.

Now, these people all knew that their forefathers had been Swedish peasants who came over on the *Key of Calmar :* or mechanics and cotters brought to his principality by Penn. But had they not founded Luxborough? That was a patent of nobility in the minds of their descendants, who clung fondly to their old oak chests and chain clocks.

The young people, it is true, had talked much, of late, of certain Scotch lords and English baronets, whom, without regard to Burke and Debrett, they declared to be their ancestors and whose crests they uneasily adopted.

Luxborough asserted itself, however, most strenuously in the Monthly Whist Club (established A. D. 1767). The mill-owners beat in vain at its closed doors. They jeered at the sandwiches and tea which were its fixed features, but their hearts were sore with envy. These homely simplicities showed a superb contempt for the vulgar splendor of their balls and costly suppers. Once a year minuets were danced at the club, the girls wearing their grandmothers' brocade gowns. The patronesses "requested the honour of your presence" on the backs of playing cards, as the club had done when Dolly Madison or Nelly Custis were its guests. These things furnished the new-comers with endless gibes. But the old Luxboroughans smiled and vouchsafed no answer. They were sure that their town, with its patrician caste, was as unique in the world as a Rome or a Damascus.

For the rest, their minds were chiefly concerned with their food and the squabbles of the High and Low churches. They were all good housekeepers and churchgoers, and, let the world rage as it would, the excellence of their hams and jellies and missionaries were firm foundations on which they stood impregnable. So deep was their complacency that if a Luxboroughan went out into the world and found success, his old neighbors scowled askance at him. Why should he go out into the world? Could he not have the best of hams and the Monthly Club at home? They would not clap their hands for him.

Young Logue was the foremost American sculptor in Rome for years, and George Parr, the philologist, was recognized by the greatest of German scholars. He was for months the honored guest of Queen Sophie in the Huis ten Bosch.

But when the two men came home Luxborough passed them with an icy nod.· No cards were sent them for the club. "They have good blood," said Mrs. Hayes, who was patroness that year. "But it is safer to keep out all artistic riffraff." She felt that they should be taught that Luxborough was its own world. Roman studios and foreign courts were but as the rim to its cup.

Naturally, men of ability who were born in the town and could not push out into the world did not find these things as ludicrous as they seemed to Doctor Parr or John Logue. They complained that they were stifled: sunk in a slough, not of despond, but of self-satisfied mediocrity.

Doctor Warrick was one of these men. The war gave him his first chance to draw a full breath of life. His wife, on the contrary, was calm and self-contained as any Luxboroughan, although she came from another city. Certain idiosyncrasies belong to all Pennsylvanian towns as though they were first cousins.

Mrs. Warrick lived a couple of miles outside of the borough. She ignored the town as the town did the rest of the earth. Her children, her garden, the cook, the turkeys—here was the world. Even the war threw but a far-off shadow through the windows of her cheerful lighted home.

She had her anxieties, however. She was forced to economize closely, as her husband was apt to lend part of every quarter's salary to some needy friend in camp. Sometimes, what with tobacco to the prisoners and suppers to the staff, he would have none left to send home.

"Your papa"—she would say, with kindling eyes, when this happened—"your papa is the most generous of men ! He is giving his life to his country, and he would give his last dollar to any body who needs it. Well, thank God, the dear soul has it to give !" Then she would go to work to nip ten cents here and there out of meat and butter bills to make up the deficit.

When the news of Lee's surrender came the neighboring women rejoiced loyally together in their sanitary committees, but she fell to cleaning house to be ready for the doctor.

Her nephew, Brooke Calhoun, a noisy boy who had rushed in from the country when the news came, hauled down the flags from the garret early in the morning. "I'll put one out of each window," he shouted. Anne, a lean child of ten, clattered down the stairs after him, loaded with nails and hammer. Mrs. Warrick came in from her crocus-beds with muddy fingers.

"No, I think not, Brooke, dear," she said gently, "not flags; it is peace, you know. Your uncle has been through such horrors in these years—knee-deep, you might say, in blood and mud—that I thought the house ought to be very quiet and clean for him. Just home. No flags— evergreen now, twisted around the pillars and over the door ? What do you think ?"

"All right," Brooke said. But he and Anne scowled as they nailed up the hemlock. Their souls were clothed upon with victory and blood to-day. Brooke banged the nails viciously. The whole North was resplendent in red, white, and blue ; why must he carry out the idea of a ridiculous woman ? As for Anne, she hid one of the flags. She intended presently to go to a window in the barn which opened on the road, and, wrapping it around her, pose there as Liberty, for passers-by to see. Sometimes she covered herself with a piece of old mosquito netting and stood there, hoping that people would take her for a bride. Mrs. Warrick, who kept her little girls apart from the villagers as if they were nuns, never dreamed of these tricks of the child.

Mildred Warrick, a girl of fourteen, stood silently watching her sister and Brooke, slowly turning her innocent blue eyes from one to the other. They never asked for her opinion in their disputes. Her mouth was as dumb as her eyes. Nobody had ever known the soft, chubby creature to have an opinion since she was born.

When they were seated at breakfast Mrs. Warrick looked around her with a beaming face. Her regency was nearly over. Surely Samuel would think she had not managed badly ?

Five years ago, at parting, the doctor had made over the property to her. "You'll make ducks and drakes of it, of course, being a woman," he said, with a shrug. "But what else can I do ? "

When they were married the house had been surrounded for several miles by the Warrick estate. But the doctor, from time to time, to pull himself out of debt, had sold farm after farm, until only the old apple orchard was left on one side, and on the other the garden where his wife worked all day among her pease and beans.

"If my wife breathes on a seed it turns into a rose," he used to say fondly, which pleased her so much that she did not notice that he never helped her to weed the rose-bed.

In front of the house a grassy field sloped to the road, and upon it three or four huge, ancient oaks threw an always grave and solemn shadow.

The homestead, like most Colonial houses in Eastern Pennsylvania, was built of black-lined English brick in a large, unmeaning square. The doctor liked to tell of the entertainments which long dead Warricks had given here to Washington, or to wandering Bourbon princes, and there was still a lingering flavor of gracious hospitality in the noble proportions of the lofty apartments and the vast fireplaces, with their unwieldy brass dogs glittering in the flame. Time had softened the florid splendors of the frescoed nymphs on the ceiling and yellowed the marble Caryatides of the mantel-pieces : even the gorgeous roses on the carpets had faded into soft, dull hues on which the sunshine fell pleasantly. The great mahogany chairs on which the children sat at the table shone in it, black with age.

"Your papa will find no change in the house when he comes," Mrs. Warrick said complacently, "and I have not sold an inch of ground, either."

"That is a pity," said Brooke. "If you had

sold Matthew Plunkett the orchard, and he had built his big villa there, it would have sent up the value of this property five hundred per cent."

"Perhaps so," said his aunt indifferently. "We have enough of money. I did not care to have the Plunketts for neighbors, or any of the new rich clique."

"Here comes Dave Plunkett now," said Anne. "He writes poetry," she whispered to Brooke. "He reads his tragedies to mamma while she plants her seeds! He waddles after her through the paths like a tame dog."

"I will not bring my tragedy, when I write it, to Aunt Sarah," said Brooks gravely, looking at the jolly face and tawdry plaid gown of the stout old lady.

An enormously fat lad, gaudily dressed, came into the room, and, after greeting them with a bob of the head, dropped into a seat and fell to work voraciously at the scrapple and hot toast. He paused long enough to mumble:

"When d'ye expect the doctor, Mrs. Warrick?"

"Next week. We are almost ready. The grates must be polished and the pictures hung."

"Why did not you keep the prints on the walls for your own comfort all these years, Aunt Sarah?" said Brooke.

"The frames would have tarnished, and besides I take no interest in pictures," she said, calmly sipping her coffee.

"And yet they count for so much to the doctor! He must have grown thin, kept away from such things so long!" the boy said.

"George ! how he will scamper around to theatres and old book-shops when he comes ! And how the money will fly ! "

" I'll go with him ! " piped Anne shrilly.

Mrs. Warrick, her cup in her hand, turned her broad red face from one to the other with a startled stare. In the last five years she had learned to look upon her husband only as a hero, facing death for a great cause.

But—. Why, of course he would run about to theatres and book-shops, irritable, voluble; in a paroxysm of rapture one minute over a first edition, and a paroxysm of misery the next over a limp collar. And she—always outside of his paroxysms ! The old days flashed up distinctly before her. His finest engraving was no more to her than black scratches on paper. Clothes were to her only a troublesome covering for the body. He had poetic ideas about color and drapery which she never could understand. How tired she used to be trying to understand, to keep up. But Samuel never saw it. He would keep her for an hour descanting on the lines of a Morghen when she was frantic to go and devil the crabs for supper.

Milly watched her anxiously. She caught her hand under the table. " Is papa like that? " she whispered. " Would he waste your little bit of money on such trash ? "

" Mildred ! " she shook off her hand. " You don't know your father. He is a man who—why —he has great ideas, great purposes! He stands head and shoulders above other men, like Cato or Nelson, or—or—Lafayette. He has been risking his life for years, and you would begrudge him a little miserable money? He lives away above us with his books and his pictures. You'll see."

"Why! I didn't mean any thing! I am sorry!" stammered Brooke, amazed at this outbreak. He wanted to laugh. Love between people of his own age was a divine thing, but the devotion of this old woman with a mole on her nose to the fussy little surgeon was like a farce on the stage.

David Plunkett, who had been watching Mrs. Warrick, broke in at this crisis:

"Calhoun, did you know I thought of going to Princeton? Father says I can, if I like."

"Well, do you like?" said Brooke gruffly, with an uneasy glance at his aunt's dim eyes.

"Better'n any thing. It seems as if I ought to have the chance, too. There's Sims the butcher's sendin' his son to Yale, an' Warren—you know Jo Warren—he's workin' his way through Harvard. If I—think of me graduatin' first honorman in Princeton!" He stretched out his huge arms with a deep breath.

Brooke looked at him a moment and then said respectfully, "It will take a lot of work, Pud."

"I don't mind work. I've got a fine brain. If I do it at all, I'll go in for bein' a professor. Why, I'd rather be a teacher sittin' up there with a lot of men before me, knowin' things that they don't know, than be President!"

"Why don't you go to college then?" said

Brooke impatiently. "Your father's reckoned an eight-million man—he can afford it. What hinders you?"

David munched a great mouthful deliberately before he spoke. "Eight million? P'r'aps. But you see, if I'm to be an oil man like pap, I've to begin now. College graduates don't count in business. You've got to be trained young."

"It does not need much training to measure tanks of oil and take pay."

"So! that's your idea of the oil business, is it?" said David contemptuously. "My father began without a dollar, sir. But he knows oil and gas. He's got the sharpest eye for indications of any man in the State. That's what brought him the eight millions. If I mean to carry on the business, I've got to go in training now. I must give up college."

Brooke laughed. "Well, go in training, then! You won't have money enough!"

David looked at him steadily, a sharp cunning creeping into his flabby white face. "Millions breed billions, is the old saying. But you've got to nurse 'em well. You can't have too much money nowadays"—his catlike eyes twinkling.

"I am ashamed of you, David!" said Mrs. Warrick. "You are going to sell your birthright for pottage that you don't need!"

"Oh! Nobody but you ever thought I had a birthright, Mrs. Warrick." David rose and went to her side, a queer tremor on his broad face. "I brought sumthin' for you to read to-day, but I guess you're too busy!"

"A poem!" she said, smiling kindly. "Come this evening, my boy. I am going to town now."

"Well, then, I'll go. 'Mornin!" he muttered, with a general nod.

"'By, Pud," said Brooke.

"Good-morning, Mr. Plunkett," lisped Milly respectfully as he passed her. He stopped short, his face red with delight, and held out his hand. She took it reluctantly, and as the unwieldy body lumbered out rubbed her fingers with a shudder.

"Why were you civil to him then?" cried Anne. "He thinks the world is made up of Dave Plunkett!"

Mrs. Warrick looked after Dave with alarm. What would the doctor say when he found this rough lad an *habitué* of the house?

Her soul was full of alarms. It was not a hero who was coming; it was—Samuel. How Milly's lisp would worry him! Anne's clumsiness would drive him mad. Heavens! why must the child wave her arms and legs about like that!

As she sat silent behind the coffee urn the world suddenly grew askew around her. It must be set straight in a day for Samuel.

If she were only one of these superior women coming to the front now, who organized sanitary commissions or lectured on the war! But Sarah was only clever in gardening. She was a good-humored creature. The knowledge of her inferiority never had hurt her as it did to-day. If she had even kept her pretty white-and-pink skin!

She glanced at the mirror. Samuel used to think so much of that !

Then a fiery passion rose in her. He ought not to ask whether her skin was white or black! If she were an idiot, he shouldn't care! She had loved him so. These things were trifles—trifles!

Sarah's thoughts as usual soon dropped to the basis of hard common-sense. She was not to blame if she had been born without the wit and taste which her husband and children had. She had at least made them live up to their own high standard.

"Why do you shriek so, Anne?" she said now, irritably; "other girls do it, but you cannot. How often must I tell you? You are a Warrick. A Warrick cannot be loud or pushing any more than she can be dishonest or cowardly. Your father will expect to find you fit to bear your name."

Brooke, who was reading the newspaper, threw it down. "They are going to disband the troops! It is to be peace, sure enough!" he cried. "I thought there always would be fighting here and there, and in a year I could go in. I've had hard luck, to be only a boy while this scrimmage was going on. Now, I've no chance."

"Oh," said Mrs. Warrick eagerly, "we may have a war with England soon, and then you can go in. A man always has the chance to do credit to his name."

"Why, I am not a Warrick, cousin Sarah. Nor you. We are Dacres."

"Yes, and the Dacres always stood by their

creed till death. There was a Dacre burned at Smithfield, and my grandfather was whipped by the Puritans in Massachusetts. On his grave-stone it says, 'He was the son of generations of fearless confessors.' You are descended from him, Brooke," said Mrs. Warrick, with kindling eyes.

Brooke laughed. "Oh, I've no doubt the Puri-tan creed was as nearly right as his own. He ought to have met them half-way comfortably, and so dodged the whipping. We've outgrown that sort of thing! You are a churchwoman, but you don't want to burn Father Riley, nor the Plunketts, who are Methodists."

"I'd as lief go to the stake myself as to Mass or to the Methodist revivals," she said doggedly.

Brooke laughed, and took Anne to feed the cows. Her mother looked after her anxiously. Would Samuel be satisfied with the girls? She knew nothing of modern training. One or two ideas had seemed to her of authority: the Church and the family honor. She had helped herself in her weeding and darning by thinking of Jane Dacre tied to the stake. But was this sort of thing enough for the girls?

"Elegance of deportment," "grace of atti-tude"—some of the doctor's favorite phrases came back to nag her honest soul.

Milly was patting her hand fondly. "Mamma, Anne does not understand," she said; "she would not be burned sooner than be a Methodist, but I would."

"Oh, yes; certainly, dear," her mother said impatiently.

If Anne had said that it would mean something. But Milly's mind was so easily filled and
emptied! When Mrs. Warrick had an opinion,
she knew as certainly that Milly would echo it /
as that a cup of water would reflect a passing '
color.

"She will be what I am while I am with her,"
she thought. " Well, I shall probably always be
with her. Even when the girls are married, I
shall look after them a bit."

She made haste now to catch the train into
town. It was a threatening day. Heavy clouds
drifted through the thin April sunshine. Brooke
walked with her to the little station. " I have
an appointment with the oculist," she explained;
"my eyes have suddenly failed. I must have
glasses before Samuel comes. Brooke, what do
you think of this gown? It is my best, but the
figures are so bold. It was cheap, but I wish I
had bought a better one—and the red ginghams
the girls wear? He has such exquisite taste."

"Don't bother! What are gowns?" the boy
growled. He could not put it into words, but if
Doctor Warrick could not see how unlike to all
other girls these were in their solitary life with
their mother; with their queer unworldly notions
about their Warrick blood and souls inherited
from martyrs? If he made it a question of
gowns? He kicked a stone viciously which lay
in his way.

"What day does he come?" he asked.

"He leaves it for me to decide. He can run
up on furlough, returning when his regiment is

mustered out, or wait and come then to stay. Of course I shall write for him to come at once, if only for a day——"

She did not finish the sentence. Brooke glanced at her face, and turned quickly away.

"Here is your train," he said gently.

Sarah Warrick is of no interest in this history. The chapter which concerns her must be brief.

She waited an hour in the oculist's outer office, her mind busy with calculations of the cost of a plainer gown and the time she would need to make it. At last her turn came, and she entered the operating-room.

Doctor Swan was an old man, whom she had known since her childhood. He was standing when she came in, and greeted her gravely. She fancied that he looked anxious. He was a sympathetic man, in spite of his dry manner. Some patient, perhaps, whose case he found incurable.

"How much longer will the examination last?" she asked. "I have been looking at these tedious letters and wheels for five days. Can you not tell me what ails my eyes to-day?"

"Yes, I think I can," he said.

At another time she might have been startled by his unsmiling face, but just then she thought of a nainsook wrapper, soft and creamy white—Samuel would delight in that, unless—was she too old to wear white?

Doctor Swan meanwhile led her into a dark closet and turned a strong light into her eyes. "I must trouble you with this once more. I must be sure that I am right," he said. As she moved her eyes up and down at his bidding, she hesitated about embroidery for the gown. It would be costly, but Samuel liked lace so much——

"Now to the left. That will do."

He drew back, wiping the little mirror that he held.

"Have you finished already?"

"Yes, I have finished."

"I am very glad. I am so busy at home. And the glasses?" she asked, buttoning her coat.

The old man still rubbed the mirror with a bit of chamois-skin, looking down at her steadily, standing between her and the door.

"You never will require glasses. I wish to say—Sarah, there is something that I must tell you."

"Yes." She waited, attentive, smiling.

"There is a peculiar fact about the eye.. You may have heard of it. There is a gray curtain—I may call it that—at the back of the eye, and on it, when I turn a strong light—— Sit down, Sarah. You do not seem strong to-day."

"I am not as young as when we went to school on the hill together," she said, laughing. "I do feel my age a little this year. You were saying?"

Why did he prose so? She would have time to buy the nainsook, if she could go at once.

"It is like a gray canvas. On it, as I said"—he turned his eyes away from her, but went on hurriedly—"on it an oculist can see the marks made by certain incurable diseases before any other part of the body betrays their presence. It is the writing on the wall. Death——"

She had taken the seat he gave her. She rose now mechanically, and stood looking into his eyes. He stopped speaking, but it seemed to her, after a moment, that he had been talking a long time and had said much.

She said at last: "What did you see? What is the disease?"

He answered her, briefly.

Turning his back on her, he began to arrange some empty vials on a shelf. Her eyes followed him. How clean his bottles were—quite shining! She must go now. The nainsook—the train——

Her jaws moved beyond her control.

Death!

"Are you going, Sarah?" He walked with her to the door. "Will you have a little wine? Water?"

"No, thank you." She had her hand on the knob of the door. She hesitated a moment and then turned:

"Can any thing be done? Is there any chance?"

"Consult your physician at once, of course. But I did not diagnose the case hastily. It is kindest to be frank, when the time is short—— What did you say?"

"How long?"

"Not more than a month."

She bowed and smiled civilly, as if he had told

her the time of day, and opening the door passed through the outer office, which was filled with patients. He followed her to the hall.

"It is raining," he said.

"I have an umbrella, thank you. Good-morning."

"Good-morning, Mrs. Warrick."

As she went down the steps he put out his hand to stop her, but checked himself, looked after her with an approving nod, and went in.

It was only a spring shower. The buds on the maple-trees shone redly in it. "They will be out early in May this year," she thought, and then stopped short.

"Why, I shall not see them !" she said.

Some woman whom she knew passed at the moment. Sarah smiled and nodded, but looked after her. "She will be here. She can see the children and talk to Samuel, and I——"

Then a sudden frenzy came upon her to be at home, to see her husband. The minutes were flying, and there were so few! She had work for their whole lives to do, and no time was left to her—no time.

But at the end of a block she turned and went into a shop. As she made her purchase she saw that they were closing the windows of the house. The saleswomen were whispering anxiously together. Coming into the street, she saw work-men busy everywhere removing the flags and decorations from the houses. Black streamers hung from many windows ; groups of excited men stood talking on the street ; some of them wore crape on their arms, and they spoke low as if in the presence of the dead.

She stopped, bewildered. Had they heard— that it was only a month?

"What has happened?" she asked some one hurrying by.

"Lincoln was murdered last night!" the woman said. "Why, where have you been not to know it?"

"Is that all?" said Sarah.

She walked on up the street. It was all so natural and familiar—the sun shining on the muddy spattered sidewalks, the bells on the horse-cars jingling. There was a policeman whom she knew: this shop was where she always bought candy for Anne.

There was no awful presence near her. No death, nor God. Nothing but the gay shops and the car horses with their bells.

Sarah had, as we know, a worried sense of the inferiority of her own small mind. She felt, with a kind of humiliation now, that she could not force herself up to the supreme moment.

"I wonder," she thought, "if I shall go before Him thinking of candy and policemen?"

She went to her physician's office for an hour, then to a telegraph station, and then home.

The car was filled with her neighbors. They greeted her cordially, but they were still excited with the horror of the assassination.

Mrs. Warrick sat silent, listening, on a back seat. She said to herself, "The whole world is shaken because Lincoln is dead. Nobody thinks of me. Yet I have lived my life in the world too. I have lived my life in the world too."

She tried to quiet herself, to think rationally. How would the Warricks meet death? She had always looked up to her husband's family as of finer clay than herself. But they did not seem real at all to her now. Their very name was an empty sound.

She tried to think of Jane Dacre and the flames, but she could not remember now why it was that Jane died. She could not remember what the Protestant creed was.

As she left the car, her neighbors nodded good-by, laughing. Would they care when they knew? There was old Peter, waiting to carry her bag. She had always tried to be kind to the poor black soul. Would he remember her? Would any body remember her?

The storm which had been threatening all day had sunk lower, a gray darkness thickened the air; suddenly, fierce gusts bent the trees. They made the stout old woman stagger as she walked. She halted under the oaks; they waved their branches wildly, with half inarticulate cries over her head. She saw that they knew what had happened to her. There was some comfort in that. She turned into the old garden, which was home to her more than any place on earth. The rain was falling now, the pale green bushes were dripping; the crocuses thrust their wet heads through the soft mould. She dropped upon her knees in it. So many years she had worked with them! She knew every leaf and root of them.

They knew.

She pulled up a weed or two and straightened the roots of the jonquils with affectionate pats, her eyes growing quiet. She had been treading on shifting seas, but now she felt firm ground again under her feet.

She walked toward the house. "I'm afraid I haven't much grit to go through with it," she said, with an uneasy laugh.

The girls were waiting for her on the porch. She sat down and drew them to her, kissing them again and again.

"Have you heard?" Milly cried. "Have you heard, mamma?"

"About the President? Yes. All the world's dying, I think. Stay, don't go away! Don't leave me."

"How wet you are!" said Milly. "What's in that bundle?"

"It is a white wrapper," Mrs. Warrick said, opening it, "with embroidery. I thought you and Anne would like to remember—to see me in it. I shall wear it every day. I am sorry I ever wore those ugly gowns."

"And papa? When did you tell him to come?"

Mrs. Warrick did not answer.

"Did you telegraph to him? When did you tell him to come?"

"I told him," she said slowly, "to stay there until his regiment was mustered out. It will be—more than a month."

"Oh, you poor little mother!" Anne said. "You wanted him so! It will be so hard for you to wait!"

"I——" She gave a queer laugh. "Papa cannot bear a fuss. You must always keep him from that. I will—wait."

She sat with her arms about them, looking out into the rain.

Wait? For what? In a month she would be gone—altogether gone. The children would grow up like their father. They were of his kind—a different kind from her. She had sometimes been taken for their nurse in the train. There was a certain air of distinction in them which she never could get, try as she might. She had often felt as if she were down on a low road in life, and these girls, the children of her womb, to whom she had given her own flesh and her own blood, were climbing up above her. They would go on climbing, now, and where would she be?

Anne, who very seldom caressed any body, saw just then her mother's troubled face, and throwing her arms about her kissed her.

"Why—Anne!" Mrs. Warrick held her back, looking at her. Her eyes gathered an intelligence which never before had lighted them. "You won't forget! I have loved you so, children!" she said, "no matter what I am. Nobody will ever love you like your mother."

She walked down the porch. "It's love that lasts!" she told herself, shivering with exultation. "Oh, I see now! On the cross—for love.

He came back to them that loved him—He came back——"

Brooke at that moment rushed up the steps. "I must pull down these greens!" he said. "Lincoln's dead! I must hang out black streamers. Every-body has black streamers out!"

"No! No black on this house!" Mrs. Warrick cried. "I will have no black—no mourning! When people die they do not go away; they are not forgotten! God is good. They stay to help their own. They stay right here!"

CHAPTER II

It was the week after the funeral. The day was chilly, and Dr. Warrick sat in front of the fire, stretching out his neat little legs before the glowing coals.

Sarah had not been allowed to creep alone out of life as she meant to do. Brooke, when he knew the truth, wrote to the doctor, who came on the instant. The little man, beneath his whims, had a heart stout enough to face this moment. The small worries which dogged him intolerably every day of his life did not follow him up to this great and solemn height. He was there alone with the one woman whom he had ever loved, watching her go from him. His love was deep and strong enough to fit him for even this.

But now she was put out of sight yonder in her garden. He felt that he must brace himself and decide at once where to go and what to do. Five years in the army had cut him completely loose from his moorings. He tried to think, but his heart was sore. He took out a bit of soft gray hair, the tears coming to his eyes. There was a certain comfort in thus lapping himself in gentle misery. But as for his practice, or the taxes now due, or these two great girls?

He shuffled irritably in his chair. There was a

feeling which did not form itself into a thought:
that Sarah had taken a most inappropriate time
to die; that it was inconsiderate in somebody to
dump this load of cares upon him just as he was
looking forward to the welcome and leisure of
home. She, thank God, had entered into an
eternal welcome and leisure! She did not choose
her time to go, of course, poor girl! Then, with
the tears rising again to his eyes, he lost himself
in dreaming of her happiness yonder. The doctor's ideas of a future life were not very lofty,
perhaps. But Sarah, he felt, had been a good
woman, and he had a vague conviction that any
one connected even but by marriage with the
Warrick family would be especially cared for
there beyond. To set a family apart from others,
for generations, with special excellencies on
earth, and then treat them like the mass afterward would hardly be just.

While the doctor sat before the fire his two
cousins, Mrs. Dane and Mr. Franciscus (Warricks by the female line), were walking up and
down the porch outside. They had come out
from Luxborough before Sarah's death to help
him in his sore strait, but now were impatient
to set him on his way and go home.

The lady was a small, alert woman of forty.
She walked quickly, spoke quickly, glancing
from side to side with keen but kind eyes. Indeed, Julia Dane was a friendly, helpful soul, too
well bred ever to assert herself loudly. Yet
something, from the creak of her shining little
boots to the coils of iron-gray hair high upon her

erect head, told you that she was an authority in the parish, in literary clubs, and in a dozen benevolent committees.

Mr. Franciscus, lingering lazily a step behind her, was a tall, spare man, who stooped deferentially to his companion, talking incessantly in a low monotone. Why the gentle "Miss Fanny," as the young people dubbed him, should have been a ruler of fashion in Luxborough through two generations nobody knew. There was an intangible *cachet* of old-time elegance in his dress and bearing, so unobtrusive that each observer believed that he alone had detected it and felt the pleasure of discovery in it.

"Really," he said, waving his thin white hand to the window, "Samuel is not ten years old! They are three children together." He paused a moment and continued gloomily: "I find that there is but a trifle of the property left. Samuel has had a positive genius for waste! But he is fairly skilful as a physician; he might resume his practice here."

"Oh, the man is well enough as a tool," said Mrs. Dane, "but there must be a hand to push the tool. In the army he was under orders. Before that, Sarah, dull as she was, was the motive power. But now—that poor little thing!" nodding to Milly, who sat crouched upon the steps. Her face was pinched and her eyes dulled with crying. Mr. Franciscus gave an inarticulate cluck of pity.

"That child is making herself ill with grief; but the other girl has not shed a tear, to my knowledge. We shall find her difficult, Julia. We must look the thing in the face. In a very few years, you and I will be responsible socially for these children. That younger one is impossible."

"Poor little Anne!" laughed Mrs. Dane good-humoredly; "what has she done?"

"I'll tell you what she did to-day. I've had my eye on her," with a shudder. "It appears these people in the village made an idol of poor Sarah; why, God only knows!" shrugging his shoulders. "This morning Anne gathered them all, hucksters, washerwomen, and gentry from the neighboring kitchens, and going through the house in a sort of dumb frenzy she collected all of her mother's belongings and divided them among them. The cook got Sarah's one satin gown; the milkman her À Kempis—a Pickering! I protested gently, and she cried, 'What are old gowns and books? If they can make her alive a little longer to the people who loved her, shall I keep them?' Well, there was a certain truth in that, but—I foresee a radical in that girl."

Mrs. Dane's boot-heels clicked more firmly as she walked. "I'll take the radicalism out of her," she said quietly.

Milly meanwhile had a very clear idea of their meaning. Why should they interfere? She and Anne could easily carry out mamma's wishes. They would always live here, taking care of dear papa. They would talk and act just as their Warrick blood required. They would be good

Christians. She had some hazy ideas of an embroidered altar-cloth and new covers for the Sunday-school books, and advice to her wicked inferiors. And so it would go on and on. And some day when they were quite old and gray, the pearly gates would open, and they would all be together again. Life seemed simple enough to the little girl in whose pure soul her mother was really, as yet, the only God or law-giver.

Mrs. Dane suddenly stopped. "We will go at once and talk the matter over with Samuel. He must wake up to real life," she said decisively. "Come, Mildred, you must be your father's helper now."

"Yes, Cousin Julia. I mean to do exactly as mamma did."

"Oh? Your mamma——" She interrupted herself with a cough. "Come. I shall expect much discretion from you, my dear."

It was the first time in her life that any body had expected any exercise of brain from Mildred. A curious flash lighted her blue unmeaning eyes.

"Shall we call her sister, Paul?" said Mrs. Dane.

"No, Cousin Julia," said Milly quickly. "I can manage. Never mind Anne."

Mr. Franciscus's prologue to her father was ponderous and lengthy. Mildred understood but little of it.

"You are most kind, Paul, most kind! and so is Julia," said the doctor, waving his nervous fingers, as if to scatter their arguments into air. "I mean to take care of the children, of course.

I had intended to give up my time to original research, in the direction of germ disease. But now, with two schoolgirls to—— I'm sure I don't know any thing about bonnets and calicoes. It was the most inconvenient time for—— But I blame nobody! God, He knows what He wants done. I shall give my life to my poor children," drawing Milly toward him and resting her head on his shoulder, with a miserable sob.

"He will help you, Samuel! I know He will!" said Mrs. Dane, the tears in her own eyes. "But there are details to consider. Paul and I are ready to do what we can to aid you in directing the girls' future. I can advise you as to schools, and Paul is really, as you know, a social power. He can aid us enormously with them when they enter the world; and also in—in the promotion of suitable marriages. One may as well speak frankly. We must face the whole matter now. Women are born to be wives, and it is our duty to place our girls advantageously. You must perceive, Samuel, that their future, the kind of education which they receive, their place in society, and, some day, their marriages, all will depend upon one consideration."

"I suppose you mean the will of God," said the doctor, vaguely remembering that cousin Julia was aggressively devout in the way of tracts and church-going.

Mrs. Dane hesitated. Milly's little white face was turned toward her, eager for her reply. Her mother had never bared her life to her in this naked fashion. What was this which was needed to help her through all that was to come?

"We all bow to the will of God," said Mrs. Dane severely. "We are not pagans, I trust. But in this case—you surely must see, Samuel, that the future lives of your daughters will largely depend on your income? On the amount of money which you can expend; and the style in which they live?"

"Money?" said Milly, under her breath, "money?"

"Yes, my dear," said Mr. Franciscus testily. "Money. That, I am sorry to say, is now the dominant power in America. Great fortunes have been made during the war. Vulgar contractors are pushing in everywhere, even in Luxborough."

"You give the child a low view of life, Paul," said the doctor hotly.

"You must look at society as it is," said Mrs. Dane calmly. "Myself—I take a philosophic estimate of it. One thing I will say. Dear Sarah brought up the children in this solitude with very peculiar ideas. They were to make their way through the world by virtue of good blood and the example of some martyr ancestor. Now, Samuel, these notions are of no more use in every-day life in Luxborough than—than the spear of the archangel Michael would be to keep off the rain. It is an umbrella you want in a storm, and it is money a woman wants to make her comfortable. I speak plainly. I always do in a crisis. Now listen to me. If there is no probability that these girls will inherit a fortune, we must give them a plain education. We will not introduce them into fashionable life at all. Nothing is so tragic as a poor girl trying to push her way in it, in her cheap silks and Rhine stones. If I have a claim to any virtue it is common-sense, and I bring it to bear now. Paul here would be for giving them, when they come out, a season at Newport or a winter in Philadelphia. But no. It would only make them discontented. We will prepare them for a career of comfort—not luxury. But—*but* if there is a chance, even the barest chance, of their being heiresses, we will strain every nerve to fit them for a brilliant position."

"What are you talking about? How in Heaven's name should my children be heiresses? My practice may return, but——"

Cousin Julia lowered her voice, glancing around cautiously. "You forget your cousin Eliza Joyce. There is no reason why you or your girls should not be her heirs."

"Bah!" The doctor sprang to his feet and paced up and down. "Do you mean that I am to spend my life toadying to the whims of a cantankerous old woman, in hopes that she may fling me her shoes when she is dead? I am poor, but I have not sunk so low as that! No, Julia!"

"No old shoes," said Mr. Franciscus, laughing, "but a very snug fortune. I wish I had your chance, Warrick."

"Why don't you try for it then?"

"Who? Me?" said the old beau indifferently.

"I am out of the running. So is Julia. She will leave it only to a Warrick by name. You have a fine chance, if you are decently civil, or allow the girls to be so. But just as you please" —concealing a yawn.

"I have quite made up my mind as to *that* point!" said the doctor doggedly, resuming his seat. "What next?"

"This is too important a matter to decide in a moment," said Mrs. Dane gently. "I only wished to suggest it. The fortune is a large one. It would give solidity and brilliancy to the children's lives. It is there, waiting for you to pick it up. But we will not discuss it now. Paul and I must go home this evening. We will come back in a few weeks, dear cousin, to talk it all over when you are settled and your heart is not so sore. That will be time enough for business."

After Mr. Franciscus was settled comfortably in the carriage beside Mrs. Dane that afternoon, he abandoned himself to reflection.

"They are an impracticable lot!" he said, rousing himself at last. "I like to help my kin to the farthest generation, but—— Now that girl Mildred is the most hopeful of the three. A dowerless woman with as marked beauty as hers sometimes marries very well indeed. Her tints are exquisite, and that dove-like softness of voice and manner is very alluring. But I'm afraid she inclines to embonpoint. There is a thickness in her lips and eyelids which suggests absolute fat at thirty. She should eliminate from her diet for a year or two all oils and sugars and starchy food. I wish you would see to that, Julia. She is your godchild. I want to do the best I can for the child. She has no mother."

Mildred just then was sitting in the wet grass beside her mother's grave. Her tears had never been so bitter as now. Anne found her there and stood beside her, stroking her head softly, at which Milly sobbed more loudly.

"I wish I could cry too," said the little girl.

"I'm glad she is here, so near!" cried Milly passionately. "I can come to her every night, to be sure that I have done just as she wished me to do!"

An hour later, as the girls walked home through the gathering twilight, Mildred stopped in the orchard.

"You can see the windows of the Joyce House from here, dear," she said. "Did you know that Mrs. Joyce is our own cousin? We ought to go to see her."

"She is a wicked old woman! She is no cousin of mine," cried Anne. "Brooke told me. She has all kinds of disreputable people at her dinners. She is a gambler—she jeers at the Bible. Mamma was afraid of her."

"Yes, I know," said Milly thoughtfully. "Mamma——" Presently she said, "The world is so big! And there are things in it," she added, with a little air of authority, "which perhaps even mamma did not know. I think we should be kind to poor Mrs. Joyce, Anne."

CHAPTER III

WE all know that Pennsylvania and her children grow old slowly; they seem to linger always in the calm of satisfied, mellow middle age.

Luxborough, for example, after eight years had passed, had not changed a whit; it had not as yet even suspected that any change could better it. It listened with silent, well-bred contempt to reports of the transient enthusiasms of Boston, the huge fortunes of New York, and the crude splendors of new-born Western towns. Luxborough had no need to pant or swagger, to clutch at money, or to grope after Christian Science or Buddha. The good folk still waged war on each other from the High and Low churches; the same Bourbon rose-bushes reddened the dusky alleys of their gardens. They pickled and preserved by the same recipes, and still danced the minuet once a year in the ancient brocade gowns of their grandmothers.

It was the identical grimy train which went lumbering up from Philadelphia through the deep gorges and perilous beauty of the Gap to Luxborough one wintry afternoon, and the same Dutch conductor, his jaws redder and his hair whiter, who called the stations as he had done for twenty years.

A young girl spoke to him in a low tone. The

old man shuffled from foot to foot, looking back at her, as he turned away, with pleased admiration.

Mrs. Dane, who sat beside her, said gently, "I have travelled with that man half of my life and I never have spoken to him."

"How droll!" said Anne. "I know Fritz well, though I have not seen him for five years. I wanted to hear about his wife and his boy Jake. Mamma knew them all."

"Your mamma," said Mrs. Dane, hesitating, "cluttered up her life with common people. She knew all about the diseases and debts of her cook and butcher. I pay them their money; that ends our relations. I give charity through organized associations. When you have studied social economics as thoroughly as I have, I think you will find that to be the easiest way of dealing with that class, my dear, and the safest."

"Undoubtedly it is easy and safe," said Anne, turning her bright eyes full on her for a moment. Mrs. Dane bridled with annoyance. What was she laughing at? She was always laughing!

Judge and Mrs. Hayes were in the seat behind her. She knew that they were eying Anne curiously. Presently Mrs. Hayes leaned forward, the beady fringes on her broad bosom rattling.

"Who is that?" she whispered. "What a distinguished-looking girl!"

"It is the younger Miss Warrick. She has been five years at school. Near Boston. With Mme. Dupont. Best class of girls in the country. So exclusive! Really, you have to enter a pupil's name while she is in her cradle to get her in. I have just been up to bring Anne home."

"Very odd, attractive face, eh?" said the judge.

"Oh, no! candidly, Anne is very ugly," said Mrs. Dane. "But she surprises me every day. She will puzzle Luxborough," she added, with a complacent smile. "She will be something quite new in the way of a young woman."

"Ah, really!" said Mrs. Hayes dryly.

The younger Hayes girls were not yet settled. Mrs. Hayes scanned this new *débutante* with jealous eyes. There were quite enough marriageable young women in the town already, she reflected.

Why could not Jenny and Matty bear themselves with that repose? The girls trained by Mme. Dupont did acquire an air !

She turned to look at the woods flying past, the pompons of her hat nodding gloomily.

"Why, Aunty Conn! I'm afraid you don't know me!" said a voice beside her. "I used to call you Aunty Conn. Don't you remember Nancy, and the day I broke through the glass of your hot-house climbing over it, and how you bandaged up my leg and gave me root-beer?"

Mrs. Dane, looking back, saw the Hayeses on their feet, shaking hands and laughing with the girl. Cornelia Hayes's broad face was beaming with hearty pleasure. They left the train at the next station, tearing themselves away from Anne with difficulty.

"I'll bring Jenny and Matty up to-morrow!" the judge called from the platform.

"And remember, my dear, dinner on Thursday, and you shall have root-beer," said his wife.

Mrs. Dane listened, amazed. "I wonder how she did it?" she thought, looking at Anne, perplexed. She could not quite master this school-girl.

Mrs. Dane had been faithful in her duty to the Warrick family. She had piloted Mildred into both factions of Luxborough society. A brilliant match was always possible to a girl of such singular beauty. Anne had been an ugly, high-tempered child. Mrs. Dane had decided to hand her over to Mme. Dupont, who was said to turn out "superior" young women. An intelligent girl, possessed of a certain amount of Latin, literature, and executive ability in church-work, she was sure would take in old Luxborough circles and soon marry a professor or one of the assistant clergy.

Such were her plans. But would Anne fulfil them? She had tried in vain yesterday to obtain some estimate of the girl from Mme. Dupont, but that lady (certainly a most eccentric person) had not the faintest ideas of the duties of a teacher. Mrs. Dane stood with her on a balcony, watching Anne in the garden below, as she bade good-by to the girls and a half dozen dogs.

"You can speak freely to me of my niece," said Mrs. Dane affably, to the little woman in black. "If I have any ability, it is a thorough comprehension of young people—a sympathy. What is she? What does she know?"

"Know?" repeated Mrs. Dupont. She nodded and smiled affectionately as she met Anne's eye. "Nothing, accurately. But she will learn more than most women as life goes on."

"I must understand her. I must plan her future."

"She will do that for herself," said the teacher quickly.

"I am quite satisfied," said Mrs. Dane, with official gravity, "with her manner. The voice is low and clear and the carriage noble."

"Oh, these are mere habits," said the other woman carelessly. "I am sorry," she added, observing Mrs. Dane's impatience, "that I cannot schedule her character for you. You see?" motioning to the crowd below. "Whatever else she may lack, she will have friends. That capital she is sure of. And there are other things— Anne gets more out of life than we do. The world is fuller for her. You understand me? I have heard of certain people," she said, smiling, "who are born without the outer cuticle. The sun is hotter to them than to us, and the wind colder. They know sights and smells and the calls of insects which are nothing to us. Anne is like them."

"Really?" said Mrs. Dane anxiously.

"She comes closer to things. At her age, naturally, she sees the gay side first—the fun. But after a while—I hope her life will not be a hard one"—she broke off abruptly

"Her father is not a rich man."

"That will have something to do with it. Not much," said Mme. Dupont. "Shall we go down?"

Hence Mrs. Dane, when she left the school, was greatly bewildered. She inspected Anne's skin keenly. It was all right. Or had the woman only been talking in allegories? Mrs. Dane hated that hyperbolic way of putting things! It was so—Bostonian; which was the term Luxboroughans used for any thing which they did not quite understand.

As they came near Luxborough, she feared that Anne's welcome would not be warm enough. She saw that this home-coming was a thing of tremendous import to her. She had been thinking of it for years. Mrs. Dane kept an eager watch ahead. Very likely the doctor would forget the time when the train was due; it would be just like him! Mr. Franciscus had boarded the car at the lower station; one could always trust Paul to do the right and courteous thing.

Anne, however, had a welcome of which Mrs. Dane knew nothing. The old fields were looking at her. She knew every foot of them, and they knew her. There was her own hedge, which the king-birds liked best. The snow lay thick at the roots of the bushes, but the leaves of some red creepers which had outlasted the winter fluttered atop. "They knew I was coming and waited," Anne thought. It seemed to her as if she and every thing about her were shouting for joy.

They skirted the edge of the town with rapid glimpses of the narrow, empty streets, running up the hill between lines of great Lombardy poplars, and near the way-side station at The Oaks. There was the orchard; the chimneys of the house rose behind the hill, and now she could see old Peter waiting by the hedge, and Bruce beside him, and——

"There is papa!" she said quietly, as the train stopped. But she trembled so that she did not speak to him at all when she came to him.

"God bless me! And here you are, my dear! And you're glad to get home to old Daddy? Tut—tut! Why—Anne?"

He had been mildly glad that she was coming home. But—nobody before had ever cried with joy to see him. His thin blood throbbed in his veins.

"Run along home together," said Mr. Franciscus, with a little quaver in his laugh. "I'll send the luggage up. Samuel, go along with your girl."

As he strolled homeward presently with Mrs. Dane, he whistled inaudibly to himself, a sure sign that he was greatly pleased.

"She is quite satisfactory, Paul?" she asked. "I should call her figure perfect, and she knows what to wear. That brown gown and hat, with the fleck of red here and there——"

"It is not her clothes. Nor her looks. But something in the girl herself, indescribable," he said, with energy. "It wasn't easy to spare the money for her education, but I am glad we did it. She does not suspect that we had a hand in it, I hope?"

"No one but Mildred knows. She is reasonable. Samuel would resent the obligation. But he gives Milly the purse to carry and asks no questions."

"It is no obligation," he said hastily. "I do not wish Anne ever to know. I am glad that we did it!"

Anne, going up the hill with her father, halted suddenly. "Where is Milly, papa? I always thought she would meet me here, at the oaks."

"Oh, don't you know, my dear?" stammered the doctor. "She is gone to New York for a month. Mrs. Joyce wished to consult a specialist, and Milly felt that she ought to go with her. The poor old woman is quite dependent on your sister now. Mildred left her love for you."

Anne did not speak for a minute.

"It must have been harder for her than it is for me," she burst out loudly. "She will have nobody there, and she knew that I would have *you*."

"Yes, yes!" the doctor held her arm tightly. His heart fluttered as it had not done for many a year. How the child loved him! He had so much to tell her. He was sure that *she* would understand. She would see things as he did. Dear Mildred could not come back unexpectedly. And they could do as they pleased for a whole month!

He gave her another hug when they were inside of the door, and ran bustling about, humming a tune.

"Make up a rousing fire," he shouted. "Let us be warm for once. Maria, come and show yourself to Miss Anne. About dinner, now?" adding some whispered orders, which sent Maria amazed and chuckling back to the kitchen. He had startled himself into a frightened silence for a minute. But no matter! The bills would not come in for a month, and surely Mildred would remember that Anne only came home once in her life.

"Well, well, my dear! How Bruce does keep close to you! Milly detests pets, but she tolerates him because—he was your mother's dog, you know."

"Yes." Anne laid her cheek down on the shaggy head in her lap. "But we must have a half dozen more. I'm very fond of dogs," she said.

"Oh? Six dogs! Why, Mildred—but run up to your room now. Dinner will soon be ready."

Anne ran up the stairs, and then down by the back way and out through the garden to a little mound among the crocuses. She knew the way in the dark! She had been thinking of coming here for five years. She threw herself down, crying and laughing and kissing the ground. "I've come back to you, mammy, dear! I've come back to stay," she cried.

The doctor skipped about, putting a rose in his buttonhole, adjusting the glasses on the table, humming a dozen tunes. How lucky it was that he had thought of decorating the house with holly! She had seen it in an instant. That girl saw every thing! He would show her the etchings after dinner. And to think that an hour ago he did not know what was coming to him! A companion for life! Mildred was a dear girl, but she understood him no better than if he were an Esquimau.

When they were seated at dinner, the holly-berries glowing between him and the young, vivid face opposite, he cackled on without ceasing. It seemed to him that he had not talked before for years.

"I am so glad that you have a good appetite, my dear. Your sister only nibbles. We don't have game or ice cream unless when Mildred entertains the millionnaires of Luxborough, but I thought that to-night——"

"She entertains a great deal then? I am so glad of that! Mamma always had a cover laid for any one who might drop in."

"Oh, Mildred says that kind of hospitality is out of date. She has to perform her social duties, you know. 'Keeping up with the procession,' they call it. She has two heavy dinners yearly for these people who only come to feed, and pays her debts to all the others by one big reception. She borrows for that day your Cousin Julia's silver and Turkish rugs and curtains——"

"Ah-h!" gasped Anne.

"Yes, quite so! I don't think it is in good taste, myself. I say—damn the millionnaires! I beg your pardon, my dear. Why go into their

set at all, or try to compete with them? That's
what I say. But Mildred manages—every
thing, money and accounts. I have my own
occupations—a kind which society don't touch.
I live my life apart. Do take this bird, dear?
Well, if you won't"—laying it on his plate.
"So it goes. She keeps up appearances, you
see. Two dinners and the At Home. But the
rest of the time it's bare, very bare! Why, I
haven't tasted partridges before, since——" The
doctor forgot to finish the sentence, anxiously
nibbling the juicy morsels until the bones were
bare, and then wiping his gray mustache and
leaning back with the air of a gourmand. "That
was really an excellent dinner!" The little man
contentedly clasped his hands over his stomach.
"Milly made out a bill of fare for each day while
she was gone. It was—not long."

His complacency increased with each moment.
The big fire burned. He had for once had plenty
to eat, and there sat Anne—young, yet belonging
to his own generation—listening to every word
he spoke with eager, trembling lips. She loved
the theatre. She turned over his etchings with
a sort of reverent ecstasy! His stories of the
elder Booth and Macready and Jenny Lind were
new to her, and when he sang a snatch of one of
the great Swede's ballads, the tears actually came
into her eyes. "Tut, tut! child!" he said, patting her shoulder. "You like it, eh? My
voice is cracked now, but once—well, well!"
Then he told her of his music-teacher in Paris,
and of Paris itself—a jumble of his tramps

through the forest at Fontainebleau, and royal processions, and dinners, when his last coat was pawned, of *pot-au-feu* and bread—fit for the gods.

"We'll go there together some day," she said, drawing a long breath when he paused.

So it came about that evening, while his heart was melted and his judgment shaken by the coming of this new affection and sympathy into his life, that he told Anne his great secret—took her up to a closet in his room and showed her a mysterious collection of glass tubes and dishes.

"This is my true work. I never speak of it to Mildred. But here is where I find my real life," he said, with a dramatic wave of the hand.

"What are they?" Anne asked, awe-struck. "What is it that you do here, papa?"

"I study the germs of disease. It is comparatively a new pursuit in this country. I purposed to give myself up to original research when I left the army, but I had to begin practice—I had a young, helpless family."

"Yes, us. I know!" stroking his arm. "And then?"

"I cannot attend to both. Sometimes I feel that I am on the verge of a discovery which will make the world hold its breath. If I could pursue my experiments, I know that I should find the germ of cholera. By inoculating for it, I should save thousands of lives."

Anne's eyes flashed. "And yet you do not pursue your experiments! You could benefit the whole human race, and you go on earning money for *us*? Has Mildred allowed you to make such a sacrifice?"

"Oh, I never have told Milly," the doctor said, with almost a sob. He was greatly excited. The cholera germ had really been a very vague idea until to-night, but Anne's faith gave it a sudden reality. "I oughtn't to have told you. But I have had this secret so many years, and you come so close to me, Nancy."

"Yes, yes! I understand. Let me think a moment!"

She walked up and down the chamber, her cheeks hot, her eyes burning. Here was a man within reach of a great triumph—a mighty gift for all mankind, and his hands were tied by duty —duty to her! On the very night that she came home, to discover such a hero—and in her dear old father! Anne's imagination, always ready to kindle, was now all aflame.

She must act at once and for the whole family. But discreetly. In her own opinion she was always as discreet as the judicious Hooker himself.

"Now, father, come and let us talk this matter over coolly. Let us go down to the fire again. We will be perfectly calm. We must do nothing hastily."

When they were seated beside the library table, she began gravely, "Have you never seriously thought of giving up your practice?"

"Oh, dear, yes! I think of giving it up every day. It's a terrible grind. You've no idea how stiff one's legs are, riding over these hills !"

"Is there any one to take your patients? They must not suffer."

"Any one? There's a dozen! The country's swarming with Bob Sawyers. But you don't wish me to stop at once?"

"In a day—an hour—if that will hasten your great work! But we must be practical, dear. What income have you outside of your practice?"

"Well, there's this house—and the land about it. Enough for chickens, and pigs, and calves, and potatoes, and that sort of thing."

"Quite enough, I fancy. Chickens and veal? We shall live like Irish kings! That is all?"

"Oh, dear, no!" said the doctor, with a little pompous laugh. "There are some government and railway bonds, bringing in two thousand or thereabouts—Milly knows."

"Why, we are rich! And now that I am at home my school expenses will be saved. Papa, you must stop at once! Write to Mildred to-night——"

"I—would it be necessary to write to Mildred?"

The doctor was being swept off of solid ground into a great flood. He thrilled with exhilaration. To discover this germ! To become famous all over the world—to be able to be done with back-breaking rides, and to be able to stay in bed all night and every night! But, if Mildred knew?

If the step could be taken while she was gone, there would be a victory!

"If the thing is right to do, let me do it!" he blustered. "Never mind Mildred."

" 'TO THINK MY FATHER IS TO DO THIS GREAT WORK !' "

"Right? There can be no question in the matter! Of course Mildred will agree with us." Her courage was so lofty and gay that the doctor's momentary bravado suddenly collapsed before it.

"It is too important a thing to decide in haste, child, " he said irritably.

"It is too important to dawdle about," she retorted quickly. "Let us talk it over in detail."

They talked it over until the clock struck twelve, one, two. The more the doctor vacillated, the more urgent Anne grew to force him into heroism.

"How can I give up my patients, my dear? We will starve!" he cried for the twentieth time.

"Mr. Greeley says the way to resume specie payment is to resume!" she said. "The way to resign your practice is to resign. Wait a moment!"

She seated herself at the desk, drew a sheet of paper toward her, and wrote a courteous note stating that Doctor Warrick, having resolved to devote his whole attention to laboratory work, must decline to receive patients after the first day of the ensuing February.

"There! That is concise and businesslike,"— looking at it critically. "Give me a list of your patients, and I will copy it to-morrow and send it out to them. You can call and explain a little, to be friendly."

"Yes, yes!" The doctor chuckled. "What

4

a breeze it will raise in Luxborough! And Mildred—— Copy it early in the morning, my
dear. Something might happen."

He gave her his list and carried her candle to
her door, kissing her good-night. She held him,
her hands on his cheeks.

"To think my father is to do this great work!
My father"—her lips quivering.

"Yes, dear. You do carry things with a high
hand! I wonder what Milly will say? We
must send her a copy."

He went, laughing to himself, to his own room.
The doctor's triumph was not so much that of a
hero taking up his life's work, as of a donkey
kicking off a load.

But Anne did not suspect that. She glanced
at the list of patients. "How few there are!
They do not appreciate him here, then? They
will, some day!" She kneeled at her prayers,
trembling with a lofty exultation. "Well, I have
done a good day's work for the world!" she
sighed, smiling happily as she fell asleep.

CHAPTER IV

THE circulars were sent out and Doctor Warrick hurried from house to house, explaining the
reason of his self-sacrifice. Luxborough heard
the news with smiling indifference. The doctor
was one of themselves, and, if he had committed
burglary, his old neighbors would have hushed it
up. They would hush it up now, if he chose to
play the fool and starve; but they had no interest
in his germs or in any such new-fangled folly.

Anne was amazed when the great deed thus
fell flat on the world's ear, but she indignantly
urged her father on to work. "You are the only
man in America who is trying to do this thing,"
she said; "you will soon be a benefactor to every
nation on earth!"

She wrote huge and ardent letters to Mildred
to this effect; the doctor also wrote to her, stating how prudent his course had been; how every
detail of income, outlay, etc., had been considered before the irrevocable step was taken.
Mildred simply replied, "I have received your
circular, dearest papa."

A certain look of alarm deepened on the
doctor's face after that. He busied himself in
his laboratory for a week. Then a new novel
fell in his way, and he began to take Anne to the
theatre in the evenings, finding that as to melo-

drama her taste needed training, and then a great event occurred, which drove germ culture quite out of his head.

During this winter Mr. Mears, the humanitarian, had been urging upon the Northern people his pet scheme for establishing colonies from the surplus population of their cities in the cheap lands of the South. He insisted, as our readers doubtless will remember, that these wildernesses could be made at small cost to blossom into creamery farms and chicken factories, whereby New York toughs and Chicago anarchists would speedily be converted into mild, church-going citizens.

Major Patton, the railway king, was one of Mr. Mears's enthusiastic supporters, and offered him a special train for a tour of inspection through the South. The major invited a few of his own friends to accompany them. Among these were Doctor Warrick, his daughters, and Mrs. Dane.

Mildred returned unexpectedly at this juncture. Anne, who had been tramping over the hills one afternoon, came home late in a heavy rain, and saw through the window a plump little woman in pale blue, quietly seated by the fire, sewing. She threw up the window and rushed in, followed by the driving gust.

"Oh, my darling!" she screamed. "Oh, Milly! Is it really you—you?" She threw herself on her knees, hugging her sister, looking up into her pleased, smiling face, stroking her soft cheeks. "Five years! Yes, five years, that I haven't had you!" she cried.

"We will always have each other now," said
Milly gently, kissing her on the forehead.
"Close the window, Peter, please. Don't be so
nervous, my dear. I am afraid I have startled
you. I really arrived at Luxborough this morning, but I had to establish Mrs. Joyce comfortably before I came home."

"I—I have so much to say to you," stammered
Anne, rising discomfited, she knew not why.

"Of course you have." Milly stood on tip-
toe to kiss her cheek again. "But dinner will
be ready in twenty minutes. Run now and dress.
You are very wet."

Anne turned at the door to look at her again,
but Milly did not see her. She was patting the
rain spots on her gown with her handkerchief.

There were a thousand things which Anne had
been keeping through these years to tell to Mildred. Was she not her own, only sister?

Neither that day, nor any day did the time
come to tell them. Milly never "talked things
over." Anne's return, the doctor's surrender of
his practice, the long journey which they were
soon to make, were accepted without comment as
matters of course. After her arrival the house
grew neat, the meals shrank into mere morsels,
and preparations for the journey were made in the
same calm silence. Anne felt her own passionate
spurts of energy feeble and ridiculous beside the
steady progress of this fair, low-voiced girl, who
handled the worst difficulties of life as if they
were bits of a dissected map; a touch of her firm
white fingers, and they fell into order.

After five weeks' delay Mr. Mears announced that he was ready to start. He had asked Brooke Calhoun to go with him. He needed a practical farmer to pronounce upon soils, methods of tillage, etc.

"You are young, Calhoun," he said; "but there is not a farmer in Pennsylvania for whose judgment I have more respect."

Brooke laughed. "Of course, you know, Mr. Mears," he said, "that it is the biggest chance that ever has come into my life. I never have had time or money to study soils or crops outside of this State. For that reason you make a mistake in taking me. I know nothing about rice or sugar culture. I'll go farther," raising his voice when Mr. Mears would have spoken, "and say honestly that I think you are making a worse mistake in trying to rescue New York thieves or paupers by dumping them out in the country. Farmers are made, not born. A clever pickpocket is not necessarily a successful or a moral potato grower."

Mr. Mears smiled. He had an obstinate feminine smile. "We won't argue, Calhoun. I never argue. I know I am right in this. In any case come with me, and keep me from going too far astray. It is settled, eh?"

Brooke hesitated. "I will give you my answer to-morrow."

Mr. Mears had a womanish dislike to being balked in a pet plan. He knew that the liberal salary offered was of weight with Calhoun. "I don't know why you hesitate," he said peevishly.

"That model little farm of yours ought to run without you for a few weeks."

"Oh, that would be all right! My men are competent."

"You have neither wife nor mother to consult."

"No. It's my brother," said Brooke.

"Edward? Nonsense! He is not a child. Much more a man of the world than you are. Do you mean to say he can't live a month without you? Why, he has been four years abroad."

"Yes," said Brooke. They walked on in silence for a few minutes. "I really can't decide without seeing Edward," he said abruptly. "You will hear from me in the morning." He turned into a shop to avoid further discussion, and Mr. Mears, shrugging his shoulders, went on.

Mrs. Dane, in the afternoon of the same day, drove out to The Oaks to talk over the preparations for the journey.

A light snow whitened the fields. Mrs. Dane hurried gladly from the gray cold without into the wide, warmly colored room. A log burned on the hearth. Before one of the windows a handsome blond young man, in a loose corduroy jacket, was perched on a high stool, painting, while Anne posed for him on a sofa, wrapped in a red shawl. She sprang up to meet her cousin, while the artist bowed impatiently and waited, scowling, his brush suspended over the canvas.

"Ah, Edward Calhoun? Sorry to interrupt the sitting!" said Mrs. Dane briskly. "I will sit here by the fire until I thaw. I came to look after your arrangements, my dear."

"Oh, they are all made!" said Anne. "Milly has set the house in order, and started papa on his farewell visits. She is over at Joyce House now. She gives every afternoon to that poor old woman. Will you not go on, Edward?"

"No," scraping the paint from his palette impatiently. "It is impossible now. The light has changed. You have lost the expression. Oh, it does not matter!" He hesitated a moment and then dashed his brush across the picture. "You are not to blame, Mrs. Dane," in answer to her cry of horror. "It is I. An artist could take up the idea again. But a poor dauber like me is dependent on the fire of the moment. The fire is such a poor flicker that it soon goes out!" with a bitter laugh.

Mrs. Dane had a long acquaintance with Edward and his griefs. "Patience, my dear boy!" she said. "We all know that some day you will do immortal work. You have sent your 'Twilight at Carnac' on to New York?"

"He painted it out yesterday," said Anne. "And his great 'Annunciation' he slashed out of the frame the day before."

"Laugh, if you feel like it." The young fellow was very pale. "The joke for you is death to me. I waken every morning thinking, 'To-day I will do great work.' I do it, and it is trash! I've no chance here," he went on irritably. "The light is hard; every thing in this country is so abominably crude and raw. If I could have stayed in Persia! I was mastering color there, when the rheumatism seized me. It was my usual luck!" with a grim shrug.

"Poor boy!" said Mrs. Dane anxiously. "Why don't you paint your cousin Mildred? You have beauty there surely, pure and simple."

"Yes, the beauty of a bit of bisque china! Now, Anne," scanning the girl critically through his half-shut eyes, "Anne is like a twilight study by Corot—it only suggests—— But what infinite meanings, possibilities——"

"He has found the possibility of every character in history and fiction in me," Anne said, reddening and laughing. "One day I am Joan listening to the angels, and the next Becky Sharp. Ned is especially unhappy this evening," looking at him as she would at a fretful child, "because Brooke has had this offer to go with Mr. Mears."

"You think I am base enough to begrudge Brooke his chance? Thank God, I am not selfish! Nobody can accuse me of that. But now, Mrs. Dane," turning to her with a nervous laugh, "confess that it *is* a little hard! The southern warmth, and color, and landscape are exactly what I want for my art. That good honest soul Brooke does not know one color from another. He sees nothing but lumber and crops in Nature. Yet—he goes, and I stay on the farm! I am so tired of that neat house, and the meals like clock-work, and Brooke's eternal drudge drudge, that if I could turn tramp and take to the road, it would be my salvation!"

Mildred had entered during this tirade, and waited until it was finished. "Brooke is coming through the orchard in great haste, Edward," she said.

The lad's face lighted, as it always did at the sight of his brother. "Brooke always rushes along, his nose in the air as if he had just heard good news and was in a hurry to tell it," he said, laughing, and went to meet him.

Mrs. Dane looked after him eagerly. He was the only man of genius that she knew. "Edward is always most interesting to me," she said, "most interesting! He has undoubtedly had hard measure in the world."

"Do you think so, cousin Julia?" said Milly softly. She had not quite lost her lisp.

"I certainly do. Here are two sons of the same father. Brooke's mother has a fortune: Edward's not a penny. Brooke has hard common-sense and business ability to earn money. Edward, who has none, with his genius and sensitive nature is helpless. I have no doubt, too, that he has much to bear from his domineering brother. The old story of the iron and porcelain pot! I consider it extremely selfish in Brooke to accept the offer and leave his brother behind."

"Papa told me that he declined it this morning," said Anne. "He saw how it discouraged Ned."

"Declined it! Really? Well, of course he was right. But such an opportunity will never come in his way again. Declined it? Rather Quixotic and young to do that. At least so John Mears will think."

The door was flung open and Brooke burst in.

"It's all right! Great news! I beg your pardon, Mrs. Dane, I did not see you. I've just had a note from Mr. Mears asking me to bring Ned. He says he probably can be of use drawing maps, if they decide upon any sites. Of course Ned will pay his own expenses. You can be perfectly comfortable on that score, old fellow. But Mears's letter is most considerate and hearty. I feel as if I could shout!" he said, laughing, his face red. "Such a lark for us all!" He was watching Anne, but when she did not look at him he turned to Edward. "You can bathe your soul in heat and color now, boy."

"Have you accepted for me?" said Edward coldly.

"Why, no; the note has just come. But I am going at once to see him."

"You can tell him, then, that I shall not go to draw his maps! What does he take me for? Any high-school boy can draw his maps! Answer the man civilly. But let him understand that he has made a mistake!"

"Don't be too hard upon him, Edward," said Anne, who was watching him with cool amusement, as he pulled his long beard through his trembling fingers.

"Oh, it is the American idea of art! I am not angry! I only pity his ignorance." ·

"All right!" said Brooke good-humoredly. "Come, Ned. Drive home with me. We will talk it over as we go."

While they waited for the sleigh Mrs. Dane talked of farming to Brooke. She prided herself upon the tact with which she always could aim her conversation directly at each man's specialty.

But Brooke, while he talked to her dogmatically of draught-horses, was furtively watching Anne. He had been in Ohio, and had seen her but once or twice since her return. He had an intense curiosity about her. She held herself aloof from him, while all the rest of the world, as he saw, even to the horses and dogs, easily made friends with her. What did it mean? Was it only the prudish school-training?

She had been a frank, ill-mannered, hot-tempered child. But he had found something in his little comrade which no other person ever had given him. Since this reticent, grave young woman had come back to The Oaks, Calhoun felt that something had gone out of his life, which he might never find again. Whenever he spoke to her, he knew that he was groping in search of it.

He suddenly quitted Mrs. Dane and crossed the room to her.

"I shall be sorry if I cannot take this journey with you," he said abruptly. "You see I don't know you any more. Sometimes I think that my little play-fellow has gone out of the world. I want to find her."

"Ah?" said Anne coldly. "I thought that your interest in this expedition lay in rice-culture and cattle?"

"Yes, of course," said the young farmer eagerly. "I always have contended that Hol-

steins will not find the grass in the far South suc-
culent enough to—— But what do you care for
Holsteins ? "

Anne lifted her eyebrows, with a shrug, and at
the moment Edward called his brother. "What
an ass I am!" thought Brooke angrily, as he went
out. "She will think that I am more interested
in cattle than in her! Well, I don't know; perhaps I am!" laughing, as he jumped into the
sleigh and waved his hat to her in the window.

Anne stood looking gravely after him. The
last six weeks had been heavy with disappointment for her. She had left school eager to see
the great struggles that were going on in the
world. Out there she supposed every man was
striving to win fame, to help humanity. Life
was a sort of hurdle race, a series of victorious
leaps to triumph. Now it was Brooke, who,
long ago, had planted this idea in her mind.
He was the only man except Colonel Newcome
whom she had ever really known. She had been
his little adopted sister for years. The big lubberly collegian had poured out his most secret
ambitions to her. She was looking now at the
very bench under the oaks where they used to
sit and plan how he would be a great lawyer, an
orator, a statesman. He might have been any
of these things. Her eyes softened with tender
feeling. In all the years in which she had been
gone, she had been planning what he might be.

She shrugged her shoulders contemptuously.
He *was*—nothing! A ploughman, content with
his turnips and pigs! She remembered how

frantic he used to be to fight for some great cause. Slavery was abolished, the Union was saved; but there was surely other great work to do?

Anne had come home on fire with these thoughts. But nobody else was on fire. Her father's noble example interested nobody—not even Milly. Old Luxborough knew of no great purpose in life except to keep strangers out of the Monthly Club. Milly's purpose was to hold her footing with the dull patricians on top of the hill, and to make her way among the dull parvenus at the foot, with as little expense as possible. There must be a bigger life than this somewhere in the world! Old Luxborough was stifling, clammy, a graveyard!

Anne played Chopin softly as the twilight gathered, the hot, angry moisture rising to her eyes. Presently her father and Mr. Mears came into the room. She turned civilly, and after a while listened. Mr. Mears was talking of a proposed Reformatory on the Lusk system.

This man had noble purposes! She looked at him eagerly, seeing as for the first time his lean, ascetic figure and pale, vague eyes. St. Augustine must have looked like that when he walked into the great Council singing the Te Deum, leaving paganism behind! To save thousands of neglected children—that was a different thing from Holstein cattle!

Mr. Mears, turning suddenly, saw the pleading eyes and quivering lips of the young girl. What a breathless interest she took in his plan! He

directed his explanations entirely to her while he
stayed, and went away with a pleasant sense of
encouragement. This fresh, childish enthusiasm
was certainly a relief after the daily sharp criticisms of his elderly woman colleagues on the
board! He wished vaguely that he had a sister
or an aunt or—something, like the younger Miss
Warrick; and then remembered with a little shock
of pleasure that she was going South with her
father.

Anne went back to Chopin, but oddly enough
it said nothing to her of the Lusk system. The
most melancholy strain expressed only sharp dislike of Brooke Calhoun. She would never change
her opinion of him! Anne knew that she was
apt to change her opinions. At school she had
vehemently sided by turns with the abolitionists
and slave-holders, aristocrats and anarchists.
But there was one kind of man for whom she had
no sympathy nor use. ·The grub, the earth-
worm. She was quite sure of herself on that
point.

Milly told her presently that Brooke was coming to breakfast the next morning.

"I do not wish to see him at breakfast or at
any other time," said Anne tartly.

Indeed, her antipathy to Brooke Calhoun, when
she went to bed that night, was so virulent and
strong that it seemed to have given a new
stability to her character.

CHAPTER V

In the meantime Brooke whistled to his horses and bowled cheerfully along. He was a stout, warm-blooded fellow; and, whenever a blast of sleet struck their faces, he whistled more loudly, and told Ned again that it was a glorious day.

"You are ready to shout in all kinds of weather," grumbled Edward, who was always too hot or too cold. "This air is death to me. Heavens! To think that you will pluck roses out of doors next week!" He waited for Brooke to answer, and when he said nothing, went on in an authoritative tone. "Understand me, Brooke, you are to go with Mears. I will not permit you to remain with me. If the man had not insulted me, I should have been happy to go, God knows! Well, he probably estimated me at my true value. I am a poor creature, as far as art goes. But a drawer of maps——"

"I can't discuss it with this wind in my face," said Brooke cheerfully. "I'm starving, too. The thing will be plainer to us after supper."

The road wound through the rich farms of Delaware County, and Brooke met several of his neighbors. They halted to give him bits of news about the rise in school taxes or the water famine. They touched their hats coolly to the young man beside him. There was a general belief that

Calhoun was spoiling the lad. One woman, in a
sleigh that passed them, spoke of his singular
beauty.

"Yes," said her father, "Ned has an uncom-
mon face. He was painted once in Rome as
Apollo, and he has been posing as some Greek
god ever since."

Ned certainly was not unconscious of the effect
of his fine head rising out of the rich furs in which
he had wrapped himself, nor of the girl's admiring glances. The talk of the farmers grew intolerable after that.

He remembered how he and some of the men
from the Latin quarter used to explore the
environs of Paris. Different evening drives,
those! At every turn their keen eyes detected a
fine shadow, a subtle color, or some picturesque
grace or squalor. These Americans had no ideas
beyond sugar-corn or calves. Even Brooke!

"Get on, man!" he said irritably. "Damn
it, get on!"

"I must stop at this house. Phipps! Hello!
Just a moment, Ned. About those pigs?"

The pig question consumed twenty minutes.
Edward sat in sullen silence until they reached
home.

The farm-house was aglow with comfort, fire-
light shone in every window. Savory smells
stole out into the frosty air. The old house, in
which six generations of the Dacres had lived
and died, stood on one of the lower spurs of the
Alleghany Mountains. Like most Colonial farm-
houses in Pennsylvania it was built of rough

blocks of gray stone, square and solid, with after-
thoughts of offices and store-rooms growing out
of the sides. Rain and lichen had mellowed the
walls into warm saffron and yellow tints; the
American ivy muffled the sides and the steep
roof, green or blood-red most of the year.

Inside of the house were no modern pretti-
nesses: the ceilings were low, the rooms large.
Even in July logs smouldered in the huge fireplaces. There was an atmosphere of large,
happy content about the place which did not suit
Edward's mood. He swore now at the boys who
rushed out to take the horses, and kicked his
way through the dogs that barked a welcome.
Brooke lingered, laughing and talking to them
all. He always welcomed himself home with
fresh delight, if he had been gone but a day.

He had seen English manors and Colorado
ranches, but in his secret soul he thought them
mean compared to this old house, and rich little
farm, which the mother whom he had loved so
much had given him.

In the fulness of his good humor he blurted
out this opinion when they were seated at supper. Edward stared at him.

"I should not select this assortment of corn-
ricks and barns as the ideal home," he said dryly.

Brooke laughed, and recommended the steak.
He felt it to be natural that Ned, with his poetic
temperament, should be fretful: it was as natural
too, that he should always be the victim of Ned's
ill temper as that he should be wet when it rained.
Nobody was to blame.

"Nothing that I say goes through his rhinoceros hide!" thought Edward. Yet it was this blind good humor which made Brooke necessary to him. He pushed away his plate and watched him make a hearty meal, with the contemptuous affection which he might feel for a dog.

"Of course they all will blame me for hindering you from going with Mears," he said presently, in an aggrieved tone. · "I suppose it would be a profitable trip to you?"

"There are plenty of profits to be made at home. Some more coffee, Dolly."

"You'll kill yourself eating such heavy suppers. I ought to say for you to go. But I cannot stay here alone. I simply cannot. You are the back-bone of my life, Brooke."

"Glad of it, boy," said his brother, glancing at him affectionately.

"I've no doubt Milly and Anne regard me as a miserable drag on you," he said, giving a dog who fawned on him an angry kick. "And so I have been. I see it. I'm not ungrateful."

"Ned——"

"I'm not ungrateful," raising his voice. "I never had a cent of my own, and I have spent your money like water. Those years in Paris, and that trip to Persia, must have cost you a pretty penny. You never could afford decent clothes for yourself. And the bric-a-brac and rugs and pictures I brought back! Why, the duties you paid on them in New York ran up into the thousands. I've been a whelp—a damnably selfish whelp."

"Once for all, Ned," said Brooke sternly, "there can be no question of money between you and me. If you had it and I had not, I would come to you for it. God has given you a great talent, and what is our money for but to develop it? Let me never hear of this again." He walked nervously across the room, and coming back, laid his hand on the lad's shoulder. "Why, Ned, you're—you're my brother," he said, his heavy face contracting.

Ned nodded, laughing excitedly. "That's so! And you're only just to me, old man, when you say that if I had the money I'd spend it on you. Thank God, there's not a mean bone in my body! I value money no more than dust—dust! I'll repay you some day. When I paint my great picture I'll put your name with my own in the corner. You shall have the credit of it through all time. About that picture, by the way; I've an idea——"

Brooke sat down, lighted his pipe, called the dogs to him, and listened while Ned dilated on Breton peasants and Alpine sunsets. He stopped abruptly. "I know what you think!" he exclaimed. "That I should find subjects at home? Lay the foundations of an American art, vigorous and novel? I agree with you."

"I know nothing about art," said Brooke cautiously.

"I have often thought of it. It is the short cut to success." He was silent a while, then jumped up impatiently.

"But what can I do here? How can I paint

American scenery shut into this little farm?
Brooke, listen to reason. We are wasting our
lives in these potato-fields. You as much as I.
Let us quit them!"

"Quit the farm?" Brooke looked at him
sharply. Most of his evenings were spent in
listening placidly to Ned's wild schemes. But
this was earnest.

"Yes, quit the farm. I never could understand why you were on it. When I went abroad
you were studying law. Your heart was in that.
When I came back you were absorbed by Ruta-
bagas and oats."

"I don't dislike farming, and I am satisfied
with the old home," said Brooke evasively.

"Ah? I am not, then. Listen to reason.
Rent the place. Then we shall be free-footed.
You can practice law in New York, and I can
travel and study American scenery. What do
you think?"—breathlessly. "What do you say
to that?"

Brooke's countenance clouded. "You have
forgotten one thing," he said, forcing a laugh.
"How are we to live in the meantime? It
would require years for me to gain a practice in
New York."

"Why, your income——" exclaimed Ned, with
an amazed stare. "Your mother left you a
fortune."

"A very small one," said Brooke hastily.
"Besides the farm I had a few railway bonds.
I have sold them."

"You have nothing but this farm?"

"Not a dollar. And I have to work it myself to make it pay."

"The bonds should have kept you until you had made your footing sure in your profession," Edward said authoritatively. He walked up and down with a puzzled face while Brooke watched him furtively. "I'm afraid," he said, stopping abruptly, "that you managed badly, old man. I never should have suspected *you* of extravagance, though."

Brooke laughed, with sudden relief, and lighted his pipe, which had gone out. "What is done is done. I must stick to the Ruta-bagas, you see."

Edward sat down, holding his head between his hands, in gloomy silence. Suddenly he started up. "I have it! You said I would pay my own expenses with Mears? Why not give me the same amount and let me go alone? To my mother's people in Louisiana? By all reports the Soudés are a good stock—worth knowing. I could study the scenery on the Gulf! By George, Brooke, that's a great idea! I would have no end of a good time. It would set you free to go with Mears. Though he's a cad. But if you like him—— Why do you look so grumpy about it? You object? I wish you to be satisfied," he said, hesitating. "What's wrong, then? Where's the difficulty? Oh, I see"—rising with an angry laugh. "New Orleans is not a Sunday-school! I may play euchre? This is a little too much, Brooke! You know that I have outgrown that folly. Come now, old fellow, don't draw the reins too tight. I'm not built like you."

" GLANCING IN AT NED "

Calhoun did not speak for a minute. "No," he said, "and I have no right to dictate to you."

"Good! I'll promise you—any thing! What a glorious idea it was! Why, I'll bring you home studies that—you'll see! It won't cost any more than staying at home either."

Brooke nodded. "Let me know in the morning how much you will need."

"I'll tell you now. I'll make an estimate. I like to be accurate about money. I'll sum up my necessary expenses"—taking out a pencil and paper anxiously. "Of course I'll take a little over; just a margin in case of accident. One likes to feel secure. I need not use it, you know."

"Don't stint yourself, Ned. We have plenty for that." He filled his pipe and sauntered out to the porch, laughing to himself. Of course the money would fly like leaves before the wind, but it would be almost against Ned's will. He was considerate; he would be a miser with his brother's money—if he could.

Brooke strolled up and down in high good humor, glancing in at Ned and his anxious calculations as an indulgent mother might have done.

The boy would make his southern studies, perhaps paint his great picture now.

"Then," thought Brooke, "he will be happy at last. He will stand on his own feet." For he always supposed that Ned's chronic miseries grew out of his dislike to be a burden on him.

Brooke, who had no taste for self-sacrifice, was heartily glad that he was free to go. "The journey," he reflected, "will be of enormous value to me in my business. And——" His eyes grew bright and tender as he thought of two months of daily life with his little comrade.

CHAPTER VI

ANNE awoke often that night, to tell herself that she would not go down to breakfast. She would make it a rule for life now not to hold any hypocritical parley with people who were uncongenial to her.

But very early in the morning she stepped out on the porch where Milly was feeding the pigeons.

"Anne! Why do you wear your best merino in the morning?" she exclaimed.

"Quite right, my child!" cried the doctor. "That crimson is a fine bit of color. I hunger for color! These hills are so gray and dull! But peaceful—peaceful! Now the Southern mountains are full of sadness and unrest—like man's ineffectual strivings heavenward. They depress you. But in these hills there is a fat, well-fed content; d'ye see what I mean, Nancy? Satisfied, phlegmatic, like their Dutch owners. Like our good Brooke coming yonder."

"I really don't understand what you mean, papa," said Milly. "Southern men do not strive for heaven any more than Pennsylvanians, and nobody's strivings need be ineffectual who follows the teachings of the Bible and Prayer Book. As for Brooke, I am glad that one of the Warrick family is well-fed and content."

"So am I. I have a great respect for Brooke. He is making money out of his calves, no doubt. I hoped once for better things from him than money or calves, but—that fellow has not a single aspiration!"

"Much better without them," Milly said, watching him as he sprang from his horse and crossed the lawn, waving his hat and calling out that he was to go, after all. The doctor ran to meet him, delighted. Nobody could long be ill tempered with the sensible, affectionate fellow. Even Anne's dignity relaxed when he wrung both her hands, declaring, "I shall be with you for two months—two months!" She smiled, but checked herself, and sat down beside him at the table, with a severe face.

"This makes the thing complete!" said the doctor. "I could not have gone at any other time, you know—but having just given up my practice—you received my circular in Ohio, Calhoun?"

"I did, and was much surprised by it."

"Yes. Every body was surprised. I may say that that announcement took the medical profession unawares, like a blow between the eyes. Even Milly, here, was greatly surprised. I determined on the course after consultation with Anne, and at once issued the circulars. On reflection, it does seem, sometimes, as if I had been rash. My income, outside of my practice, is really very small. And here are the girls——"

"But you thought it expedient to give it up?"

"No. I can't say that Anne and I considered

it in the light of expediency at all"—knitting his
brows anxiously. "Ever since Davaine began
his work in 1850, I have been experimenting. I
am a mere amateur in science, but Anne thinks
that I shall become more; that I am upon the
verge of a great discovery which will benefit all
mankind. Now, I could not experiment and
practice medicine at once. Just at the critical
moment for my microbes a flood of neuralgic
women or croupy infants would set in, and there
was an end!"

Mr. Calhoun's dark face flushed. "It was
Anne, then, who persuaded you to leave her and
Milly with a pittance, in order that you might
make a great scientific discovery! It was like
her!" He gave a short laugh. After a moment
he turned to Mildred, his eyes twinkling.

"And what did you think, Milly, when you
came home? You pay the monthly bills, I
think?"

Milly shot a warning glance at her father's
vague, troubled face, and said sweetly:

"Whatever dear papa decides is best. And
besides," lifting her delicate eyebrows, "it was
done. Anne moves like a cyclone. I never fight
against what is done."

"Poor little thing!" thought Calhoun, looking at her tenderly. He was used to the horrors
of coal and meat bills, and no money in the purse.
And this soft creature would be so helpless before
such trouble!

"Papa," twittered Milly's sweet voice, "papa
tells me that he hopes to discover the cholera

bacillus and to inoculate for that disease. So when the cholera comes to this country, he will make immense sums inoculating for——"

"God bless me!" shouted the doctor. "Do you expect me to take a fee, child? You are like Simon, wanting to sell the gift of God for money!"

"I was only joking, papa," she said.

The doctor hastily changed the subject. Milly sat silent, watching him with a bewildered look, as a physician might a mad patient.

When they rose from the table Anne hurried out of the room. The doctor laid his hand on Brooke's arm. "Of course," he said, "practical men will call me a fool in that matter. But there are higher objects in life than money-grubbing, thank God! Besides, I am not going to let the girls starve. Reports of my experiments will be well paid for—if one must take a paying view of it!" His thin nostrils dilated with a fine scorn. "I expect letters to-day from a publisher. By the way, that fellow Peter has not gone for the mail. You'll excuse me, Brooke?" and he hurried away, twitching his gray mustache.

Mr. Calhoun looked at Mildred. "It is more serious than I thought," he said. "What can you do?"

Mildred came closer to him. "It is not as serious as you suppose," she said, in a low voice. "Papa's paying practice never was large. It was nearly all gone now. He did not see that, dear soul; but *I* saw it. He had plenty of work which paid him nothing. Now, he is done with paupers. If he writes about his vibrios and things, it will bring in more money than they did, and if he should make this discovery, it would help our social standing outside of Luxborough enormously. The distinction of learning pushes a family forward almost as fast as capital." She was silent a moment, her forehead knitted anxiously. "I can manage for a year or two," she said at last. "We have a certain income, and the rates of living are lower this year—beef is but sixteen cents a pound, and flour——" She checked off item after item on her little fingers.

"You poor child!" said Brooke.

"Oh, I have been going through a narrow alley for years! It costs to keep in the front of Luxborough society, I can tell you. To have dinners and receptions that are both charming and—cheap! What should I do without you, cousin Brooke? I run to you with all my troubles!" She looked up at him with pleading eyes.

"Poor little girl!" Calhoun thought her the most guileless of women. She had the habit of carrying the flighty vagaries of . her father and Anne to him, as one would carry a faulty watch to an expert, to be regulated. In fact it was a relief for her to bare now and then her anxious little soul, whose movements were so carefully hidden, before the kind eyes of this reasonable cousin.

"I have to make Anne's way in society now," she said. "She will not lift a finger to help herself."

"No," laughed Calhoun. "I believe that."

"No. Anne's intellect is not acute. I shall have to manage without help for a year or two."

"What help will you have then?"

Milly, who never blushed, grew scarlet; her eyes dropped. "Some door always opens to those who wait," she said at last, smiling.

Brooke felt that a blank wall had suddenly risen between them. He talked uncomfortably of the weather, and, after glancing around, vainly searching for a glimpse of a crimson gown, bade her good-by.

As soon as he was gone, Anne reappeared.

"You are very confidential with Brooke," she said. "He is a most uncongenial person, I think."

"He is very kind; the only one of the Warrick connection that I know who has common-sense. He has just promised to buy my beef at wholesale prices. He is very useful to me."

"Yes, he is quite competent to buy beef," said Anne. "But he will not be useful to *me*. He does not interest me in the least."

Milly left the room, but Anne stood by the window. He was crossing the lawn. The man was utterly unworthy! He had chosen low, ignoble work. How strong he was! What a hearty, kind voice, even when he talked to the dogs!

If he was only the old Brooke, who used to hold her hand and comfort her.

She needed comfort now. She knew that her life was to be a total failure.

Anne's mother, at eighteen, had a definite work and hope before her. The work was to learn how to keep a house; the hope was for a husband, children, and a house to keep. But Anne, at eighteen, belonged to another generation. The doctrine that work for the public was the highest duty for women had begun to creep into sight in this country. She had been taught that a woman must hunt for a nobler errand than to marry and bear children. These were accidental, secondary tasks. If she had lived now, she would probably have had the prevalent desire for notoriety and mistaken it for an inspiration, and have written an indecent novel to set forth a great truth, or rushed before the public to show how feebly she could kick against Christianity, or marriage, or the Tyrant Man.

But the old decorous trammels were still upon her, and her soul was devout.

" Here am I," she used to pray, upon her knees, every day. "What wilt thou have me to do ?"

There really seemed nothing for her to do. She meant to compose an oratorio which was to lift up all starved souls. But she never could get through with her scales correctly. She began two long poems, but her grammar always failed her at a pinch.

A month ago the butcher's boy had sprained his leg and was laid up. Here was her opportunity. Every morning she tramped through the snow to his house, her eyes shining, her heart thumping with zeal. " He that shall save a soul from death," she used to whisper to herself in awe.

She had Tom at advantage. He could not budge, his legs being in splints, while she lectured him.

But Tom was cured. He had brought the chops for breakfast just now, swearing as hard as ever. It hurt the girl like a blow. Would God have none of her help? or was that lower class really no better than the brutes?

Once she would have gone to Brooke to make it all clear. Bah! She turned angrily from the window. Was she to make a man her guide and confessor because he had broad shoulders and eyes that held her, and hurt her as they held?

She went down to Mildred. The house was in order, the trunks and satchels piled in the hall. Milly was quietly seated at her desk, daintily dressed, her curly hair knotted high from her white neck. She nodded when Anne asked if every thing was done, and ran to meet the doctor, who came puffing in, out of breath, from the frosty air. "Sit down, dear papa!" she cooed. "You are worn out with this preparation! Here is a cup of hot bouillon."

"I do feel utterly tired out," said the little doctor, with a groan of exhaustion.

"But really, sir," said Anne, standing bolt upright before him, "you and I have done nothing. Milly has had all the work and worry. She always has them."

The doctor set down the bowl angrily.

"Mildred, have you been doing menial work? I gave all necessary orders to the servants. We may be poor; but the women of my family shall never labor, please God!"

"Of course not, dear," said Milly, stroking his grizzled hair. "*Et moi, je suis Papillon!* You shall work, and I will be *Papillon* to the end of the chapter."

He rose, grumbling, and went out into the hall.

"Now, I've no patience with that!" said Anne. "You a butterfly! You carry the whole family. You work like any grub. Why do you fool him so?"

"Because! Oh, you do not understand men. They want to manage—to be at the head. Well, why not let them think that they are at the head? Papa thinks he is keeping us in idleness as his ancestors did their daughters. And he shall think it!" Her pink cheeks paled a little. "I love my father, Anne, and I'd lie every hour of the day to make him happy."

Anne laughed, with a shrug, and said nothing.

"If I could make papa into an energetic business man, then indeed!" said Milly. "But I haven't lived twenty-two years without finding out that you must take folks as God saw fit to make them, and do the best you can with them." She sat down again to her accounts, and presently closed the book, with a nod of satisfaction. She had a surplus from last quarter, in spite of the money flung away on scientific books, tubes, and microscopes. It surely would not be long before her father would discover something. "And I'll see that he has his royalty on the 'gift of God'!" she thought. "Dear me!" she said aloud, "what is papa doing now? He has

6

not looked at his tubes nor written a line for two days. What is it, dear?" she said affectionately, when he came in.

"I am looking—something I have mislaid——"

"Some of your notes? Are you at work now on your papers on etching, darling? Or on germs?"

The doctor grumbled an answer between his teeth. It was, in fact, "Esmond" which he could not find, which he was rereading for the twentieth time. "Well!" he sighed, "I'll go back to my grind," and toiled up the stairway. Milly called out that she would gladly take notes for him, but he thanked her, and hastily shut the door. "Milly's a sweet girl," he groaned, "but she certainly does drive like the devil. Where is that book?"

He could not find it, and appeared again in the hall. "Going out, papa?" said Mildred.

"Going to church, my dear." The doctor polished his high hat and drew on his worn gloves. "It is St. Thomas's day, you know?"

"No, I did not know."

Milly considered herself a good Christian. No storm could keep her out of the pew on Sunday morning, and she paid promptly their assessment of church dues. But churchgoing on week days in her opinion argued a disordered intellect. The doctor bustled about the room uneasily.

"Daughter? my dear?"

"What is it, papa?"

"The—the collection? For the hospital, you know? I really—I am quite out of money——"

Milly opened her desk, turned her few notes over wistfully, and at last gave him, smiling, a scrip note for twenty-five cents, kissed him, and hurried him out of the door. Then the smile faded.

"People will think it is a dollar, perhaps," she reflected. "St. Thomas, indeed! What right has the Church to take me by the throat for money in that way? As if people at my age did not know how their twenty-five cents for charity should go!"

The doctor trotted down the muddy hill, keeping a close watch on his polished boots. He began to plan how some day he would send turkeys and ice cream to every hospital in town. Other people could send meats and bread on Christmas. "I'll surprise them with something to make their mouths water on common days." He entered the church, his eyes twinkling as he saw himself carving the turkeys and giving out the candy, for he had no idea of being anonymous in this thing. He liked to be praised and thanked. In this glow of benevolence the shinplaster in his pocket felt small and cold and greasy.

The girls stood together on the porch, watching him. It was a cold, sparkling morning, the air full of vigor: the bare trees glittered with rime; the river flashed out between its hummocks of muddy ice; the red blood showed in the maples. The world to Anne breathed out a sudden new splendor; even the clouds swept over the hills as if hurrying to some wider life beyond.

She looked down to where the crocuses were planted in the garden, her eyes slowly gathering tears as they saw the raised mound.

"I ought to have gone with father," she said. "I thought I'd begin the Spanish grammar to-day. What do I want with Spanish? It is just this crazy, longing to do—something. If I were a boy, I'd run away to sea!"

Milly looked at her, perplexed.

"I'm a fool!" Anne broke out. "I ought to be satisfied. This dear old house, and you keeping every thing so comfortable, and papa doing a great work for humanity! Very few women have such a full, happy life." Her breath came short; she stood silent.

Mildred watched her. The sudden throbbing of her own heart choked her. Was not the girl right after all? Had not her dead mother talked in just that way? But to get money, to rule in society——

Yet they had a happy home. They had enough. Her father's and Anne's wants were few. Simple food and clothes, a few good books, a few good friends. Why not sit down with them in quiet?

A sudden loathing of the sham fashionable life which she had tried to lead overpowered her. The imitation Persian rugs, the terrapin made from mutton, the Warrick crest emblazoned on plated dishes—all her frantic efforts to vie with the women yonder who had millions pressed upon her; her soul for the moment was filled with disgust.

But she rallied. Why should she not eat real

terrapin from solid silver, like these others? "Why should I wear this coarse homespun?" Milly demanded of herself savagely. "Velvet is softer. Why should Anne and I creep through life afoot, without great houses, and carriages, and pearl necklaces and winters in Paris, if I can get these things for us?"

All the little envies and rages of her life against richer women flamed up in her breast` at that moment. But she answered Anne presently, with the usual slow lisp.

"You are quite right, dear. Of course we are greatly blessed. Yet there are a few good things in the world which I should like you and papa to have. I mean to try to give them to you."

A man in a sleigh at the moment turned into the avenue.

"Who is that?" said Anne, seeing her sister's startled look.

"One of Mrs. Joyce's men. Something is wrong."

"I thought you bade her good-by this morning?"

"I did. I thought I had arranged every thing," said Mildred anxiously. "I left written directions for servants, nurse—every-body."

"Papa tells me," said Anne, "that you have cared for her all of the years that I have been gone as if you were her daughter."

Milly's laugh had a bitter tang. "Not all daughters would——" she began, but checked herself. "She is very old and very ill, and she is one of our blood, Anne," she said meekly.

Anne suddenly stooped and kissed her. "You are the best woman that ever lived, Milly!" she said energetically. "My idea of a saint is not a starved ghost with lilies and a halo, but a plump little woman in blue serge."

"Hush!" said Milly sharply. She was silent a moment, and then added gayly, "Mrs. Joyce owns a mountain tract in Carolina. She wants us to visit it when we are there, and bring her Doctor Mears's estimate of its value. They say," she continued, her blue eyes kindling and the red deepening in her cheeks, "that the mountains in it are full of iron and corundum. The farming lands in the valleys are rich: there are mineral springs, mica mines. They have found gold and rubies—oh! it is a principality in fairyland!" She ended with a shrill, nervous laugh. "Rattlesnakes and moonshiners hold it now. But one could easily drive them off!"

"Has she never seen it?"

"Seen it? No! She cannot even name a tenth of the things that she owns! Shares in silver mines in Montana, in wheat farms in Minnesota—in banks—in railways——" She stopped, craning her neck forward, her eyes half closed, drawing her breath with a whistling sound through her narrowing lips.

"Milly!" cried Anne, amazed. "What are you thinking of?"

"I?" recovering herself. "Nothing. Poor Mrs. Joyce! She will not have these things but a year or two longer. Ah, here is Paterson. A note for me?" She read it hastily. "I will go. Wait, Paterson, until I bring my wraps."

Anne followed her. "Is she worse?"

"No. But she writes in an odd way. Affectionately. She is never affectionate. She wants something. Perhaps she wishes me to give up going with you?"

"Mildred! You will not do that? You are not her slave."

"Hush–h! I will do it, if she asks it."

"Why must papa's wishes and mine be sacrificed to Mrs. Joyce's whims?"

"Because——" Milly looked keenly at her sister. Then she said gently: "She is very old and ill, dear. It is my duty."

It was but a short drive to the Joyce House. Mildred entered the door, and passed through lofty halls and rooms where the plenishing told of the taste and wealth of many generations. Mildred knew the value of each picture and cabinet. She had had time to learn it. One corps after another of cooks, footmen, and nurses in these years had found Mrs. Joyce's rule intolerable and left her. But Milly stayed. She could not ask for her wages and go.

She found the mistress of the house in her wheel-chair beside her bed. She was an old woman, made enormous by disease. Her broad flat face, from the same cause, resembled an immovable mask of yellow wax, in which her small black eyes moved incessantly, hungry, challenging.

"Are you worse, cousin?" said Milly tenderly.

The negro nurse, a large, powerful woman in white cap and apron, drew back into a corner, seizing a moment's relief.

"No, I'm no worse. Unless the devil has possession of me more entirely than usual," said Mrs. Joyce, with a barking laugh, in which, had Milly the ears to hear, there was a certain miserable pathos below the ill temper.

"You should not slander yourself so," she said amiably, with a perfunctory smile. "I thought perhaps you meant to bid me to stay? That you could not spare me?"

"Not spare you? Bah! There is nobody and nothing that I cannot spare. You will be more useful to me there than here, if you get proper estimates of the capabilities of that land from these men. Go and bring me some broth. No, Jane," as the negro started forward. "Miss Warrick will go." After the broth had been brought and taken, she leaned back, yawning. "I really don't know why I sent for you. You've done all you had to do, and said all there is to say. You can tell Jane again about that night draught. She makes it too hot."

"I will, dear."

"I'm a great deal worse," Mrs. Joyce went on fretfully. "Not since morning. I told you that. But since last month. These queer flutters in my head—I am certainly growing weaker every day. You will not find me here, Mildred, when you come back."

"Let me stay then, darling," said Mildred, in a voice which, in spite of herself, was tired and bored.

"Yes, I'll be gone! And even Jane will say, 'A good riddance!'"

"Don't hurt me so, dear cousin," Milly murmured, kneeling before her and caressing one of her great hands. "Don't talk of leaving me." She managed to force the water into her eyes, but it was hard to wring it out. She had heard of this fast approaching death for so many years!

Mrs. Joyce was watching her keenly. The cold wintry daylight struck full on the rose-tinted face.

"Wait!" said Mrs. Joyce. "Don't go! Stay where you are. Mildred——" She leaned forward, her eyes searching the fair, sweet countenance upturned to hers with a fierce eagerness. Milly was bewildered and annoyed. She wanted something from her? This was why she had sent for her. But what?

It seemed as if all of the years in which they had been together had led to this moment. The clammy hand trembled in Milly's firm little fingers, the coarse mouth quivered. Out of the intolerable solitude of her great age, without a friend and without a God, with the chill of death on her, she turned to this girl for—what?

Milly smiled sweetly. "Is there any thing I can do for you, dear?" she said, in her amiable little pipe.

Another breathless pause.

Then Mrs. Joyce pushed her back roughly. "You? Nothing! There is nobody! I drove them all away long ago." She leaned back, closing her eyes, while Mildred stared perplexed, at her bald head and waxed face. What did the woman want? In what had she failed?

Mrs. Joyce then gave herself up to unusual ill temper, and during the next hour spared Milly no menial service. When Jane interposed, declaring that "de wohk wan't fit foh de young lady," her mistress smiled grimly.

"The young lady loves to wait on her 'dear cousin,'" she said.

At last Mildred closed the door of the Joyce house behind her. Her habit of feeling was naturally kind and amiable, but she would have been glad just then to see this old woman lying dead before her. As she passed the negro maids she thought they eyed her with contempt. She grew very pale, and her teeth chattered as with cold.

"I am a servant, too—unpaid!" she said.

On the road Mrs. Judge Hayes passed her in her victoria, her men in livery. Milly bowed and smiled sweetly and walked on, still smiling mechanically. Some day, she too—she would not always trudge in the dust! Her liveries, her horses should take the lead, in Luxborough. Some day——

But the price to pay was heavy—heavy!

CHAPTER VII

OF all the little company who journeyed through the South with Doctor Mears, Anne found most keen pleasure in the adventure. Every-body was kind to the shy, dark little schoolgirl, who was so ready to help and so quick to catch a joke. She was perpetually meeting, too, remarkable people. Mildred, who never saw any thing remarkable in any body, was bored by her excitement, and Anne soon learned to keep it to herself.

This certainly was an enchanting world! The demonstrative Southerners paid such homage to her father's learning and to Mildred's ' ravishing beauty.' Anne felt that she belonged to a royal race; her heart glowed when she awoke each day, warm and comfortable within her.

She had satisfaction, too, in showing Brooke Calhoun her disapproval of him and his ignoble life. True, she was not sure that he perceived her contempt. Whenever they made a halt he was engrossed with Doctor Mears and committees, and, she fancied, avoided her. Very well; she was glad that he knew how obnoxious he was to her. But—did he know it? He ate heartily; she heard him singing in the smoking car sometimes, and he was eager enough, examining soils and minerals, smelling and tasting them.

She raged at herself that she could not rid her mind of him as the weeks went by. Mankind was a hazy whole to her. Why should she listen to catch this one man's bass voice in the noisy throng on the platforms, or watch to find into which car he was going, or concern herself about the ugly bend on his nose, or the mole on his hand? She was amazed and ashamed within herself at these things. The whole trend of her teaching at school had been toward the great work waiting for her somewhere in the world; her own hot ambition pushed her on the same road. So did all the talk of Professor Mears, and he talked much to Anne, on a wide range of subjects, from the proper treatment of the insane to tobacco culture. What had Brooke's mole or crooked nose to do with these things? Or with her?

Nothing at all. She knew that so certainly that, when she accidentally met him one day face to face, she only bowed, not being able to speak, and hurried away, shivering with sudden cold.

"She treats you," said Milly, who was with him, "as if you were her one enemy in the world."

Calhoun nodded, smiling good-humoredly.

"Are you to blame?" Milly scanned his face sharply.

"No!" But he said no more, and soon left her. Going into the car, he seated himself behind Anne, and for a long time watched the thin childish profile turned toward the window. He wondered stupidly why she disliked him. He

had tamed a dog once that had taken an un-
reasonable dislike to him. Nothing living loved
him as Wolf did now. If—his eyes kindled.
" Next station—Mobile! "

Brooke looked at his watch. At Mobile he
surely would find letters from Ned. He had
heard but twice from him, each time by wire, asking for more money. Was he working so hard ?
Paints—models—these things were costly. Or
was he ?—Brooke pulled his coat over his ears and
fell into anxious thought, in which his little comrade had no share. Mr. Mears came up to talk
of the Alabama Black Belt, but Calhoun answered
curtly and soon left the car.

Mr. Mears took the Black Belt to Anne. For-
tunately, he never wanted an answer. She looked
at him as if she were drinking in his words.

But Anne had seen Booth in *Richard* the
night before, and she was thinking of how he had
paid suit to another Anne—of his fierce vehe-
mence, his passion—abasing himself before her.

" I could have loved a hunchback and mur-
derer, if he had wooed me so. It was worth
while to be a woman then," thought Anne, lifting her head haughtily. " But now men think of
their cows or fertilizers for twenty-four hours of
the day, and of a woman about ten minutes."

Brooke found no letters at Mobile. But his
relief was great when one of the first men whom
he met at the Battle House proved to be a
cousin of Edward's—John Soudé, from Louisiana.
Soudé was a tall, robust young fellow, evidently

used to fill a very big place in a very little world. His broad negro inflections made his slow talk almost unintelligible to the Pennsylvanian.

"Edward Calhoun? Why, certainly. He is recuperating now, sir, at Le Reve des Eaux, our old plantation, on the Gulf. A lee-tle tired—*ennuyeux—en voila tout!* He will be well taken care of, I assure you. My father, General Gaspard Soudé, is there, and my cousin Theresa, of whom you no doubt have heard. Probably the most charming woman in the South. And you are his brother?" shaking both his hands. "You must meet all my friends in Mobile!"

"Is Edward at work? Painting?" asked Calhoun anxiously.

"Painting? Possibly—if that amuses him. But the shooting at the plantation is fine. The general, no doubt, will urge that upon him."

"All right!" said Brooke. He was much comforted. Mr. Soudé, seeing him smile, insisted upon drinking some very black brandy at once to Edward's health.

The Northern guests received much hospitality from the best people in Mobile; more effusive perhaps because of the memories of the war, which were still bitter and poignant. Balls and dinner parties were given to them, and young Soudé met them at many of his friends' houses.

"I am glad to do it," he said to Louis Choteaud, a former brother-at-arms who was with him. "I never met a Yankee, except in the field or in gambling dens at Natchez, until

Edward Calhoun came. I should like to see what the decenter class in the North is like."

A day or two later he told M. Choteaud that he was much impressed by Doctor Warrick. " He is a gentleman, Louis, wherever he had the misfortune to be born. I shrewdly suspect that he is one of the foremost of Northern statesmen. Why, sir, he repudiates carpet-baggers! He is going to induce his friends to invest in Southern industries."

" I should guess from his costume," said Choteaud dryly, "that it is his friends' capital which he will invest."

Mr. Soudé, who was a big, slow man, stared down, bewildered, at his companion. Louis' sharp little gibes always amazed him. The man's wizened face actually grew like a ferret's when he so far forgot himself.

" I fail to perceive," said John gravely, "how the fact of his position in life is affected by his clothes or his money."

"Ah-h? We shall not quarrel about him. You always had queer likings. I did not expect you to adopt a comrade of that species, however. *Ohé!*" with a suspicious laugh. "He has two daughters—not ugly!"

" I did not observe them," said John.

"So much the better!" thought Louis. Any adventurer could impose upon poor credulous John. He was a child—a lamb! Yet Choteaud, with this pitying contempt, had an awed respect for his friend as a man of genius. There were thousands of men who could fight for the South;

but he knew only one who could write for her. He had been going about Mobile for days, telling every-body that John was the author of those brilliant papers now appearing in the *Picayune*, descriptive of the hunting and fishing in the Gulf States. "The finest bits of word-painting, sir, in our literature!" He was especially pleased to trumpet these masterpieces to the Northerners. The North had been insolent long enough with its Irvings and its Hawthornes! Now it would be forced to recognize men of real genius in the South land!

That very afternoon Louis met Doctor Warrick and his daughters driving out to Spring Hill, and eagerly joined them. He soon managed to tell the doctor of Mr. Soudé's pleasure in his liberal sentiments.

"Soudé?" said the doctor eagerly. "I remember! Tall dark young fellow, with a tremendous laugh? And he is ready to bury the hatchet, eh? Good! It only needs the combination of a few leading men to bring the country into peace and prosperity. I am working to that end, Monsieur Choteaud!" And the little man puffed and frowned anxiously.

"John Soudé's aid will be of immense importance in calming the South," said Louis, pushing his horse closer. "A man of great power, sir!" touching his forehead. "The Soudés have been a ruling family since the days of Bienville. Men of master minds and enormous estates!" cried Louis, in crescendo.

At these words Milly suddenly leaned forward,

listening eagerly; and M. Choteaud pranced to
her side of the carriage to pour forth laudations
of his friend, whose verses Mildred praised
warmly.

At the next turn of the road Fate brought them
up against the poet, who was on horseback. M.
Choteaud proudly presented him to Miss Warrick.

The carriage had stopped before a mass of
live-oaks. Before this sombre background,
John saw a small face of dazzling fairness looking up timidly to his own. Mildred's lap was
heaped with pink blossoms. John spoke but
a word or two, and rode on. But the pale,
scented flowers, and the meek face went with
him.

He began to think of the sweet dunce, Cordelia, and of hidden snow-drops. These were
the kind of ideas out of which he pieced his
poetry, for the newspapers.

"That scared little girl is very sweet," said
Louis presently. "But I like a woman with
more knowledge of the world. Her sister,
now?"

"Was there another?" said John.

"Mildred," said Anne, when the men left
them, "how could you praise those verses?
They were pure bombast, and you know it."

"Hush-h, Anne. No, I don't think they were
all bombast. And if I did, I need not shout it
out on the highway. They were pretty imita-
tions of Poe!"

"Poe! Cannot the man see that Poe's work

7

was done once and for all? Poe could not found a school."

"Oh, my dear! Somebody will hear you!" She glanced at the hedges. "Mr. Poe was a man of great ability. He could have found a school, I'm sure, if he had wished to teach."

Anne laughed. "And as for this man Soudé," she said, "I have read his letters. They are turgid and commonplace. Yet they call him the Scott of Louisiana."

"Very well, dear," said Milly soothingly.

"No, it is not well at all! How are the Southern people to have a literature if they set up such cheap gods as that? They fall in adoration before every man or woman who writes tawdry verses as they might before a saint who worked miracles."

"Don't be blasphemous. Why are you so aggressive with these people? They have been so hospitable! We have hardly had to pay for a meal since we came to Mobile. Yet you differ with every Southerner you meet on every point."

"Why do they differ with *me?* Can't they see what is right?" She checked herself to watch the off horse, while her father jerked and scolded, growing red.

"Give him the whip, papa!" shouted Anne. "He'll have us in the bay! Here, I'll take the reins!"

"Keep your seat!" thundered the doctor.

Anne seized the whip and gave the vicious brute the needed cut. When he trotted quietly again, the doctor said, in an aggrieved tone, "I know I am an ignorant old man in your opinion. But I did think I knew how to drive. These old Southern statesmen," he added, with a forced laugh, "consult me about the management of the country, but you won't trust me to drive you to town."

"Papa, dear, we would trust you to drive us to the world's end!" cried Milly anxiously.

"I wouldn't, when he pulls the off horse like that," said Anne doggedly. There was a long silence after that. But presently the doctor glanced back, and Anne, her face scarlet and the tears starting, scrambled up to the front seat and whispered to him, crying and kissing his hand. In a few minutes the doctor's face was beaming, and they both were laughing as usual at their own bad jokes.

Milly, leaning back, watched them, wondering why, with these incessant squabbles, they were such close comrades. She, who never broke the peace, was outside of the alliance. The gentle little woman had found Anne a heavy burden to carry on this journey. Travelling had brought out her crude opinions and her dogmatic certainty that she was always right. Milly thought it hard that her father should prefer this uncomfortable child as a companion to the daughter who for eight years had carried the family on her poor little shoulders.

Milly's brain suffered a strange revolution that afternoon. She suddenly loathed this eternal plotting and managing! She felt strangely alone and neglected. Some women did not need to work, or plan, or think of social success or money. They simply sat tranquil, and were—loved.

She leaned back upon the cushions as they sped swiftly on. On one side the air stirred the trees drowsily, on the other the bright wide deeps of water softly lapped the beach: the sunshine held all in its warm grasp. Through it, there came to her again the flash of dark eyes, startled, enraptured by the sight of her—*her*. There was in them the promise of something which life never yet had given her. Milly's brain was sharp and practical, addicted to dealing with bills and other small hard facts. But this new fantasy warmed her shrewd thoughts as the golden sunshine did the hard pebbles yonder. She lay back silent, a smile on her half open lips, her soft blue eyes moist. When Anne spoke to her, the voice sounded far-off. Some power, delicate and more vague than any dream, held her. Could they not leave her with it, in peace?

As they neared the city the doctor saw the lank figure of Professor Mears racing on before them, his light hair flying in the wind.

"Hello, Mears!" he called. "Let us drive you into town. Here is a seat beside my daughter."

Mildred roused herself, and made room for him beside her. The professor settled himself, well pleased. Anne was his companion, but he approved of the elder Miss Warrick. He felt her guileless, transparent character to be very sweet and restful. She was most anxious now to hear about his work.

"Yes," he responded to her soft questionings, "I talked to-day with several influential men; effectively, I hope. But capitalists are as shy of philanthropic schemes here as in the North."

"There is a Mr. Soudé here," timidly suggested Milly. "I hear that he has a wide newspaper influence, and large property. Is that true?"

"John Soudé, you mean. He could be of use in Louisiana! But that is too far South for a colony. The climate—" and he discussed climate in every phase while Milly listened with rapt attention.

When he had ended, she said, "Mr. Soudé's plantations are in Louisiana then? Cotton or sugar? I have heard that his wealth is something fabulous?"

"Oh, I don't think of buying land there. My field is in Kentucky."

"Assuredly, the first colony must be in Kentucky. Oh, if it only succeeds!" clasping her little hands. "Then you think," after a pause, "that the reports of this Mr. Soudé's wealth are exaggerated?"

"No, I fancy not. The plantations are on the Gulf. There was a Victor Soudé, a brilliant lawyer in New Orleans. I knew him at the Virginia springs. He ranked as a Crœsus then. He was killed in the war, I believe, and this lad is his son or nephew—heir probably, in either case."

Miss Warrick's eyes were wandering indifferently. "Now," she cried, when he paused, "tell me what men you can count on in Mobile."

They talked earnestly until they reached the Battle House. The professor then rushed away to find Major Patton and to ask him to remain in Mobile another week.

"Why, this morning you were eager to push on! What has happened?"

"Nothing. But it has been suggested to me that Mobile will probably be the largest seaport in the South, and that I can find employment here in the future for many workmen. I have still much to do here."

That night Doctor Warrick told his daughters that Professor Mears would detain the party a week longer in Mobile.

"I thought he would," said Milly quietly.

CHAPTER VIII

DURING the week that followed, Mr. Soudé met Miss Warrick at one or two dances. The plump little girl was, he decided, vapid and commonplace. In fact, John liked bold effects. He adored Hugo and Dumas; he used coarse perfumes; he cared for no music but that of a brass band; he often warmed his black costume with a red necktie or purple fez and nodded delighted approval as he looked in the glass. Naturally he preferred picturesque women; *poseurs* who could take and hold the centre of the stage. However, he danced once with Mildred and found her light in motion as a bird. But he saw that she was too timid and too young to make her way among these experienced matrons and maids with whom he flirted habitually, whispering dangerous nothings to each, his blood rising for the moment hot and thick in his veins.

"Why does that little Warrick girl muffle herself up to the chin?" M. Choteaud said one evening.

"Damnation! You would not have *her* undress like these others!" cried John. It was as if Louis had asked a child to sing an indecent song.

"The woman is nothing to you. Why do you attack me about her?" retorted Louis.

Soudé did not know why. It was a mere mascu-
line instinct. She was so helpless—·so altogether
a woman.

But it did not occur to him to dance with her
again; and, if she had left Mobile, he would have
forgotten her as soon as he would a dog that he
had noticed kindly.

In fact John was not a marrying man, nor a
man about whom there is any story worth the
telling. Some of his comrades in the New
Orleans clubs were, as one might say, perpetual
heroes. That was their *métier*. Dort, for
example—all the world knew of Dort's hopeless
passion; and Sennele, once a priest and now an
atheist; and D'Orveto, fighting his way up
against an incurable disease. These men played
out their dismal tragedy of life in full view of the
town, cheered by its sympathy or applause.

But John Soudé had no play to play. He was
as idle, happy-go-lucky a fellow as could be found
in the Gulf States. He had never been troubled
by a religious doubt in his head nor a keen emotion in his heart. Even as a motherless boy,
running wild with the negroes over the plantation, he had borne the diseases and discomforts
of childhood with the lazy indifference of a good-
humored dog, an indifference which might grow
out of high courage or brutal stupidity.

As for love—"I had a thousand grand passions
when I was young," he was used to say. "But
I am thirty-six now. I love all women alike."

Nothing could make him see ugly teeth or
tricky ways in any woman. At the Mardi Gras

balls he was just as likely to waltz with old fat Miss Lachean as with one of the *débutantes*.

Sometimes indeed, after dinner, he would tell the story of his grandfather, Mad Jean Latouche, who, finding that the woman he worshipped was listening to another lover, picked her up one day as she was walking in the street in Charleston, threw her into his gig, drove to the house of the nearest clergyman, called him out, and with one pistol at the head of the parson and another at the head of his bride, then and there married her.

"And I am told that it was a divinely happy marriage," John would say, thoughtfully. "He adored her, gentlemen."

Something in this story always fired his slow blood. If he could find an exquisite creature like that and win her in such fashion! Yet when his cousin, Miss Soudé, once asked him the truth of this old story, he denied that he knew it. It was not fit for her pure ears!

Sometimes he would ruminate vaguely on the chance of his marrying that rich Cuban widow, or a certain stout heiress whom he knew in Savannah. If he did that, he could always smoke the best cigars, and the dear old general could stop the mouths of that hungry pack of tradesmen.

But he was always ashamed when these mean fancies nibbled at his ordinary calm content, and regarded them as vulgar baits of the devil; just as he was sometimes tempted to call for made drinks instead of brandy or whiskey straight.

It was from M. Choteaud that Miss Warrick

gradually obtained the facts of Soudé's history.
He also gave her copies of John's letters in the
Picayune. She read one of them aloud to Anne
one morning—the account of the sudden death
of a child in a train, but broke down and could
not finish it.

Anne looked at her in amazement. Milly's
tears were always ready. But her sister had
never seen her sob in this fashion. She took the
paper and finished the story, amused at the faulty
grammar. But she too felt a lump in her throat
before she had finished it.

There was a lawn party that afternoon and a
dance at night at one of the large houses upon
the bay. Mr. Soudé arrived late, and found that
some of the guests had wandered out upon the
half-ruined galleries, and to the lawns sloping
down to the beach. The sun was hidden by a
silvery fog, a damp wind stirred the blossoms of
the magnolias and the veils of gray moss upon
the trees. There was a hush in the air, a sad
significance of decay under all the soft splendor,
which touched Soudé, who was easily moved by
the moods of nature. He wandered down alone
to the beach. In the far distance the heaving
plane of water was covered by dull mists, out of
which white sails flashed and disappeared. Suddenly he started forward.

A woman was walking out upon a rotten pier,
her eyes fixed upon the distant sails, unconscious
that the timbers were crumbling beneath her.
The water below was deep and slimy.

John climbed out on a beam below her.

" A WOMAN WAS WALKING OUT UPON A ROTTEN PIER "

"Don't look down!" he shouted. "Give me your hand! Quick! There!"

He caught her just as the timbers fell with a crash into the water.

"Why, bless my soul! Miss Warrick! What on earth—? Don't cry! You are safe. You poor child!" He seated her and stood between her and the house. He wanted to take care of the poor little thing himself. He could hardly keep from stroking her soft fair hair.

At last she controlled herself and looked up. "You have saved my life."

"Nonsense! Nothing of the kind! You might have been a little wet." He dropped down on the grass beside her. There was an awkward silence. He was thinking, as he watched her askance, "She thinks I saved her life. And so I did. Very cleverly done, too, John, my boy!" He said aloud, formally, "I hardly hoped to meet you again, Miss Warrick."

"No; but I hoped to see you." She was making a great effort to control her voice: her little clenched hands rested on her knees, her anxious eyes were fixed on his. "There is something I wish you to do, Mr. Soudé. Very important."

"Me? Now, what can that be?" He smiled kindly down on her upturned face. What a sweet, babyish creature she was!

"I wish you," she said earnestly, "to come to the old town in Pennsylvania where we live. To write about it. It is an historic place. And the hills are very beautiful. I have read your letters, Mr. Soudé."

"Oh! That nonsense!" The big fellow grew hot from head to foot. He shouted out a laugh, and instantly was dumb and solemn.

"Oh, yes! I have read them," said Milly, with a grave little nod. "Why should not our hills be given a place in literature? That last letter, Mr. Soudé! That story of the baby! I used to think the death of Paul Dombey the finest thing in the English language, until—that dear baby!" She stopped, with a sob.

John shuffled uneasily. His heart gave great thumps of delight. "Ah, that little incident?" he managed to say with dignified composure. "It was true. Any body could have described it."

"Any body?" She turned her mild, reproachful eyes on him. Tears stood in them. A woman's tears always unnerved Soudé, and it was his own genius that had drawn these from the child. Child—yes! But what an intellect she had! What unerring perception! He stared at the drop of salt water creeping down into her round chin. Some day a man would kiss the tears from her sweet face, he thought, a strange tremor passing through him.

Soudé had always spoken of his work with a shy sensitiveness. He was not sure whether he had earned immortality or only made a fool of himself.

But now while Milly kept up a gentle patter of questions, certainty blazed upon him. This fire within him was genius! He stood upon the same plane as Shakspeare, Gayarré, Christian Reid!

And this innocent girl had been the first to detect it.

Do not set John down as a vain fool. He had put into these poor letters and verses his secret thoughts—his best. The woman who understood them was no alien. She trod a hidden path straight to his heart.

They walked side by side, for a long time, under the live-oaks. The sunset threw a daffodil glow above the mist; at their side the waves muttered to them, like cautious whispers: from a ship far out on the bay came the melancholy notes of a French horn.

Mr. Soudé was skilled in flirtation with all kinds of women, from school-girls to hardened widows. But it did not once occur to him that this Northern girl could be complimented or wooed. He felt such a strange respect for her that, when he talked to her, his tongue grew stiff; his arms and legs lumbering and heavy.

CHAPTER IX

THERE was to be a dance in the evening, and the girls flocked to their chambers to change their gowns. Doctor Warrick stopped Anne as she hurried past him in the hall.

"David Plunkett has come," he said anxiously. "I met him at the hotel. He heard we were in Mobile, and ran down from New York on his special car."

"Just what one would expect from him," said Anne angrily. "I shall not tell Milly that he is here. Let her have her dance in comfort."

"Why should David make her dance uncomfortable? If a woman dislikes the presence of a man, she can easily dismiss him," said her father.

"Yes. But Milly——" Anne checked herself. She was not at all sure that Milly would deal so promptly with the young man whose wealth gave him such large space in the world.

She passed on to her room. Milly joined her, and sweetly declining the aid of the chattering mulatto maids, shut the door upon them.

"They would tell all Mobile that we have no maid of our own," she said.

"What if they did?" said Anne. "But I do not want them. I never wish to see one of the color again." She perched herself lazily in the window-seat, while Milly rapidly unpacked their satchel.

"I had great hopes of the negroes before I came South," continued Anne. "I thought of teaching in the freedmen's schools at Port Royal—— You did not know that, Mildred?"

"Oh, yes, I did. Pins? Yes, here they are."

"I am wretchedly disappointed in them," continued Anne. "A human being just given freedom ought to be full of the highest ambition. But a good fat meal and finery—that is all they think of."

"Really, you have not spoken to a dozen of them since you came to the South," said Mildred placidly. "When you were twelve, you intended to go out to India, as a missionary. You wanted to see the temples and queer dresses. A good many other nervous women want adventure in a picturesque country and think it is a Heavenly Call to preach the Gospel," she said with a laugh, shaking out her snowy ball-dress. "Papa told me yesterday that you wanted to go into the freedmen's schools. He was miserable enough. But I said, 'Don't worry. She has been planning heroic flights since she was born. But when the time comes, down she falls flat.'"

Anne laughed, but said nothing. If she had fallen when she had tried to rise, it was the fall that hurt her, not Milly's little gibes. How could poor little Milly understand?

The next moment she jumped from her perch. "Just look at the carving of this bed," she cried excitedly. "And this crucifix! I was told that the mistress of this house six years ago was the owner of a thousand slaves. She has not a dollar now. I wish papa would spend the winter in Mobile. I love these Southern women—they are so thoroughbred, so helpless. I know I could teach them our practical ways."

"Anne, you have not brought the waist of your dress!" interrupted Milly, in dismay.

Anne ran to her, held up the crimson skirt and stared at it. "Too bad! Too bad!" she said, her lips quivering. "Well, I don't care for the dance. I'll sit here until you are ready to go home."

"Nonsense! Wait, let me think," said Miss Warrick. She did not scold. She never had scolded in her life, and besides, nothing that Anne did ever surprised her.

"That black silk fits you exquisitely," she said anxiously. "What a noble figure you have, child!" She passed her hand caressingly over her sister's shoulders. "If I had any waist at all! Sit down, I will put your hair into high puffs. And for your neck——"

Anne pulled out some fresh linen.

"Collar and cuffs at a dance! Absurd! I brought that old lace fichu. I can arrange it as a high ruff. You will look like Mary Stuart."

Anne smiled complacently into the glass. She was quite willing to look like Mary Stuart. Milly skilfully rolled her dark hair about her face with many affectionate pats and admiring nods.

But—the lace?

She had intended that lace to give the final touch of meaning to her own clinging drapery. So much might depend on her looks, to-night of all nights! She finished her work, and surveyed her sister's head with genuine admiration.

"Ah, you dear thing!" she said, kissing her. "You can wear the linen collar, after all, Anne."

"Very well," said Anne, pinning it on awry.

Milly was dumb with anxiety as she dressed herself. Anne watched her with amazement rushing nervously about, for Miss Warrick was a reticent woman, even in her motions. No human being ever had guessed what Milly thought of Milly. She was dissatisfied with herself now. She knotted the curly hair high, and lowered it to her neck. She trailed roses over her breast and threw them away. At last she lifted the candles high and breathlessly scanned herself in the mirror.

"Ah! how stout and vulgar!" she said, shivering.

Mrs. Dane tapped at the door. "Come, girls! Oh, my dear!" surveying Milly with delight. "You certainly are an exquisite creature, Mildred. Heavens, Anne! Black and linen! Why did you let her make herself such an object?"

"Oh, come! Let us go down. I will explain presently," Milly said, running toward the stairway. Then she shrank behind Mrs. Dane, lingering. She never had been diffident for a minute in her life. But now she was afraid. She panted for breath.

Doctor Warrick met them at the foot of the

staircase. Anne went with her father into the ball-room, as unconscious of the observant crowd as if they were trunks of trees, but Milly clung to Mrs. Dane's arm.

"One minute, cousin Julia. Give me a minute."

"Yes, come aside. I must tell you. David Plunkett is in the room. He found that you were here and asked me to bring him."

"To bring him?" repeated Milly in a dazed tone. "Here?"

"Yes. It is a bold move. He is very much in earnest, Mildred,"—looking at her curiously, as they entered the room. "He makes his money, I hear, by bold movements. *Toujours l'audace* usually wins in finance—or in love."

But Milly, cool on the instant, turned from her to meet her hostess and made no answer. M. Choteaud and some other men crowded around her.

Milly smiled sweetly up in their faces, but her fierce little brain was busy elsewhere.

There was the hideous creature in the doorway, eying her, as he might a horse he thought of buying. Cousin Julia would be glad to do the selling. She looked at Mrs. Dane and hated her. She was a worldly, wicked woman, who cared for nothing but money!

Money was nothing in this life, Mildred told herself in her dumb rage—nothing!

A soft, pleasant warmth crept over the little woman; her eyes glowed. There was no need that she should be sold, thank God! At home they had enough—enough!

Who would care for luxuries when they could have *that* which was coming to her soon? She knew that it was coming. Why, a woman could live in a hut, if—— The men buzzed around her, but she saw only a look which once had fallen on her. It seemed as if she had been all of her life waiting for that look. If he would come now—if he would dance with her! Milly felt that she could die to-morrow just to have him touch her once and know that he belonged to her—to her.

At last!

He was coming in! Milly turned her back on the door and in a moment floated away in a waltz, smiling indifferently on him as she passed.

CHAPTER X

MR. SOUDÉ was startled to find a crowd of vassals about Miss Warrick. He had looked upon her as his own discovery.

He was staring at them angrily when Louis touched him. "Let us be off to Orleans to-morrow, John. There is nothing to keep us here."

"No. I'm ready."

"How well that little Northern girl dresses up to her character! Lace and roses. You never see her in jetty armor or tailor-made gowns. Her curly head and thick lashes make me feel as if I must stroke her, like any other little furry, stupid creature."

"Stupid?" Soudé laughed. But he would not discuss her with poor Louis. He must bid her good-by, if he were going to Orleans in the morning. But the sight of that crowd of men around her shook his decision about going back to Orleans in the morning.

Not being able to come near her he went to her father, who was in a corner looking over some engravings. He found a singular charm in the little man's prattle about epidemics and a vegetable diet, though it reached him as through a fog. Ha! what was that he was saying?

"And if you should come to the North, you

will find plenty of material for your pen in Phila-
delphia. Birthplace of the Nation, you know.
We live in a suburban town. A shabby old
Colonial house, but you will find a welcome in it."

"I thank you," Soudé said stiffly, bowing low.
He was amazed. Why had he been chosen out
of the mob of dancing, brandy-drinking young
Southerners for this favor? Had she prompted
her father to—— Did the girl really care for
him so much? He glanced at her, on fire with
delight and conceit and some other passion which
he did not recognize.

"Dear child! As innocent as a babe! But
really—a Northern woman?" he thought, biting
his mustache. He turned again eagerly to the
doctor. Heretofore he had thought his father's
friends, the old French cotton planters on the
Gulf, the finest gentlemen in the world. But this
little man, with his bristling white whiskers and
military air, was, John thought, the most patrician
figure that he had ever seen. He heard the
doctor urge a dozen other Mobilians with their
families to spend next summer with him, and
though Soudé secretly felt snubbed, his respect
for him increased.

He lent an attentive ear as the doctor talked
of the engravings, handling them tenderly, as a
mother would her infant.

"Ah, how satisfactory these are, Mr. Soudé!
Masterly lines there! You have some fine collec-
tions in the South. In Richmond I saw an undoubted example of the early work of Vertrie
—undoubted."

"I know very little about those black-and-white things," said John. "A good portrait in oils, now—I have a friend, an amateur, who can knock you off a likeness in half an hour."

"Oh, yes!" said the doctor hastily. "You like color. You are of the age to like it. *You* live. What have you to do with faded etchings? Leave them to us old fellows, who—do not live."

Soudé stared at him, bewildered. "Oh? certainly! I suppose," after a pause, "your own collection is very fine?"

"No. I only own one good print. That is a treasure. I am a poor man, Mr. Soudé. But my love for engravings brings me in great pleasure. All the dealers in the cities know me, and when they have rare proofs to sell send me catalogues. Then I go to see them, and mark on the catalogues the ones I should buy if I had the money. It is very pleasant! I always keep the catalogues."

"Say, doc!" interrupted a young man who had been standing unnoticed beside him; "show me the catalogue next time there is a sale, and by gosh! you shall have the pick of them!"

"Thank you, David," said the doctor, with the flicker of a smile. "Mr. Soudé, may I make Mr. Plunkett known to you? One of our foremost business men in Pennsylvania."

The doctor a moment afterward extricated himself from the crowd, and left the young men together.

Plunkett was a huge, shapeless lad, badly dressed by a London tailor in the extreme fashion. As he waddled to a seat, something about him suggested to John that Nature had started to make a man and left the job incomplete. His neat little feet were too small for the mass they carried; a faint line of down struggled irresolutely over his wide upper lip; now and then a manly, sonorous tone broke into his piping treble, or a look of keen intelligence peered out of his watery eyes like cray-fish from a pool, to disappear suddenly and leave unmeaning vacancy.

"Hoh!" he said, nodding kindly as he looked after the doctor. "The old man undervalues himself. The Warricks are poor, but what of that? Money isn't the only valuable goods in the market, I say. They have had scholarship and gentility for generations, and I don't rate them things low, sir. No, I don't! Though of course a sharp-witted American with a good bank account can afford to do without them." As he spoke he clawed complacently at his flabby chin. "I for one appreciate them in the old doc, sir, or in any man. You take Dave Plunkett's word, there's things of more value than money in the world."

Mr. Soudé paid no attention to him. He was watching his chance to penetrate the black ring of men around a little white figure at the other side of the room.

"Some of your Southern women are infernally pretty, d'ye know?" continued Plunkett. "Yes, I think so, really."

"They are grateful to you," said Soudé, scowling at him.

"A little lean, hey? Too much chalk and

rouge on 'em, too. But they light up well, hu! hu!"

Plunkett always ended with a fat, complacent chuckle, which gave you the impression that he was chewing and gorging the subject. After a leisurely survey of the women who lighted up well, he turned, and seeing his companion's fixed gaze, followed it.

He gave an annoyed grunt, and his eyes suddenly had the watchful stare of a dog that had hidden a bone which he feared would be taken from him.

They were playing a waltz. Mr. Soudé crossed the room. A flash of angry intelligence glinted into Plunkett's eyes. "It's Milly! I hit the bull's-eye! He's going straight to her!" he said to himself. He stood in the way of the dancers, his hands thrust into his pockets, staring at Milly. Another man would have concealed his dismay, but David never concealed any thing. He pursued his object as a hound its prey, unconscious of lookers-on.

Soudé did not ask Milly to dance. When she glanced shyly up at him, he had a mad impulse to snatch this innocent child to his arms and carry her away out of sight of the coarse crowd. He stammered a word or two and stood still, looking at her. At least he would not go spinning around with her before this miserable mob!

"It is very quiet on the veranda," he said. "Will you walk through this dance with me?"

She laid her hand timidly on his arm, and they

"PLUNKETT DREW A STARTLED BREATH"

went out. As they walked to and fro, on one side were the windows of the ball-room, with their flashes of color and light, and on the other the heavy night, with the mysterious waste of star-lit water quivering yonder on the horizon.

David Plunkett stationed himself on one of the windows, where he could catch glimpses of the two figures passing in the darkness. Once the light fell full upon them. Plunkett drew a startled breath. He had never seen Milly's face look like that, so happy, so—honest. "The little devil's telling the truth now, for once in her life," thought David. What hold could this strange man have on her?

"He is coarse and dingy as his own mulattoes," was his verdict, glancing complacently at his own pasty, broad face in a mirror. Then he looked from the reflection of his bulky, dwarfish body to the shapely figure disappearing in the shadows.

"Dave Plunkett has a better card than figger to play," he thought, with a grim smile. "Let her have her fun out to-night! When it comes to marryin' she'll tramp him down as if he was a spider—if he's poor."

Meanwhile partners whose names were on her card searched wildly for Miss Warrick, but she was not to be found. David saw that she and Soudé were sitting in a hidden recess of the veranda. He caught the man's tones in a long monologue. Milly was silent. Such an escapade by the correct, conventional Miss Warrick was equal to an outbreak of madness in another woman.

Was she mad ?

David's countenance grew more leaden in hue. "I'm not afraid," he told himself. "After all these years! All Luxborough believes that she will marry me when I ask her. What right has she to fool with that man, damn her!"

He went to the supper-room and drank a glass of brandy, but it did not warm him. His blood was like ice.

Milly was in the ball-room when he went back, chattering gayly to Mr. Soudé, her blushing, sweet face aglow with delight. John observed that when she saw Plunkett she stammered, and held her roses to her lips, looking over them at him with a sudden terror. But David made no motion to come near her, and in a few moments she left the room with her father.

Soudé turned to watch David with jealous curiosity. He saw that the huge lad was treated with homage by the Northerners. Old men bowed respectfully when he spoke to them, and women, when they danced or sang, glanced at him, for approval.

" Who is that brute ?" he asked Choteaud.

" Brute indeed! But I hear that he is a suitor of Miss Warrick's, and that he is worth thirty millions."

Soudé laughed. "And what would she care for his thirty millions ?" he said.

CHAPTER XI

ANNE, as she went into the ball-room that evening, had a sudden access of disgust at fashionable life. What a decorated pen it was, full of
adult human beings capering absurdly about!
Milly laughed at her wish to teach the freedmen
or the pariahs in India: but Milly never had
understood her. Professor Mears recognized the
immortal longings in her. He was a man: men
had the chance to make great sacrifices, to rise to
great heights in life.

The room was filled with smiling people who
all knew each other. She stood beside her father
behind a large table covered with engravings.

Now, in spite of her spiritual ambitions, Anne,
since she was a baby, had expected to be crowned
sometime a queen of love and beauty. What
if she were homely and awkward ? Sometime,
somehow, there would come for her a sunburst
of triumph when all the world would wonder.
She liked to fancy crowds of lovers abased before
her, and she turning haughtily away.

It might be to-night——

The violins played a waltz. The other girls
were led out by eager partners.

" Nobody is going to ask me to dance! "

Her heart gave great throbs, her face burned.
She fancied that the Southern girls, for whom

her heart had ached with sympathy just now, glanced at her with an amazed pity in their eyes, as she stood fumbling the prints. Anne caught fragments of their conversation with their partners. How insipid it was!

"I am not stupid! I am a clever woman!" she thought indignantly. "I know more than most of these men. Why do they neglect me? Am I so hideous?" glancing in a mirror at the dark, eager face. She tried to drag up Epictetus to comfort her.

"What matters any thing that can happen to me, if my soul is above it?"

But her soul just now would have none of Epictetus. She looked at her sister surrounded by a crowd of men. She nodded gayly to Anne, who smiled bravely back. Thank Heaven, Milly was not neglected!

"Why are you not dancing, my dear?" said the doctor. "Young blood should be young."

"This child's blood is young." It was Professor Mears who spoke, smiling kindly down on her.

Anne grew red, guiltily. If this wisest of men knew that she was wretched because nobody had asked her to dance! She knew that he had been born heir to a life of luxury and ease, and had chosen to spend it in hard labor for others. She burned with contempt of herself. But high purposes nauseated her to-night. Professor Mears, his mouth a little open, was standing, his pale, vacant eyes fixed upon her sad, pleading face. The thought came to him again—what a companion would this sensitive creature be to him when he was fagged to death by bureaux of charities!

Brooke Calhoun saw some such meaning in his foggy gaze. He suddenly crossed the room. "Will you come out with me to supper, Anne ? " he asked abruptly, offering his arm.

Anne took it, her eyes sparkling. "Oh, yes, indeed!" she said. Then the recollection that this man was obnoxious to her put her joy to flight. No doubt he came because he pitied her: he had seen that no girl in the room was so neglected as she.

"Have you met any of these lovely Southern girls ? " she asked, hesitating.

"I don't wish to meet any body but you," he said simply. "Will you have oysters ? "

He did pity her; he had seen how she was ignored by the men—had noted angrily her dingy gown and crooked collar. "Poor little girl! I wish her mother were here!" he thought, with a tug at his heart.

He found a table in a corner and placed her beside it, brought a foot-stool and shawl to keep away the draught. Then he heaped her plate and, sitting opposite, watched her contentedly. The honest fellow liked to feed any creature that he loved. And this was his little playfellow—his own, for a minute, for the first time in many years.

Anne was warm and happy. She had not known that she was so hungry. She had never been so taken care of—like a helpless little queen.

Brooke told a great many funny stories, at which they both laughed till the tears came, and then they discussed certain dogs and horses dear to them both years ago. High purposes, pariahs, and Epictetus all retreated out of sight. She forgot that this man had sold his birthright for a mess of pottage. This was Brooke, her old comrade again—Brooke.

But he was not eating any thing, she saw anxiously. And the drive would be long into town. She sprinkled salt on his oysters and herself put the sugar into his coffee, and as she reached forward to give the cup to him, it flashed upon her how homelike was the little table, with its cups for two—she looked up, red and trembling, and met Brooke's laughing eyes.

In old times they had an odd habit of thinking together. She began to talk incoherently of Professor Mears's great schemes. Brooke did not seem to listen. His eyes shone, looking at something which she did not see. It was the little breakfast room at the farm, with the fire crackling and the sun shining in at the windows and the little table laid—for two.

Could it ever be? Was it possible? Why was it not possible? He answered her vaguely, scarcely knowing what she said:

"A wise man? Oh, yes! Young, too, to have achieved so much."

"I wonder," said Anne, moving restlessly under his steady gaze, "why he never married? A woman who could throw herself into his work would be of great use in the world."

"Use?" Brooke laughed. "If I were Professor Mears I would not marry a woman to be a charitable agent. She should be just—my wife."

It was the commonplace idea of a commonplace man; the kind of idea which Anne always trampled underfoot with fierce contempt. But now she rose unsteadily, pale and breathless. Brooke had not looked at her; yet it seemed, when he spoke, as if he had taken her in his arms and kissed her.

He led her out into the corridor. He did not know what he was doing nor where he was going; but he felt that of all his warm, comfortable life, this was the moment most keen with happiness. He was possessed with the thought of the old fields and the old house at home—the pleasant centre of this pleasant world. If he could seize her and put her into it for life! Had the good God any such wonderful thing as that in keeping for him?

The new delirious thrill of passion which shook him was, it is true, mixed with thoughts of the house and cornfields and cows, but Anne did not know that, which was perhaps as well.

He halted beside a window, poring hungrily over her face in the moonlight.

"My little comrade! you were gone from me so long," he said. "It has been lonely."

"You could not have missed me," she faltered. "You had your brother and your work."

"Yes, of course. I have been very happy with Ned and the farm. I'm afraid," looking at her anxiously, "that you don't appreciate Ned?"

"Oh, thoroughly!" said Anne, with a short laugh.

"If you don't like him it is because you don't understand him. I hope I can make you know him some day, if——"

He did not finish the sentence.

"I think," said Anne, trying to speak carelessly, "I understand Edward—and you."

"Perhaps so. Your intuitions were keen, even as a child. You were appallingly clever. I have always been afraid that you would outgrow me, do you know?" His dark face burned; he leaned over her. "In all the years that you were gone, I used to wonder whether, when you came back, you would give me again——"

She drew back, looking around to escape. If she could fly and hide somewhere! She trembled with dread. Yet she did not move an inch. What was it he asked her to give? What?

Her eyes, her whole life, hung upon his lips. She could not breathe, waiting for him to speak. She saw, far off in the bay, a white sail flicker up out of the mist and slowly disappear; but still there was silence.

Until an hour ago Calhoun had never known what it was he wanted from this woman. But he knew now. He had needed it when he was a boy—when he was a man. Bare and poor enough life had been without it.

It was coming now! She would give it to him. He saw it in her eyes. He would take her to the dear old farm—he would be her drudge—her slave——

The honest fellow choked when he tried to speak, the water stood in his eyes.

"Anne," he said, laughing hoarsely, "you see. I am as blundering and slow as ever."

"Calhoun!" called a voice behind him. "Ah, here you are!" David Plunkett came down the corridor. "Here is a telegram which has just been sent out from town for you. No bad news, I hope? Open it, man! From New Orleans— Ned, probably."

David, who always had a childish curiosity about the affairs of others, watched Brooke keenly as he read the despatch.

"What is it? Is he dead?"

"No. He—needs me. I must go to him at once. If there is a train to-night——"

His eyes were fixed on Anne as he led her back to the ball-room. She was not deceived by his mechanical answer. He had had a blow. It had struck hard and deep. "Deeper than any thought of me," she thought bitterly, as she hurried to her father.

Brooke stood motionless a moment, looking steadily at her. Beneath his trouble he was in a dull rage with himself. He was so paltering and slow! He had always been slow. It was unstable, feather-headed Ned, after all, who had always made his life; pushed him here and there —as now. He turned, without a word of farewell, and left the house. Plunkett followed him.

"Is Edward dead, Calhoun?" he said.

Brooke handed him the despatch. David mumbled it over, half aloud:

9

"I have broken my promise. I have ruined you. To-night ends all."

He folded the yellow slip carefully and gave it back.

"Been gambling, eh?"

"I don't know. What does that matter? He means suicide."

"Stuff! Threatened men live long, especially when they threaten themselves. But you must go to him, or he'll make himself the talk of New Orleans somehow. There is no train to-night, but my car is here. I'll send you down by special. Not a word! Easiest thing in the world. Brace up, Calhoun."

"I've neglected the boy lately. I've not written regularly——"

"More likely you've been too indulgent. Ned's a shallow fellow, and he needs a tight rein. Here's my trap. I'll drive you in."

Brooke had a vague comfort in the presence of the shrewd, huge lad, who, whenever he saw man or beast in trouble, was the kindest of human beings, though he usually drove the victim mad with fuss and dogmatism.

They bowled along the wide shell road without speaking.

"Ned's a sheer idiot as regards money," Plunkett said at last. "I would not lend him a dollar. But if *you* need any, Brooke, telegraph me. I'll see you through the scrape. And," he added in a louder voice, cracking the whip pompously, "I'll not charge you one darned cent of interest, either. Heh? What d'ye say?"

"I shall not need it. I have property to cover Ned's losses. But I'll not forget that you offered it, Dave."

Special trains do not take the road at a moment's notice. Hours passed while Plunkett gave orders and Brooke paced up and down the platform at the station.

Doctor Warrick and John Soudé came to him, but he scarcely understood what they said.

"I hear that your brother is ill or in trouble?" Soudé asked anxiously. "Is he in New Orleans? Has he left the Reve des Eaux?"

"Yes. I suspect that he has incurred heavy debts in the city."

"Oh, is that all? He was playing high. That was why my father urged him to go to the plantation. All fair and among gentlemen, you know, but our men play better than Edward."

"I am going to satisfy them," replied Calhoun irritably.

"Of course," said Soudé, smiling. "One can give a cursed tradesman the go by, but debts of honor must be paid, more's the pity!"

Doctor Warrick drew Brooke aside and excitedly pressed into his hand a hundred-dollar bill. "Take it, my dear boy. I wish I had more," he whispered. "I can borrow from Mears until I reach home. They cannot have fleeced the poor lad of more than that."

Brooke thrust it back. "No—no! It isn't money—if I find him alive"—he gasped.

Plunkett, the next moment, hurried him into the car and waved good-by while the train steamed down the track.

"If he finds him alive?" stammered the doctor, staring after the vanishing car. "Has poor Edward been driven to despair? Do you think he will attempt his life?"

"No such good luck!" replied David promptly. "Go home, sir, and to bed in peace. Ned Calhoun will devil his brother until he is gray. That sort live long."

Mr. Soudé offered his arm to the doctor, and led him homeward with the most reverent deference. He, too, took a consolatory view of the situation.

"I cannot imagine," he said gravely, "that any rational man would end his life because he could not pay his debts: and Edward Calhoun impressed me as a most rational and practical man."

Meanwhile Brooke was whirled along through the gathering darkness.

The chance that he would find his brother dead had stunned him at first. But when he had time to think, this chance, even to Brooke, seemed improbable. Ned was one of those men who delight to dance the skeletons in their lives daily before their friends, and he had threatened suicide ever since his first whipping at school.

"I'm not really afraid of *that*," Brooke said half aloud, glancing miserably around the empty car. "But—ruin?"

There was in fact but one way to pay the debts in New Orleans.

"The farm must go: the farm must go." He said this over a dozen times, trying to make himself understand it. He got up, and walked unsteadily up and down the car.

"The farm must go. After that, Ned and I must depend on my labor from day to day."

Hitherto, Brooke had believed in a brilliant future always at hand for his brother—fame, fortune. To-night, this fond dream vanished like a wrack of cloud. He saw Ned as he was, a dead weight, to be lifted and carried to the end—or to be left to perish by the road.

He walked up and down, up and down, looking at the ugly facts steadily. Brooke had no sickly love of martyrdom. If he could win that dear child yonder, and take her to the old house which was almost as dear to him as she, no man on God's earth would be more content.

It would only hurt himself if he gave her up. She had but a childish friendship for him. Professor Mears was more of a companion for her. He stopped for a moment, and then fell again into his slow walk.

No, he could not do both. He could not put the burden of Ned's life on any woman's shoulders.

He sat down, wiping the cold sweat from his face. "It must be Ned and I alone," he said, with a long breath. "There will be no place for any other comrade."

When the train rolled into the station at New Orleans, a lank figure rushed up to it, and a pale unshaven face was thrust into the windows.

"Thank God, you have come!" Edward cried, wringing his hands. "Twice I have had the muzzle of this pistol on my forehead, but I could not die without your forgiveness."

"Give me the pistol now, Ned." Brooke uncocked it and dropped it into his pocket. They walked out of the station, Edward glancing wildly from side to side, and muttering that there were "other ways—other ways."

"How fat and composed you look!" he broke out presently, savagely. "The same complacent smile you had at home, while I've been in hell—hell!"

"We'll try and bring things straight now, Ned," said Brooke quietly. "It doesn't matter how either of us look. Where is your room? We must go somewhere to talk over this matter."

"You're in a devilish hurry to look into my shortcomings," said Edward, with a bitter laugh. "One thing you must understand. These men must be paid. They are gentlemen. I want no sanctimonious cant either—or trying to dodge a gambling debt. You must lend me plenty of money. You needn't be afraid. I'll pay you." His voice rose to a shrill shriek.

They were crossing Canal Street. The fruiterers, arranging their baskets on the banquette, stopped to listen.

"They shall be paid. Come on."

"How will you raise the money?"

"I will sell the farm."

"Thank God for that! I hate that old house, and the cursed cows and pigs." In a few minutes

"'GIVE ME THE PISTOL NOW, NED'"

he said, "Forgive me, Brooke. I know you like the place. Mortgage it. I'll pay you the money to redeem it as soon as I get to work. One picture will buy a dozen such farms."

He walked a few paces and stopped again. "I've had no money since Tuesday," he stammered. "I'm faint. If I had some food, I should not be so nearly mad."

"Hungry! Great Heavens! Come, boy, come!" But when Brooke with a shocked face dragged him toward a café, Ned hesitated.

"Mme. Eugènie's is just around the corner," he said. "You really ought to taste her crab patés. This way, Brooke."

When they were seated at a dainty table, a pot of flowers in the centre, the French waiter bowing, menu in hand, Ned flirted his napkin open, with a sudden beaming smile.

"That place you were plunging into was good enough. But I do like sparkling glass and roses, and all this sort of thing. It's weak, I suppose, but I can't help it."

"No," said Brooke. "You can't help it. It was born in you. I understand."

And he too smiled.

CHAPTER XII

According to their consciences, Mr. Franciscus
and Mrs. Dane were faithful guardians to Doctor
Warrick's daughters. The doctor himself, they
regarded as a babe in the ways of the world; a
babe clothed upon only with a few paltry hobbies
and rags of useless knowledge.

"Samuel," Mrs. Dane often said to her friends,
"is a mere pawn on the chess-board of life that
never will reach the kings' row. But Paul and
I are heartily fond of the girls. We will spare
neither thought nor effort to establish them upon
solid ground for this life and the next."

By solid ground she meant marriages into old
Luxborough families; incomes that would warrant
a pair of horses and a man-servant; and a mem-
bership for themselves and their descendants in
the Monthly Thursday Club. To ensure them
these enduring good things Mrs. Dane and her
cousin Paul had spent money as well as time and
thought. But of that they never spoke. Naturally, however, they kept a keen watch over the
affairs of Mildred. .Mrs. Dane wrote frequent
reports to Mr. Franciscus.

Three days after the ball she sat in her parlor
at the Battle House, scribbling one of these
bulletins.

"We are likely to remain in Mobile during this week. Mildred has persuaded Mr. Mears that it is a good base of operations for him. I fancy she does not know why she delights in Mobile. She is as unconscious and naïve in her first passion as a girl of fifteen. She and young Soudé live in each other, regardless of all lookers-on. Milly is oddly altered by this new flirtation, or love, whatever it be. She has became frank, talkative, and even quarrelsome. She will have nothing to say to poor Plunkett, who, in his turn, says nothing, but bides his time. Really, Paul, the idea of any woman's marrying that monster is quite too terrible!

"This Mr. Soudé is, I hear, of old French Louisiana stock and, they assure me, has large estates—probably in Spain! It is impossible to find out any thing with certainty, here, on questions of income. These Southern people pride themselves on their lack of visible means of support—especially if they lost them during the war. I am certain it never has occurred to this young man to enquire what *dot* Doctor Warrick can give to his daughter. Do tell me, Paul, precisely, what Mrs. Joyce's condition is. Of course, I pray God to grant her long life. Anyhow, I hope she may have time to repent. But Milly has done her duty to that old woman, and deserves her reward. When she does go to a better world— or some world—poor Milly can afford to marry her long-legged Louisianian in his old-fashioned clothes. Perhaps Doctor Weems could give you a hint as to Eliza Joyce's health just now. I

confess I am most anxious about Milly. With
her beauty and 'faculty,' as the Yankees call it,
and a good income, she could take a foremost
place in any society. I like a girl to be able to
please herself in her husband, if possible, too.
Being Milly's godmother, I feel responsible for
her future. Try to see Weems, soon."

She folded the letter and, as she sealed it,
glanced at Mildred and Soudé, who sat on the
opposite side of the room. John was supposed
to be reading the morning paper aloud, but in
reality he was watching Milly's fingers as she
sewed.

Neither John Soudé nor Mildred could have
recalled the doings of the last few days. There
had been walks and sails on this unreal earth and
sea, an enchanted air about them, a hazy cloud
of witnesses around. That was all. It had never
occurred to Soudé to compliment or make love
to Mildred. He never thought of love. She was
his friend. Her whispered questions touched his
most secret thought; her soft eyes looked upon
his naked soul. She believed him to be a Shakspeare or Bacon, and John slowly began to believe
that he was both. She raised him to a throne
and sat down at his feet. From day to day he
grew more delirious with this homage, and the
pure contact with his one little worshipper. A
brilliant warmth and triumph had suddenly suffused his life—as for to-morrow he did not think
of that at all. Probably he might go North with
Doctor Warrick and spend the summer in Penn-

sylvania. Men of genius were appreciated there. He might spend every summer in Pennsylvania.

But he went no farther. Marriage, for years, had not occurred to him as a definite factor in his life. It did not occur to him now. He was so happy that it seemed to him that he had always been a cautious old man and had just become a boy. He tried awkwardly now to show Mildred this deep content in his soul.

"If I ever write a great poem," he said, "it will be your doing, Miss Warrick. You have brought me such a divine courage. I wish you could tell my cousin Theresa what you think I can do. She always laughs at me."

Mildred's delicate brows contracted, but she said nothing.

"I wish you could see Theresa. She is considered to be the most charming woman in the South."

"I have heard you say so—many times," Milly replied, with a sharp laugh. "All of your Southern women apparently have been born into the superlative degree. They either are dazzling beauties or 'brilliant wits,' or ' they have finer voices than Nilsson.' "

"But you!" said Soudé, his sultry eyes kindling. "What are they all to you? Do you know my whole life seems to have been a kind of stairway up to this day when I know you? I often wonder what Theresa will say when she sees *you*."

Mildred was silent, and Mrs. Dane, having finished her letter, began to talk to them of the last new novel. Mrs. Dane, like other clever women in Luxborough, liked to fire off opinions as impromptu, which she had polished ready for use in the sanctity of her own chamber. Mr. Soudé listened courteously, his half-shut eyes on Mildred's quick white fingers. Presently, having disposed of the novel, she summed up Mr. Mears and his work.

"That good man, I suppose, is one pure flame of holy zeal," she said, "but really he kindles no answering heat in *me*. I found poor Ned Calhoun's work much more interesting. Oh, of course, you can argue, Mildred, that it is a nobler mission to change the human garbage which all Europe dumps into Castle Garden into good citizens than to cover a bare canvas with a pretty picture. I can only say it does not interest me. Besides, Mr. Mears is jerking the work of civilizing roughs out of the hands of the Church. I cannot think the salvation of people's souls wholly a matter of wages and ventilation and drainage."

"I know nothing about Mr. Mears," said Milly placidly. "He has chosen Anne as his adviser. It is the queerest co-partnership. He rushes to her with every difficult point, and she takes the topmost idea in her brain and gives it to him, and away he goes, ecstatic. And you know, Cousin Julia, nobody can tell what idea will be uppermost in Anne's brain."

David Plunkett, who had entered the room while they were talking, chuckled. "Mears may choose her as permanent counsellor," he said.

"Nonsense!" exclaimed Mrs. Dane. She sat

rubbing her forefinger anxiously over her chin, and said: "There is nothing ridiculous in Mr. Mears's charitable pursuits. In spite of them he has always been well received in society in Luxborough."

"Really?" said David, with a shrug. "And you're exclusive in your little town, ma'am—you're exclusive! Why, Mrs. Judge Hayes said to me the other day, 'Who is this Ralph Waldo Emerson, anyhow? He is never called upon when he lectures in Luxborough?'"

"No, I suppose that he is not. We are very careful," said Mrs. Dane. "No doubt Mr. Emerson has ability. But ability is, if I may say so, an annual plant. We insist upon long-rooted merit." She glanced around, smiling, pleased at her little metaphor; then added gravely, "We have had to be rigorous in the Monthly Club. Its doors open only to descent."

"They opened to me, ma'am!" David broke in, with a brutal laugh. "I wonder why? You wouldn't like to say why; now, would you, Mrs. Dane?"

Cousin Julia forced a smile. "Don't make the discussion personal, Mr. Plunkett," she said feebly.

"Oh?" He laughed again insolently. "I had cards of invitation for two years to your Club-minuet, sent by Mrs. Hayes, Patroness! I wonder if it was my descent that moved her? Why, you must have known my grandfather, old Zack Plunkett? A beastly old devil! It was my father that made the money. Zack peddled salt fish and canned oysters all through Pennsylvania. Yes, he did. Now don't pretend you never heard that, ma'am. I'm not ashamed of it! I don't care a rap what my grandfather did, so's *I* don't have to peddle fish and oysters!"

Soudé stared dully at him, amazed. Mrs. Dane nervously adjusted her papers on the desk. Milly stitched on, with downcast eyes. The silence lasted uncomfortably long. David broke it with a loud laugh.

"No. It wasn't my descent from the old pedler that opened the door of your club to me. I know what it was, well enough! So do you. I tore up the cards and threw them in the fire. Mrs. Hayes may look elsewhere for a gilded calf to set up in your club!" The huge lad gathered himself to his feet, standing erect with a certain clumsy dignity. "If she couldn't see that I should have been asked for other reasons than my money—other reasons——" He touched himself upon the breast, and stood silent a minute.

"God! It's a mean world!" he broke out, turning his back on them and going to the window. Mrs. Dane started up, with a motherly impulse of pity, but catching the look of cold disgust in Milly's calm eyes which followed him, she sat down, abashed.

John Soudé lazily reflected a moment upon the discomfort of having any thing to do with underbred people. Who cared to hear that the fellow's grandfather sold fish? It never had occurred to John in his life to talk of his grand-

father. The world knew the Soudés as it knew
the signs of the zodiac. He sank back into
meditations on Mildred's darting needle. The
silence was unbroken.

Presently Miss Warrick, searching for her
silks, took a small ivory box from her basket and
opened it.

John started forward, alive, tingling through
all of his lazy body. Great Heavens! His
letters! The poor newspaper slips, folded away
among her little treasures! He leaned forward
and touched them with his finger, breathing hard.

"Do you—is it possible, Miss Warrick, that
you really care for these things?" he whispered.

Milly flushed, looking ready to cry. "Of
course I care for them," she said, forcing a laugh.
"You have been so kind to me, and I—I never
had a brother."

A brother? Soudé did not answer. Mrs.
Dane began to flutter her papers at the other
end of the room, and that vulgar mass, Plunkett,
came closer, and as usual seemed to choke and
foul the atmosphere for all about him.

John started up, took his hat, and went out.
He reached the quiet street and walked down it
in a dull heat of anger, he knew not why.

But one thing was certain, he was no brother
for her!

In a few minutes he rushed away breathless to
a little shop in St. Francis Street, where he knew
that some sketches of the suburbs, made by a
poor artist, were sold. He turned them over,
breathless.

Ah, it is—the very spot! The old pier from which she fell, the rippling bay, the live-oaks! The shopman, eying him keenly, doubled the price of the picture. John carried it to his room, chuckling triumphantly.

CHAPTER XIII

M<small>R</small>. S<small>OUDÉ</small> had been asked to go with the Northern party that evening, down the bay. While he smoked his pipe delirious visions thrilled him of the boat drifting through star-lit mists, of a soft figure scattering the perfume of roses. When he boarded the boat there were the starlight and the mist, but instead of the soft white figure, Cousin Julia, lorgnette to her eyes, stepping about like a drill sergeant, and Plunkett everywhere, a mass of offence.

Soudé pushed through the crowd of laughing girls and men. He hated them all. Was he never to have her for a moment to himself?

The boat was in motion. From the farther end of the deck came, he fancied, a faint scent of roses. The women were all in dark travelling gowns, but yonder, in the shadow, was a little drift of softness and silvery gray, and a childish face peering out of some airy whiteness.

A lamp overhead threw a single beam of light upon her. John leaned over her, and laid the little picture on her knee. "I thought," he said, "that sometime you might like to remember how happy you had once made a poor fellow for a day."

Milly held it for a moment, and then, without a word, looked up at him. Were ever eyes so meek and so innocent?

10

David was watching them. "Does Milly accept presents from strangers?" he demanded of Mrs. Dane. "D'ye see that scoundrel?"

"Hush-h! Dear Mr. Plunkett! It is nothing—some worthless trifle," she said.

David thumped across the deck and bent over Mildred. "Specimen of Southern art, eh?" he grunted contemptuously.

But Milly held it tightly. He should not pollute it with his touch or his look!

David understood her plainly. He drew back, and when Soudé hurried her away to the bow of the boat, stood staring after them with no more self-control than an animal, not caring who saw the hurt and rage in his face.

"Come away!" panted John. "Can I never see you alone? What right has that brute to speak to you? To assume authority over you?"

He was on fire with a sudden mad jealousy, but Milly looked quietly up at him, saying nothing.

They were far apart from the others, in the shadow; the vast plane of shining water parting before them, as they came, the blue heavens listening overhead.

In this great silent world, they two were alone together, at last. His fingers touched her warm hand as it lay on his arm. Poor little girl! Was that old Jezebel selling her to that beast for his thirty millions? John clutched the soft hand in his. He did not think. He was frenzied with hate of yonder fat boor. He would tear the girl out of his clutches—he would kill her before Plunkett should lay a finger on her. She was so helpless, so dear!

So dear ? Was it *that*?

The whole world seemed to swerve and change about him. It had come! It was she for whom he had been waiting all of his life. Theresa would say so. Theresa had always laughed at his loves and fancies, but she would be in earnest now about this girl.

He talked fast and incoherently; he did not know of what, and neither did Milly know. She was out of herself to-night. Her self was in Luxborough, a middle-aged woman screwing a penny from the butcher or slaving for old Eliza Joyce. Here, she was a child—a child! The warm air kissed her cheeks, the heavens stooped to listen, the vast enchanted water was parting before them as they came, and this man was close to her, so strange, so much better known to her than any living creature.

But if he knew her as she was at home!

Soudé was pouring out words with furious haste.

"I have no right to tell you this. The time is so short. Two weeks ago you did not know that I was in the world. You don't know any thing about me now, only that I am a well-born pauper; but I love you. I love you so much that it seems as if you must give me something"—his whole big frame panted; the fingers that touched hers were cold.

"If you will be my wife. I—what ? What did you say ? "

"The short time doesn't matter," Milly said, with a sobbing laugh.

He stooped to see her face.

It might have been minutes, it might have been hours, that she floated on through space, with his arms about her and his whispers in her ear.

Suddenly she tore herself out of his arms passionately.

"I'm not good enough! Oh, I'm not good enough!" she cried. "You don't know me. I'm such a miserable little fraud."

John laughed, and began to soothe her with yet tenderer words and caresses. He felt very old and masterful. He knew how to control any nervous little girl!

The honest fellow talked on while Milly sobbed and trembled, watching his face wistfully.

Up to that moment she had marched complacently on her measured little path. Even when she had knelt to pray, or when she had taken the sacred bread and wine into her lips, she had never had a doubt of her own complete excellence.

But now, when this coarse, commonplace man put his faith in her, she thrust it back—she could have shrieked aloud in shame and humiliation.

The Holy Spirit makes its way to some souls through queer by-ways.

But Milly, after all, did not speak again of her shame. After a few minutes, she was sorry that she had spoken of it at all.

She began to find her footing again in the cyclone. While John's heart was choking him

• with its throbs of passion and pride, hers fell
back into its calm, steady beat, and left her alert
brain to its usual work.

"Come, we must find your father!" he said.

He would have swept down upon them all with
his triumph. He wanted to take the whole world
into his joy.

But Milly tugged at his arm, and held him quiet
by main force. "Oh, no! You must tell nobody!
Promise me that you will tell nobody for a week!"
she said breathlessly.

"But your father? I must speak to Doctor
Warrick."

"Oh, not for a week! He will do as I wish—he
always does. But I have a reason—a week. Give
me my own way in this, Mr. Soudé."

"Call me John, then. Now, look at me—in
the eyes. Now!—'John.'"

She had her own way, of course. He loved
her all the more for the sweet shyness which
would keep their engagement a secret to themselves.

When they left the boat that evening with the
others, however, he suspected that every-body
guessed it, and led her ashore with a proud sense
of ownership, the more exultant because of the
attentive crowd and of Plunkett, standing near,
dumb and watchful.

When Milly reached the hotel she hurried to
her room and locked the door. Anne tapped at
it gently, but she gave no answer.

What was Anne, or her father? Strangers—
aliens! There was but one human being in the

world, and he loved her! She wanted now to be alone with him. She paced up and down the room, pressing her hands to her face. Here he had kissed her, here and here! The blood yet leaped to the spot.

Presently she sat down to think out her plan. It was all to give him happiness. What else did she care for now on earth?

He had called himself a "well-born pauper." Even in that first moment when she knew that he loved her, she had heard the words and keenly noted them. She was glad that he was poor! She would make him rich!

Mines in Montana, railway shares, government bonds, rivers running gold—he should be richer than Aladdin! She would give all to him!

Mildred threw herself down upon the floor; her hands were clasped about her knees, her eyes up-lifted as she counted over these things as a starving saint might reckon the joys of Heaven. Her eyes glittered, her lips grew white in an ecstasy. She reckoned them over again and again.

She had received yesterday a letter from Doctor Weems saying that Mrs. Joyce was sinking fast. She had kept silent about it. She could not go to her in time, and there was no use in breaking up the boating party. Mrs. Dane and her father, if they heard it, might think some show of mourning proper. What good could that do?

In a week—to-morrow?

All these things would be hers and she could pour them into his hands.

"PRESENTLY SHE SAT DOWN TO THINK OUT HER PLAN"

She had a fancy that no one should know of their betrothal until she could openly come to him with this royal dower.

"What do I care for money?" she muttered as she crept, shivering, into bed. "It is nothing— nothing, but to make him happy."

CHAPTER XIV

How was John Soudé to keep silence about this miraculous triumph for a whole week? He got out of bed the next morning, feverish and angry. Why must he be muzzled?

Then a thought struck him. He hurled his boot across the room with a shout of delight. He would take her to Le Reve des Eaux! He would show her to Theresa! to the dear old General! He could roar out his joy at home, thank God! Why had he not thought of it sooner?

He rushed to the telegraph office, and breakfast brought to Doctor Warrick a long and courteous message from General and Miss Soudé, urging him to bring his daughters and Mrs. Dane to the plantation, and to consider it their home while they remained in the South.

"Really! Most kind, I am sure! Most thoughtful!" buzzed the doctor, greatly pleased. "Well, cousin Julia? What do you say, girls?"

Mrs. Dane darted a keen glance from Soudé's glowing face to Milly's downcast eyes.

"Is the party here to be broken up?" she asked.

"My father would be delighted to receive them all," said Soudé eagerly. "But Mr. Mears with most of the men is going to the coal region.

Do not refuse, dear Mrs. Dane," he pleaded. "It is but a few hours' journey. The scenery on the way is wonderful."

"Ah, you know how to tempt me!" Mrs. Dane smiled and bridled. "If I have any gift, it is a keen comprehension of nature. What do you think, Mildred?"

"We will go," said Miss Warrick quietly, "on Wednesday."

"Then I will be off at once and bring down the horses and traps to the station for you," said John, jumping up excitedly. "I have just time to catch the train." But he lingered, hat in hand, talking to Mildred in a low voice.

It was a rainy day; the dingy room lay in shadow; these two by the window made a little centre of brightness and meaning in its dulness. The meaning was clear enough. Soudé's eyes glowed as he leaned over her, and Milly's face drooped timidly, like a frightened child's. Even Mrs. Dane found something sweet in the picture and turned away, her lips trembling a little.

But David did not turn away. He watched them steadily. His broad face was leaden in hue, and there was an ugly glitter in his usually kindly eyes.

"The mulatto plays a bold game," he muttered to Mrs. Dane.

"Faint heart never wins, Mr. Plunkett. You have been playing the game for years and he for weeks," she said tartly.

David made no answer. He drew back farther into the dark corner, staring at Milly. "Yes, for

years!" he groaned inwardly. Since he was a
boy. If he could only understand her! Sometimes she was so kind, so tender—he had been
sure that she loved him; and as he thought of
these times now, his huge, unwieldy body glowed
and burned. If it could be? He would be such
a good, noble fellow! It was in him to be good
and noble. He would give money to all these
poor devils around who needed money; he would
give up all the sins which his gross flesh made so
near and easy. Milly would make him a decent
man and a good Christian. He would go to
church with her and read the Bible——

Yet there were times when she seemed to him
only a mercenary little devil.

John was gone at last, and Plunkett came up
to the table where the doctor and Mr. Mears
still sat at breakfast.

"I'm sick of this place!" he broke out. "I've
had enough of the South! I'm going back to
Luxborough. You don't know the Luxborough
folk, Mears? You'd enjoy yourself in the new
set. It's the fashion to sneer at them,"—with a
furtive glance at Milly.

No one spoke.

"Yes," Plunkett continued in his shrill, rasping
tone, "folks call 'em vulgar and mercenary. But
if they do worship the dirty dollar, they ain't
ashamed of their religion, like some I know."

"I have heard that it was a very wealthy com-
munity," said Dr. Mears politely, winking his
pale eyes gravely over his egg.

"Wealthy—I should say so! I gave a little

spread there th'other day, only six of us, and we sat down a cool hundred million at the table. Yes, they've lots of style, too. I don't go in for style myself. The Plunketts come up from the bottom, as every-body knows. But them Luxborough girls have plenty of beauty and go in them!" staring defiantly at Milly. "Any man would have satisfaction in hanging diamonds on one of them an' settin' her at the head of his table. And talk of intellect, they're on top!" he went on, with growing excitement. "They write plays and act 'em, and they pick the banjo and are infernally horsey. They'd make their mark in any furrin court. An' they've got money already. They needn't look out for it in marryin'."

Mr. Mears broke the silence which followed. "Naturally, you dread women fortune hunters, I suppose, Mr. Plunkett?"

"Me? No, no!" with a cackling laugh. "Dave Plunkett's eyes are pretty wide open. No woman will take me in! If she did——" He rose and stood for a moment, his jaws working nervously. "If I found, sir, that my wife had married me for money," he went on deliberately, "I'd throw her into the street. I'd treat her like any dog that was stealing from me."

"Come, cousin Julia," said Milly's cool, sweet voice. "Let us have a tramp in the rain. The air is close here. Good-morning, Mr. Plunkett. We shall find you in a less belligerent mood presently, I hope," smiling radiantly up into his big face, round and white as that of a circus clown.

He winced as a clown would at the cut of a whip. "I dunno; I may go to Birmingham to-day with the rest," he stammered.

"Oh, no, you will not. I shall find you here." And she tripped smiling away.

"The man is a beast!" Mrs. Dane exclaimed angrily, when they were in the corridor, but Milly turned her cold eyes on her steadily.

"You do not know him," she said quietly.

Nobody could close the door on a subject so gently and so effectually as Mildred.

CHAPTER XV

JOHN'S train that day shook and joggled uneasily by turns through wet, glancing sunshine or
dark hurries of rain. He looked out anxiously.
What would she think of these villages of tumble-
down houses hidden under rose-bushes and the
men and women loitering about in clothes of the
last century? Here was his own country—his
own people. He had always been proud and
fond of them. But what if she did not like them?

The great swamps, with their myriads of
cypress knees glaring through the mist like
dwarfish ghosts, had always seemed to him like
the entrance into Hades—but perhaps she preferred meadows and apple orchards. Then came
the Gulf, a vast leaden plane to-day, heaving
sullenly up against the rain. Heavens! what if
she did not approve of the Gulf! It would seem
petty to her. She was used to the Atlantic.

He was in despair—the material was so poor
which he had to make her life beautiful and rich.

When he reached New Orleans he rushed to a
shop and chose a dozen worthless prints, which
he sent back to the doctor. "It will please her
to know that I have given the old man pleasure,"
he thought, glowing with pride and delight.
Then to a florist's, from whence magnificent
baskets of roses were despatched to Mobile by

every train. He could not send her any thing but flowers—now. But as he seated himself in the train again, visions of diamond tiaras, of ropes of pearls, floated in his brain.

He sat up suddenly on the seat, thrust his fingers into his pockets, drew out a single torn one-dollar bill, and spread it over his knee, looking at it with a laugh. Then he put it back, and, dropping his head on his breast, sat motionless. For the first time in his life John knew that he actually was a pauper.

So far his feeling for Milly had been an ecstatic dream, but now he faced facts. How could he give her the things which his wife must have? He was dependent on his father for every penny. He had never quite understood it before.

Yet John was neither a boy nor a fool. He was a man of the world, after the fashion of Southern men of his day. He had joined the Louisiana Tigers at sixteen, and gone into battle with no rage nor shouting, but with a good-humored intention to kill or be killed. After the war was over he had never had any especial intention of any kind. Life was one long gay adventure. One day his pockets would be stuffed out with bills: the next neither he nor the General would have a picayune between them. Meantime he saw thoroughly the upper and under side of life in the Gulf cities. He had flirted with the coarsest women and women as pure as Cordelia ; he had risked his last cent on a horse and had lost. But he had always kept his head through it all. Now, for the first time

in his life he had lost his head. Never before had he felt this dumb frenzy to do—to do! To take a grip on the world and shake it as a dog would a bone.

It was intolerable that her life should be cramped or balked for lack of a few dirty dollars. He kicked out his legs in his rage, and struck his shin. As he rubbed it he grinned at his own folly.

He would force things to come right somehow. Things at the plantation had been going wrong for years. He would look into them. The General left the entire management in the hands of a mulatto overseer, and John had resolved a hundred times to examine into it, and had put off the evil day. His father had a blind confidence in the fellow. Why make the old man uncomfortable ?

But it must be done now.

The fact was, that John had never but once before seriously faced this difficulty of money. He was not used to face any difficulty, if he could lounge around it. Stretched out again now on the seat, slowly puffing his cigar, he recalled with grim amusement that one great effort of his life.

We will know him better if we recall it too.

It was on a spring day years ago, when he and his father suddenly perceived that Theresa was grown up. John swore that she should make a brilliant *début* in New Orleans that winter. Money would be needed for dress, jewels, and balls.

The General had none.

John would make it. Nothing could be easier.

He took the train for New Orleans, and set to work in a fury of zeal, as sure of carving out a fortune in a few weeks as he had been of hewing down the Yankees, hip and thigh, at Shiloh.

You are not to suppose that he actually worked with either head or hands. How could he? He had no profession, no craft. His first vague idea had been to go into a mercantile house, and step up to a partnership at gigantic strides. But Louis Choteaud, whom he consulted, burst into derisive laughter.

"What do you know of coffee or sheetings? When you go into trade, *mon bébé*, the very draymen will have their pickings and stealings out of you! Conceive, too, the General finding the name of Soudé on a box of millinery or a ham! It would kill him!"

John nodded assent, and slunk away down the street as if he had been caught stealing.

But no time must be lost. He went to work in the ways in vogue with men of his caste and time: borrowed a few thousands, bought stocks; lost on Tuesday, on Wednesday won; invested on Friday in an orange plantation in Florida, which he had never seen, and sold it the next week for one-third the money.

Le Duc, his neighbor, had gone out into Kansas and bought a ranch. He had conjured a railway junction on to it, and cleared a million of dollars on town lots.

"Go to Kansas, my son," said the General, when John went home to consult him. They sat smoking together on the gallery of the old house—before them a vast prairie sloped down to the Gulf. "If you must have a million also, go to Kansas. You have capacity, more than Le Duc. In my day it was not the business of gentlemen to make money. If the sugar crop was large, we spent more: if small, we spent less—*c'est égal!* Damn it! what d'ye want? Diamonds for Therese? St. Paul tells us all to beware of covetousness." He groaned, stroking the long gray beard that swept over his huge stomach. "*Bien!* My day is over. A boy of your age must have his horses, hunting—how do I know what? Therese, too, lace, jewels! And so she ought. If I could wring money for you children out of my blood I'd do it. God knows I'd do it. But go—go with the others. You evidently have a head for finance."

"I think I have, General," John said modestly. "I ranked Olave Le Duc in college, and if he has made a million—I suppose it will be infernally rough in Kansas!"

"It is good for a man to endure hardship in his youth," said the General, his foggy brain as usual filled with scraps of Scripture. "When I was your age, I have fasted for days and days on a buffalo hunt. No shirking, sir! You've put your hand to the plough——"

He shouted to one of the women to mix his toddy, and leaning back in his rocking-chair in the hot sun, thought of John hazily during the afternoon as going forth on some sort of religious crusade.

He knew, as his son did not, the desperate need that there was for the money in the household, increasing with every year. Indeed, every morning, when his head was clear, the old man would resolve to go himself down to Orleans and make some grand coup to mend their fortunes. Other men of his generation had gone to this unclean work of money-grubbing. Elliott of Bayou Sara had started a cotton-seed oil factory and Vallue was a partner in an iron furnace. Southern men doubtless would now have control of the business of the country as once they had of its politics and society.

"Garoche!" he would shout from the gallery, "bring up the mules, to take me down for the noon train."

But after he had gorged an enormous breakfast and was seated in the gallery in the blazing sun, the dogs asleep about him, he would forget all about the mules and the fortune he was to make. The idea of money or work dropped as quickly out of the brain of a Soudé as does a pebble through water.

John, on his way to Kansas, had stopped in New Orleans to tell the men of the magnificent luck awaiting him. They agreed with him that if that idiot Le Duc could make a fortune, Soudé's success as a land speculator was sure.

They waited eagerly for good news, as soon as he reached Emporia. But five weeks passed— no letter, no telegram. Then he walked in upon them one day, while they were at dinner at the club. He would eat nothing—he told none of his experiences. But he borrowed money to take him home.

Louis drove him down to the station and anxiously suggested absinthe and cognac, hoping to rouse him from his defeat.

"I'm not drinking now," said John irritably.

"And he kicked my setter across the ferry-boat," Louis reported, when he came back. "When a gentleman sets out to make money he heads downward, straight."

The General's chair had just been carried to the west gallery, following the sun, when he caught sight of a horse crossing the prairie. The old man's eyes were as keen as a hound's.

"That's John, Therese! Tell Viny to have gumbo for supper. He likes the mess! Coming home to his old dad, eh?" He snorted and mumbled to himself, as John sprang from the horse and ran up the steps. "Well, sir, I looked for you in two weeks! It is six!"

"Why, I went to stay altogether, General. You forget."

"In Kansas? Bah!"

"I come back empty-handed," John said gloomily.

"Oh, the money?" said his father, with an effort at recollection. "Didn't make it, eh? That's unfortunate. That's more cursedly unfortunate than you know. I'm going down to town myself to-morrow, to—so you fell among thieves, eh?"

"No. They're as honest as I. But they are sharp and keen as steel. I haven't the brains. I give it up. I never shall try again!"

John, recalling this old disappointment now, drew himself up into a sitting posture with a nervous yawn. "I will try again, and I'll not give it up!" he said. He could succeed—for Milly.

Yet it hurt him to remember that little Therese had never had her laces or balls. Things had dropped to their old level, after his spasmodic effort. Therese made life very jolly without money, and he and the General had loved the girl dearly. The days had galloped by.

"And now we three will take Milly in," he said, smiling to himself, as he thought of the welcome which Therese would give the strangers to-morrow. "Viny must have gumbo—her gumbo is incomparable," he reflected.

At the next station a portly old man came into the car. John gave a shout of delight and dragged him into his seat. M. Paramba was the nearest neighbor and closest friend of the Soudés; the very man to consult about his new enterprise!

"Yes, I am going to give your father his revenge at whist, but I can only stay a couple of days. What has kept you so long at Mobile? We had to play dummy all last week. Little Therese plays a very fair hand now. She—— What is the matter, John? You look distrait. Nothing wrong at home, eh?"

"Nothing that has not been wrong for years. You are the man above all others that I wish to see to-day, major. I have a plan—or—it is hardly a plan yet," the words tumbling out headlong. "I have been a lazy dog. Done nothing since the war."

"What do you mean to do?" eying him with vague alarm.

"I think I shall look after things on the plantation a little. That fellow Farro——"

"Oh, Farro?" M. Paramba's face instantly gathered a keen interest.

"You have noticed that things were going wrong, then? You are a sugar-grower. You know what the plantation ought to yield?"

"There is no finer plantation than yours on the Gulf, John. Nor one that is more skilfully handled. Farro knows his business."

"Where does the income go, then?"

"Ah, where?" M. Paramba shrugged his shoulders. "That is what every planter in Attakapas has asked for years. The whole parish is whispering about it. But nobody, not even I, would dare speak of it to your father. Now that you have opened the matter, however—why, it's an outrage, boy! The old house is tumbling to pieces, and not a picayune is spent in repairs. The other ladies bring back fals-lals from Orleans to make their homes pretty, but Therese, nothing."

"I have been extravagant," said John, reddening. "The establishment is large——"

"So is mine, with half your income. No. There is a leak—a chasm somewhere down which the money goes"—shaking his head solemnly. "D'ye know, sir, I am tempted to suspect some

occult influence at work ? I have heard of
inferior creatures, like that whelp of a mulatto,
throwing a spell over their masters. Not voodoo-
ism (though there's something in that, too) but—
eh ? What d'ye think, anyway ? "

John laughed. " No, Farro is only a cool,
greedy beggar, commonplace enough. He is
storing the money away for himself no doubt.
I've been a fool to stand by idle so long." He
was silent a few minutes, and then said, lowering
his voice, " But you have no idea how far my
father's infatuation for that man goes. He stints
himself at every point to give Farro money. He
gave up his hunters, you know; he never goes to
his club in town now. I saw him a few weeks
ago looking longingly at a little pearl brooch for
Therese in a shop-window in Orleans. But he
turned away with a long breath, without it."

" Of course then, sir," the major said, " you can
do nothing. It is not for a son to meddle with
a father. Unless Farro could be sent to the
whipping-post——"

" The day for that is over, unfortunately.
Besides, the fellow gives me no excuse for punish-
ment. He always keeps in his place."

" Where did he come from ? He was not on
the plantation before the war."

" No. He belonged to my Uncle Victor—
Theresa's father."

Major Paramba unconsciously touched his hat.
" A great man, sir! "

" So I have been taught; I scarcely knew him,
you know," John replied.

" There never was such an orator in this country," pursued the major. " He was never known to lose a case, when he would stay sober long enough to attend to it. But Victor incessantly threw up the law to go to fighting—wherever there was a blow to be struck for freedom, sir. Here, there—all over the world! He was with Garibaldi in Greece, with Walker in Nicaragua; God knows where! Why, John, that man ranked far above Clay or Calhoun for eloquence and statesmanship. But adventure, duelling, playing high—that was his life! One day living like a Sultan, entertaining hundreds during the Mardi Gras—the next without a dollar. But always gay! Ah, boy! There were giants in the land in those days! We have no Victor Soudés now."

John shook his head mournfully. The major drew out a silver flask, and they drank some brandy in silence.

" Poor stuff ! " sighed Paramba. " Yes, I saw your Uncle Victor last in December, '61. We were in Paris. He had been playing higher than usual. I, too. When South Carolina went out, we borrowed money to come home. I thought the difficulty would easily be bridged over. But Victor knew that war was coming. That fellow could smell a fight half round the globe. We parted in New Orleans. He wanted to fit out a company, but had not money to buy his own uniform. I heard of him next year at the head of a regiment that he had equipped. Did you not see him then ? "

"No. I was with my brigade in Alabama. He was shot, you know, in the first battle."

"Yes, yes! Louisiana lost no such son, sir, as Victor Soudé. And this fellow, Farro, you say, belonged to him?"

"Yes. He bears a strange, hideous likeness to him, too. But of course I never enquired into that. About '54, my uncle freed four hundred of his people. You must have heard of it at the time. Probably in a fit of temper, or he may have been drinking. But this boy Farro refused to leave his master or to take his free papers. That was just the sort of thing to touch my uncle. He made a major domo of the fellow. After he died my father put him in as overseer. It may be that it is for my uncle's sake—this infatuation of the General's for him. The likeness—you know? My father's feeling for his brother is passionate; he will not speak his name even now."

"I know that! I know!" nodding gravely. "Your father always humored Victor; too much, I used to think. It will be difficult for you to broach this matter to your father, John—very difficult. If I can help you, I am ready to back you."

"I must put it off for the present. Some friends from the North are coming to us to-morrow. As it has waited so many years," said John, with a laugh of relief, "a day or two more can do no harm."

The hours and minutes of the day following crept slowly by for Mildred.

Before leaving Luxborough she had arranged with Doctor Weems that he should privately keep her advised of Mrs. Joyce's exact condition. Until now his letters or telegrams had reached her regularly: but to-day none came. In the morning she must go with the others to Le Reve des Eaux. If she only could know that the poor old creature was at rest, she could give herself with that noble heritage, to him, in his own home!

Milly was no murderess at heart. "God forbid," she told herself a hundred times that day, "that I should shorten her life by a single breath!"

But she watched the door all day with quick, furtive glances. She feared to leave the house for a moment: she listened to each step in the corridor, and when it passed without stopping, talked breathlessly to Anne of the tortures which Eliza Joyce had suffered, and of the relief which death would be to her.

The evening, the night passed. No letter, no message.

Breakfast was over: they were to take the train in an hour. She saw no possible chance for delay. Cousin Julia, in high good humor, brought her maid to fold Milly's gowns.

"Such a charming expedition!" she chirped. "Mr. Soudé asked the whole party, but only we are going. But the Soudé house must be enormous and the *ménage* much more perfect than ours in the North, to enable them to bring in thirty guests at a few hours' notice. I am glad I encouraged the advances of that young man at first. I take a lee-tle credit to myself for the intimacy and all the results of it. Do you hear me, Milly? All the results," with a sly glance and laugh. "I think I know a lovely chatelaine for a great princely establishment! Ah-h?"

"You are partial, cousin Julia." Milly's icy politeness suddenly drove Mrs. Dane out of the friskiness of youth into middle age. She talked gravely of trains for a moment and left the room.

Anne waited until she was gone to break the silence.

"Shall we stop in New Orleans?" she asked.

"Only for an hour," Mildred replied.

"I thought——" Anne ventured timidly. "Brooke is there. I thought he might join us."

"Brooke is not there. He is to meet Mr. Mears at Birmingham and go on with his work. High time that he did! He has played the spend-thrift long enough. He cannot afford to idle away any more time."

Anne, who was twisting up her hair, turned on her. "What do you mean? Nobody told me. What has he done?"

"What is that to you, child? Papa told me. What do you know of business? Brooke has mort-gaged the Dacre farm to its full value to pay Ned's gambling debts. He has stripped himself of every penny. Ned has gone back to the Soudé plantation. We shall no doubt see him to-morrow, carrying himself *en prince!* Brooke is an idiot. He will never rise above the level of a day laborer as long as he shoulders that scape-

grace. Oh, for Heaven's sake, Anne, don't look
so miserable! What are the Calhouns to us?
As if we hadn't trouble enough of our own!"

Anne turned away and arranged her hair in
silence, while the usually placid and methodical
Miss Warrick tossed her gloves and collars into
the trunk with shaking fingers.

She told herself that the letter or message
would soon follow her, but she could not quiet
her quivering nerves. Her fancy for playing
Queen Cophetua to this man was the first gleam
of romance in her bare, hard years, and the delay
frightened and enraged her.

A mail was brought in just as she and Anne,
ready for their journey, came out into the corridor. A negro boy went from door to door,
distributing the letters. Milly held out her
hand. He shook his head and passed her.

"Come, Anne," she said sharply. "The carriage is waiting!"

، Mrs. Dane was standing by a window reading
a despatch which had just been handed to her.
It was from Mr. Franciscus.

"Mrs. Joyce died on Friday, and will be buried
to-day. I shall be present at the reading of the
will on behalf of the Warrick family. Will telegraph you the result."

"Come, Mrs. Dane," called the doctor, "we
shall miss the train."

"In one moment." She hurried to the clerk.
"Send all despatches on to me at once in

General Soudé's care. I'm coming, Samuel, I'm coming!"

She thrust the yellow slip into her pocket, with a furtive glance at Milly.

"No. She would grieve so sorely for the old woman!" she thought. "Let her have her happy day with her lover."

CHAPTER XVI

THE sun was setting that evening, when the train drew up in a cluster of wooden cabins on the prairie. The hamlet was there only for the convenience of the planters in the parish, but it made a cheerful little swagger of its own in the world. Each hut threw up a huge sign, red-lettered, Ste. Barbe Station, Ste. Barbe Bazar, Hôtel de Ste. Barbe: and thrust out a hospitable pillared veranda, and covered itself in spring with masses of yellow and pink roses. The salt perfume of burning sea-weed weighted the thin air—and hedges of the Cherokee rose stretched aimlessly for miles across the pale green prairies.

John Soudé boarded the train before it stopped.

"They are all here to welcome you, sir," he said, grasping Doctor Warrick's hands, with a furtive, excited glance at Milly. It did not suit his French ideas of propriety to go near her. No *jeune fille* could be made the object of remark in public, and as for Milly—that sacred creature!

Outside was a tumult of trampling hoofs and shouting drivers, and whoops and yah-yahs from the swarming black piccaninnies. Ste. Barbe always turned out for the train, to guy the engineer and stare at the passengers. It had nothing else to do the year round. But to-day it was rampant. This was an occasion.

Here was the General in his landau, and
Garoche with the van, a huge coach lined with
ragged yellow satin, and Miss Therese herself, a
human chunk of good luck in which every man,
child, and dog at Ste. Barbe thought he owned a
share. Two or three of the other planters on the
bayou had ridden over to greet the General's
guests.

After the train steamed away, the entire population looked on with affectionate interest as
the strangers were welcomed by the Soudés:
even the negro postmaster, who could neither
read nor write, and had been run into office by
the carpet-baggers to plague General Soudé,
beamed down on his old master from the forge
door, delighted with the pomp of "de old
famblies."

It was the first time since the war that the
General had met a Northerner. Hence, despite
the heat, he had put on his fur-lined cloak of
state, and had driven down to the station to welcome them. His puffs and gurgles, his lofty high-
shouldered bows and waves of his pudgy hand,
each said, "We have drawn the sword against
each other. Behold! To-day we bury it."

The doctor was amazed and a little scared.
He did not quail, however, but stood up stiffly
before the ponderous mountain of flesh, and
returned his bows in kind. Both of the old men
felt, now that they had clasped hands, that the
war was over. North and South to-day had
formed a league. Then the ladies held audience
on the little rickety platform, and the General

presented his friends, Hachettes, and Dutrys, and Fontaines, who bore themselves with as stately dignity as if they were all at the court of Madrid.

Anne's eyes sparkled with delight and fun. Nobody could have expected any thing so fine as this red sunshine and world of flowers, and the friendly .good humor and high punctilio. The soft clamor of their low, thick voices left her no time to speak. She would like to have kissed every one of the white-haired old men, and to have sworn friendship with every young one. Mildred, to her dismay, stood coldly apart, answering in monosyllables instead of her usual sweet murmurs.

Edward Calhoun sat on the fence with some of the loungers about the station, paying no attention to his cousins. He knew that he was a criminal in the eyes of these priggish Warricks and Danes. They no doubt discussed him *en petit comité* every day. He had no mind to play the prodigal son and come to beg for forgiveness. Hence he sat upon the fence with his new comrades, to show his indifference. He wore white flannels like theirs, and a wide sombrero of a maroon tint, which set off well his reddish curls and blue eyes.

The colonels and majors who had just welcomed their new friends were now busily quarrelling as to who should first have possession of them for a dinner party.

" You will all come to us to-night," said Miss Soudé, "and then you can settle your disputes. The flag is out." She explained to Anne that each family on the Bayou, whenever they had an

attraction in the way of a strange guest, or un-
usually large red fish, or any new plat, ran up a
flag, which was a bidding to all the planters'
families to come to dinner at once. "Of course
the guest or the fish is only the excuse. We must
see each other every day."

"Ah! You don't know how new all this is to
me! I never felt so welcome in any place before!" cried Anne, pressing her palms tightly
together as she sat down beside Therese in her
little cart. "And did you see my father and
General Soudé meet? It might have been
Charles and Francis in the Field of the Cloth of
Gold. How funny and dear they are!"

Therese nodded and laughed, with a quick
glance at her.

She held in her horses until the van and the
landau had gone, filled with the elder of the party
and escorted by the horsemen. It was she, indeed, who had ordered the little procession, but
without a word; directing Garoche where to
turn, and holding back the escort of riders with
smiling, significant glances.

Now Mildred, too, saw that every-body, even
John, waited to take these silent orders from the
young girl. She had been under a high tension
all day, baffled and disappointed. This trifle
kindled a white heat of anger in her usually amiable soul. She was coming home—the bride.
John was the heir; she was his wife, coming to
his house, her heart full of love, ready to rain
down prosperity on it.

Who was this woman welcoming her with such

show of hospitality ? To her own house, her own carriage ? Even John waited for a sign from Therese before he took a seat in the old gig beside her. Mildred's blue eyes rested on Therese with a childlike smile. She decided in a very short time that that penniless dependent should soon learn her own place.

"You should have prepared me to meet Miss Soudé," she said sweetly to John. "You did not tell me that she was so homely. It quite shocked me."

"Homely? Therese?" He stared at her. "Why, she is the only girl in the family! Our Therese homely?"

"And a cripple, too? You did not tell me that: such a pity! She limps quite perceptibly."

Soudé's face burned a dark red. "Yes," he said, in a low tone. "We all know that. But never before in my life have I heard it put into words."

Milly, frightened, hastened to pour out the sweet babble that he loved, but he did not hear her. Therese homely? The girl of the Soudé family! Some of his own blood and life was in her. To hurt her was to wrench him to the quick.

Therese, with Anne, meanwhile, skimmed lightly past them, or fell into the rear. The drive was a long one. Anne was soon chattering to this strange girl as if she had known her from her cradle. An odd freemasonry between them told her at once that Therese understood her flighty talk better than Milly ever had done. She was something like Brooke in that.

" Did you see Edward Calhoun upon the fence yonder ? " Miss Soudé said presently. " He has ridden on in advance."

"I saw him—yes," said Anne dryly.

" He is my cousin—yours also," said Therese. "You did not speak to him—no ? Poor boy! He feels himself to be the black sheep among you—oh, quite the black sheep! Can you not forgive him, a little ? "

" He has disgraced the family and ruined his brother," Anne said vehemently.

" Ruined ? Was it so bad then ? Poor Ned! He was born so. He cannot help that." She looked enquiringly into Anne's hard-set face, and laughed softly. " No. He cannot help that. It is so with every-body. One has a crooked nose, and one has an ugly temper, and Ned—has a flabby will. Come, now, be merciful to the poor boy. His brother did not blame him."

"No. His brother——" Anne said no more. She sat looking out at the monotonous sweep of prairie, over which low, rolling clouds from the Gulf were driven incessantly. She turned at last suddenly. " You are very merciful to that vaga-bond. It is in your nature, I see, to be merci-ful," she went on garrulously; "it is not in mine. I never forgive. I have no doubt that you try to defend all the weak, scampish people you meet. And of course when Ned cheats——"

"One moment!" Miss Soudé checked the horses, in her sudden earnestness. "Edward is weak, but not dishonorable. That is impossible. You forget. His mother was a Soudé—one of us.

"ITS ROWS OF LIGHTS GLEAMING THROUGH THE DARKNESS"

He could not be dishonorable." She gave a quick little decisive nod, and flecked the horses with her whip. They darted forward. In a moment she turned, smiling, to point out some birds to Anne, but her lips were pale.

" If we had been men, she would have drawn a pistol in defence of the family honor," thought Anne, and liked her companion better than ever.

" Yonder is the house," said Miss Soudé a moment later.

John had forgotten his momentary trouble long before they reached the house. He was watching Milly's face breathlessly. This was his home. Would she ever care for it as he did ?

The vast prairie, an uneven sheet of pale green in the fading light, sloped to the Mexican gulf, seamed with misty bayous. Here and there on the plain a congregation of gigantic live-oaks gathered in council; long gray moss covering them from head to foot like spectral garments.

On the top of the hill rose the towering front of the house, massive and impressive, its rows of lights gleaming through the darkness. There was a strange, uncanny beauty in the scene which reached even Milly's perceptions.

" I feel as if we were travelling through a dream," she said, thrusting her head forward curiously.

" You like it, then? Thank God! I was born here, you know." The place was so dear to him—she was so dear, that the big lubberly man could not control his voice as he spoke. His honest eyes beamed down on her, he found her hand and held it close. "I don't think God ever made a place like it on earth—or a woman like you!" he said, gathering her into his arms and kissing her.

Milly's eyes were full of tears when he released her. She was very happy, and did not remember for a few minutes how happy John would be when she poured the great fortune into his hands. When she did think of it, it no longer seemed of so much importance. The Soudé estate, she decided, was of enormous value. She and John would probably not need Mrs. Joyce's money, after all, to make their happiness.

CHAPTER XVII

Cousin Julia had borne herself with aplomb
and credit in visits to one or two foreign courts
during her life, but she was perplexed and ill at
ease at General Soudé's dinner-party that night.

"If I understand any thing," she told Doctor
Warrick, "it is human nature. I have got on
comfortably in my time with Grand Dukes and
Sioux squaws. But this place and these people
are outside of my experience."

"I never met more cordial, simple folk," the
doctor retorted testily.

Mrs. Dane said no more, but her puzzled gaze
still wandered over the lofty apartments, which
were those of a decayed palace, while the mildew
stains on the carved ceilings showed where the
rain yesterday had dribbled through. The hang-
ings were embroidered satin of the Louis XVIII.
era, but they were ragged and faded; the silver
sconces held tallow candles; the linen napery
woven with the Soudé crest was of exquisite fine-
ness, but it was full of holes, darned and patched.
Here, on the great glittering table, were Sèvres
plates, and there, stoneware. Mrs. Dane drank
her hock from a priceless Venetian glass, and her
claret from one which would not cost a dime.
Some of the women wore marvellous old velvets,
and some, cheap muslins.

"But their old point," Mrs. Dane told Anne afterward, "was a revelation to me! Southern women may have sacrificed their husbands and their happiness in the war, but they held on to their laces! Perfectly right, too, my dear! The fichu which that old Spanish dame near me wore was four hundred years old if it was a day. Just the woman to wear it, too! She looked as if she had the blood of a hundred Castilian hidalgos in her little body. Yet she told Miss Soudé that one of her sons had just found a place as conductor on a railway and the other was minded to set up a milk-cart; at which they both laughed."

"Oh, of course, they laughed," said Anne, her eyes dancing. "I love them! Even the old women are so gay and friendly! I believe they came smiling into the world, and will go out laughing and kissing their hands to it."

"I think their chief quality is intolerable conceit," said Mrs. Dane crossly. "They are so sure of their patrician place in the world that they are no more ashamed of their milk-carts and stoneware than the Venus de Milo would be of dust blown upon her."

"You are very unjust," said Anne.

She felt as if these people were a big family to whom she was in some way akin. Had not the Hachette girls told her all about their sweet new baby—the youngest of fifteen? Was she not to be driven over to-morrow to see it? And had she not heard of two engagements to-night with the promise of all of the details in the morning?

The only fault that she had to find with these pretty, babbling girls was that they had set up Edward Calhoun as a hero. Ned posed willingly enough as a young man burdened with secret sorrow. Even General Soudé, observing that Doctor Warrick greeted Ned coldly, took him apart, and said to him anxiously, " Don't be hard on the lad, sir. He has been sowing his wild oats. Ta—ta! What of that ? You and I too, once, perhaps! He has a nature so sensitive, so delicate! One must deal gently with him. Like a fine instrument, easily jarred, you know. My niece and I have struggled to cheer and encourage him, poor boy! "

Naturally, Ned was aggrieved at the sudden irruption of Danes and Warricks with their bigoted, sour notions into this genial world which he now regarded as his own. He relished keenly the unreal glamour of the scenery and of the decayed old house: Viny's sauces made life a happiness, and the General's rugged generosity and tenderness touched him sometimes like fine music and brought tears of delight to his eyes. He found himself as comfortable among these people whose habit it was to be happy, as a jellyfish afloat in a warm summer sea. The jellyfish, probably, admires the sun, though it never warms its own clammy body.

After dinner the young Hachettes and La Fontaines, who had voted Brooke to be brusque and coarse, clustered around the gentle, melancholy lad on a moonlit veranda, enchanted with his tinkling guitar and scraps of French chansons, which he breathed forth in a weak voice full of pathos.

Mildred, who chanced to see his little court, gave a meaning smile. Edward's day here would be short! She would tolerate no lazy parasites in the house, either of her own or of the other family.

It was not a pleasant evening for Mildred. She had commanded John to keep her secret, yet she was secretly irritated that nobody had guessed it: that she was received as an ordinary guest and not the bride—the new queen, soon to rule over all. She was placed half-way down the table among the *jeunes filles*, which she knew to be proper and right. But she watched the little brown girl who presided with such an odd, quiet charm, with fierce dislike.

"She has them all under her thumb!" she thought. "John watches her eye for directions as much as the negroes do. She thinks she has her place for life—*plantée là!* But I'll unseat her—I'll unseat her!"

Milly's love for John Soudé filled all her narrow heart, but her intention to be the legitimate head of this household was quite as strong. In a day or two she would enter into possession. She would make short work then with this complacent intruder, who held the sceptre now as a matter of course. Besides, Mildred was a neat, thrifty housekeeper, and she suspected that Therese was quite the reverse. She saw the rough patches on the tablecloth, the undarned holes in the satin curtains, and the five lamps burning where but one was needed. She promised herself a full tour of inspection of the premises in the morning.

John contrived to find a minute with her, apart, after dinner.

"And so my little girl is satisfied with her new home?" looking into her face with burning eyes. "I was afraid you would think it mean and shabby. But that doesn't matter, of course. There is the General—you see what he is. And Therese is—Therese! Nobody is like her. You will be like sisters——"

"Yes; dear girl!" sighed Milly, clinging close to his arm.

"I wish you would let me speak to my father," John said anxiously. "To-night—just a word——"

"Not yet. Give me a day——"

"Well, you know what is best. I feel like a traitor to him, though. I never have secrets from him—or from any body," added stupid John, with a laugh.

"I wonder how you—*you* ever came to care for poor little me?" Milly said, suddenly looking up at him, with a humility which for the time was real. Even the kisses with which he answered her did not bring back her smile nor drive away the fierce contempt of herself which sometimes came upon her.

If he ever found out how little, how mean she was! She glanced up at him, her face contorted.

But she did not forget to make arrangements,

before they parted, for their tour of inspection in the morning.

"Could we not steal away for an early walk ? " she said. "I have not seen my home yet. I want *you* to show it to me, first."

John went to sleep that night, glowing with delight. Certainly darned curtains and wasted oil were not in his thoughts, though in Milly's they bore a large and important part.

CHAPTER XVIII

THE next day dawned soft and hazy. John waited for Milly on one of the verandas. He fancied that the morning was waiting for her too; it had put on this rare, dewy splendor for her. The old plantation surely never had looked so fair! He paced impatiently up and down. He wanted to show her the silvery patches of torn mist still lying on the prairie, and the dew shimmering on the gray robes of the trees, and the color of the purple fleur-de-lys that banked the creeping black lagoons. It seemed as if all these things were happy with him to-day. There were red lights on the surf that beat upon the distant beach, as if even the waves were glad, and brought good tidings from some other part of this joyful world.

John was pleased with his little fancies. They seemed genuine poetry to him. Why did she not come so that he could tell them to her?

Presently Miss Warrick appeared on the veranda, her delicate blue draperies fluttering about her, her fair curly hair blown by the wind. He ran to meet her. How soft and clean and rosy she was! But he did not show her the red gleams nor the mist. His fancies somehow suddenly seemed foolish to him.

"No, do not let us go wandering over the

prairie," she said. "I saw the plantation quite thoroughly as we drove through it. I heard judge Hachette tell my father it was most skilfully worked. You have a negro overseer?"

"A mulatto, Farro."

"*I* shall call him Mr. Farro. I mean to do all I can for the freedmen. He is faithful, then?"

"Oh, yes! Faithful enough," John replied, with a grim laugh.

"Then we need not concern ourselves with the plantation as yet. But—show me the house, John—my home!" She looked up, with all the tender meaning of the word in her eyes.

But the next minute she put her eyes on guard: she needed a sharp sight to-day.

"There are no farming operations near the house?" she said, clinging to his arm.

"No. All this land in sight is Therese's domain. She follows out her own fancies, here."

"Not even a garden? I cannot imagine a farm without a garden"—glancing superciliously at the flowers, which did not grow in beds and borders as elsewhere, but in fields: masses of mignonette and sweet-peas and poppies shouldering the walls of the house, and stretching down into the orchards. There was an atmosphere of lazy, heedless munificence about the place which girded Milly's economic soul.

"I should think Miss Soudé would at least have a poultry yard, and vegetables?"

"The negroes of the parish bring her these things to sell. They depend on their little earnings."

"And they cheat her, probably?"

"Oh, that, of course," John laughed.

Milly nodded significantly. "We will see to that too," she murmured, and then briskly stepped along the slope, glancing from side to side at the sweep of velvet turf through which the lazy streams oozed their way down to the Gulf.

"If I were your farmer," she said, turning her head, "I should try high-grade cattle on this land. But it is given up to—nothing! Such hedges! Look, John! Messes of roses and black-berry-bushes and birds and worms! Neat barbed wire fences, now? They would save so much ground."

John laughed, lounging after her, listening bewildered, yet fondly as to a child's chatter.

Milly led the way to a point from which the whole of the house could be seen.

The huge structure occupied three sides of a square, in which had once been a fountain and statues. But the fountain was dried long ago, and the stone gods were green with mould. The house, which was imposing at night, by day bared its age and decay shamelessly. There was no effort at concealment. The front of the building was entire, and in tolerable order. But the great side wings were roofless. Masses of climbing roses, cloth of gold and white, could not hide the rotting timbers nor the broken win-dows, some of which were stuffed with straw and rags. The great ball-room, its frescoed nymphs yellow with mildew, was used as a

laundry, and a sow and her pigs rooted tranquilly under the gallery.

Milly's lips closed tightly, and her blue eyes
were full of calculation, as she walked silently
around the ruins. Suddenly she stooped. "What
is this house built of ? I never saw such bricks.
They are rounded in front, and each one has a
different figure on it."

John gave an uneasy shrug. "You have keen
eyes. My grandfather had beds of clay on a
plantation in Mississippi, and the slaves made the
bricks by hand, one by one, when the field work
was over. It always seemed a cruel business to
me. Each man and woman put a sign on their
bricks. Poor nameless wretches, trying to be
remembered after they were dead! I hate to
look at these walls, when I think of them!"

"You are too fanciful," she said, laughing as she
ran her finger curiously over the bricks. "Here
is one with a heart, and this has a knife, and ever
so many have crosses! How funny! Such ridiculous creatures! People with colored skins somehow always are ridiculous to me. I think that
your grandfather was quite right, though, to
get the full amount of work from his slaves.
Only, if he had trained them to make bricks
properly, it would have paid him better. But
understand me, John," gravely, "I don't approve
of slavery. It was a great moral evil, in my
opinion."

"Very well," said John, his eyes twinkling.
"We won't argue about it, little girl." Nothing
could be more delightful, he thought, than a pretty

"SHE RAN HER FINGER CURIOUSLY OVER THE BRICKS"

woman prattling of these high matters which only men could understand.

Milly drew him along the path. "There is a little group of huts—quite a village. Who live there?" she asked.

"Oh, I hardly know. Old maumers and uncles—who were too decrepit to go with their children when they ran away to Butler's army."

"Who takes care of them?"

"The General—Therese, rather. She gathered them all together, close under her eye."

"Their children should be made to support them," said Milly decisively. "This lax almsgiving is a mistake, always."

"It would be a mistake for me to turn out an old horse that had served me to die by the roadside," said John coldly.

Milly glanced at him quickly and hurried on. "That is a pretty cottage. Who lives there?" she said.

"An old neighbor of ours who went to the dogs after the war. Took to opium. My father found him in New Orleans, absolutely barefooted, and brought him home. Therese fitted up that little cabin for him. She keeps him busy and—sober. Oh, she is a regular martinet! Won't allow him even a drop of claret! I am afraid," he said, with a chuckle, "that our Therese does not agree with you as to charity. Her system is to gather a lot of incapables and to pay them wages to keep up their self-respect. Her kitchen is filled with the lame, the halt, and the blind."

Milly's lips were compressed more tightly, but she said nothing.

Stopping at the end of the building, she looked back at it thoughtfully a while. Then, her face flushing, she turned to Soudé:

"A very little money would restore it! It has grand capabilities, John! It could easily be made into a palace for us!"

"Do you want a palace, my darling?" said John soberly.

But Milly was quivering with excitement. The story of her boundless fortune trembled on her lips. If the moment had only come to pour it into his hands!

"A little would make it habitable. But if we had a great deal we could bring a Northern architect and—towers at this end now—an archway here—Gothic windows—why, you would not know the old house!"

"I am afraid my father would not know it," said John gravely. "He spends days in planning how, when he has the money, he will restore it again, every brick and beam in place as it was when he was a boy. You would scare him and Therese with your towers and arches."

Milly gave a little smile of defiance as they turned to go in. John watched her uneasily. "I really care very little about money," he said anxiously, after a pause. "But I mean to go to work and make it for you, dearest. You shall have your palace or a little nest. It does not matter which to us, if we have each other."

Milly, as she ran up the steps, looked back, saucy and sparkling. " I prefer the palace, sir," she said. "And you will not have to work for the great fortune. 'Whistle and it will come to you, my lad!'" she sang, tossing him a kiss merrily, and then disappeared.

CHAPTER XIX

MRS. DANE sat with a knitted brow during the long, dawdling breakfast. She had fully expected to find a telegram from Mr. Franciscus beside her plate. When at last the interminable courses of fruit, fish, and hot cakes were ended, she went out with the group of chattering girls to the broad shaded veranda and sat silent, her eyes fixed on the levee, a high, crooked road which wound between the pools and bayous across the prairie, waiting for the messenger who was to bring the great tidings.

A queer old calèche came up the levee presently, but it only brought the Hachette girls, who came to carry Anne away to see the baby. Horsemen followed, by twos and threes, but they were some of the neighbors from ten or fifteen miles distant, who had dropped in to know how the ladies had slept.

Cousin Julia listened to the gay gossip and laughed with the others, but her black eyes did not relax their keen watch for an instant. Her nervousness increased as the morning wore on.

If a letter or message should reach Ste. Barbe for me," she asked Miss Soudé at last, " it would be immediately forwarded, of course ? "

" No; not of course at all," Therese said, smiling. " Simon, the postmaster, will probably send it, if any one chances to come over. But I do not know whether any one will chance to come over to-day. And sometimes Simon forgets to send it ; " and she proceeded to disentangle her floss with the calm of a woman to whom letters and despatches were matters of no possible import.

It was Milly's soft voice that answered. "Then I must ask you, Miss Soudé, to order me a horse and cart. I expect letters, and I will drive over for them."

"Certainly. I will drive you both," said Therese, nodding lazily. "It will be a good way to kill the morning. No, John, we do not want you with us."

John, when the wagon was brought up, helped them into it, joking about the energy of ladies in business affairs. "I'll wager Miss Warrick expects a new pattern for her embroidery, or a—a hat-posy," he said, looking fondly up into her face.

She smiled down at him. He seemed very young and stupid to her. If he could guess the meaning of the letter that she expected! The enormous interests which she soon would have to look after, the real estate, the bonded property! For, though Milly meant to give him the whole of her fortune, to pour it into his hands, as she said, she always thought of managing every dollar of it herself.

Cousin Julia asked no questions, but she watched Mildred wistfully. Did she too expect to hear from Eliza Joyce? If the fortune came to her, what would she do with it? Would she give Anne her share? How much would she consider a reasonable share for Anne?

Mrs. Dane discussed flowers and snakes as they drove over the green slopes with Therese, who had an intimate acquaintance with all kinds of wild things, but she watched Milly's gentle eyes speculatively, all of the time. Her father, of course, she would provide for. But what would she do for Anne?

Mildred's energetic action this morning had pricked John with a desire to be up and doing also. He must uproot Farro, and that soon. Why not to-day? He lighted a fresh cigar and looked at the hammock. No! If it must be done at all, the sooner the better.

Besides, there really was nothing else to be done just now. The other men had gone to the lake to fish until luncheon. Doctor Warrick, with his drag-net and tin box, was busy with the green scum on the bayou.

Farro was in the stables. He would drop in and tell him that he would assume full charge of the plantation next Monday, and then join his father and Paramba and explain what he had done. The whole affair would be settled in a few moments; he would put on the harness for his life's work, while Milly was bringing her fal-lals from Ste. Barbe.

It was with a half smile of tender meaning that he lounged into the stables. Farro was not there. Surely, there were no stables so clean in Louisiana! and none so empty! He glanced down the long rows of stalls. The Soudés had owned a famous racing stud before the war; the names of seven champions of the turf still were on the silver plates over their vacant stalls. One after another had been sold by the General at Farro's instigation. John surveyed the few horses which were left, swore at them under his breath as worthless beasts, and took his way to the Works with quicker steps. The family had been disgraced by the rule of this mulatto long enough. It was high time, as Paramba had said, that he took the matter in hand.

The Works and the quarters of the men wore an exceptional air of neatness and prosperity. John had often been congratulated in New Orleans upon the reputation of the plantation. No sugar brought as high a price in the market as that of the Reve des Eaux.

" He knows how to make the money ! " Soudé muttered, as he walked slowly to Farro's office. " *Chut!* He can go on making it, but I will spend it. He must content himself now with a salary instead of the earnings."

He climbed a rickety ladder, and reached a loft in which stood a high desk and an office stool. Before the desk a man stood writing. He looked up when Soudé entered and continued to look at him for an instant without speaking, but that was the only sign of the consternation which he doubtless felt. Then he quickly removed his hat, and humbly motioned the young man toward the stool.

"So this is your den, Farro ? " John said, leaning carelessly against the jamb of the door.

"Yes, M's John. You have never been here before," the overseer said submissively.

"No. I shall come oftener now." John glanced at the man curiously, thinking that he was but a mean little rat, after all, to have gained such power.

The mulatto was past middle age, but his size was that of a stunted, lean boy. There was an odd disagreeable lack of color or definite significance about him. His skin was pallid and covered with brown splotches ("as if," John thought, "the negro in him were fading out!"); his eyes were pale blue, staring vaguely through reddish lashes; his hair, hanging long and lank behind his ears, was of the same sandy color. "Like my Uncle Victor's," John remembered. He wore a long duster of faded cotton, and his hat was a dirty white felt. He held it now in both hands, as he stood before the young man. A singular fact about this freedman was that while he had never unlearned the manners of the slave, his voice and pronunciation were those of an educated white man.

Soudé, observing the fellow now more critically than he had ever done before, was struck by this peculiarity. That and the likeness to his Uncle Victor influenced him in his attack upon him. Instead of charging him with his crimes as he had meant to do, he stood looking at him with a pitying contempt.

"Poor devil!" he said to himself once or twice, before he repeated aloud, "Yes, I mean to come here oftener in future."

"To the Works? Yes, M's John. I often wondered you didn't take an interest in the Works.
Would you like to see the new engine, now, sir?"

"No. I don't care for machinery of any kind.
I intend——" He looked up at the overseer.
Farro was watching him intently, curious to
know his errand. The candid expression on his
mean face startled John. He might be a thief,
but his smile was kind and sincere.

"A gentleman—one of us!" flashed through
Soudé's brain.

Bah! He made haste angrily to say what he
had to say.

"I know nothing about machinery. I am quite
willing to leave the management of the Works—
men and engines—to you. I am satisfied with
the way you have managed them."

"But, there is something you are not satisfied
with, M's John?" the overseer said gravely.

John knew him to be a miserable negro thief,
yet he hesitated and answered him with respect,
almost against his will.

"I make no charges now. I mean to examine
farther. I think it would be proper that one of
the family should examine regularly into the
income and outgo of the plantation."

Farro nodded slowly. "It would seem proper,
in ordinary circumstances. On this plantation——"

"There are no circumstances which can make
it fit that you should hold control on this plantation, as you have done," John interrupted sternly.
"On next Monday I intend to take charge of the .

books. You will be paid a salary thereafter, and your receipts will be confined to that."

"Salary? I have never received a salary, I believe," Farro said, with a queer smile. He was silent a moment, looking eagerly into John's face. "You have not told General Soudé your intention?" he said at last.

"No. But I shall do so to-day. He will agree with me." What if, after all, his father took part with the mulatto? "He will agree with me," John said again loudly.

"I hope he will, M's John," the overseer said. "It would be better if he did." He turned mechanically to the books, and shut them. "It would be better if he did," he said again in a low tone, as if reasoning with himself.

John felt as if there was no more to be said. He had made the attack and there had been no resistance; the man had not even resented the hint of his guilt. Yet, as Soudé stumbled down the rickety ladder, it was with a sense of defeat.

As he walked down the levee homeward, it was not of Farro's thefts that he thought, large as he believed them to be, but of Farro himself.

"That fellow has great ability!" he said to himself. "I see it in the gleam of his eye. And his hair—it is the very color of—of Therese's!" His jaws shut tightly, as he stamped along, his head bent, kicking the lumps of mud down into the bayou. "God! To think of a man like my Uncle Victor shut up in the same skin with a negro! That's hard luck!" he muttered, stretching out his arms with a groan.

CHAPTER XX

JOHN was more moved by this talk with Farro than he cared to acknowledge to himself. He resolved not to broach the matter to his father until after luncheon, when he should be cooler.

The messengers to Ste. Barbe returned " without letters," as Therese announced gayly.

" What can letters matter?" John whispered, as he lifted Mildred from the wagon and looked into her pale strained face. " What do you want with letters? Have you not *me*, my darling?"

After luncheon was over, seeing that she was still pale and silent, he strolled with her down to the orange grove, trying to amuse her, but in vain.

In the evening there was a dinner at the Dutry plantation. Hence it was midnight before John was free to go to his father and tell him of his resolve to oust Farro.

Garoche was in the habit of serving a late supper for the General and some chosen crony, " to ensure comfortable sleep."

John therefore went to the gallery outside of his father's private rooms, and throwing himself down on the steps, stretched out his legs, clasped his hands behind his head, and waited for him. After a few moments of blissful quiet it occurred to him that he would eat supper first, before broaching this unpleasant business. Paramba would probably come in, and it would be much easier to drink and smoke with the two old men, as he had done a thousand times, than to grapple with problems of business and marriage.

The moon was mounting the sky, and the great plain before him, darkened here and there with its groves of ancient trees, lay motionless in the white light like a land of enchantment. As John looked at it the slow tears rose to his eyes.

God had made it for her—her: that he could make her happy in it. He did not hear his father, who came out on the gallery with his pipe and sat down behind him: but the old man was watching him, his red eyes, peering through folds of fat, growing more uneasy, as the silence was prolonged.

He leaned forward at last and touched John on the back.

"What has happened, boy? Something has hurt you?"

"Me? No!" John laughed to himself. "Nothing could hurt me now, I think."

"What has happened?" The general bent closer, curious. "You did not use to have secrets from the old man, John."

"No, father." John's face was aglow with the whole story, but he remembered Milly's command and checked himself. "In a few days I can tell you all, sir. Just trust me till then." He edged along the step until his broad back leaned against his father's knee. "I was thinking just now that there was no more beautiful home in the world than this, and that when I bring her to it——"

" Her?"

The General sat upright, staring at him. "Do you mean—— Are you thinking of—a wife, John?"

"Why not, sir?" John laughed consciously. "I am old enough for such thoughts, surely."

"Certainly, certainly!" General Soudé pushed him away, rose, walked to the door unsteadily, and came hurriedly back. "Pardon me, my son. You startled me. I did not receive your intimation as I ought. But you have never spoken of marriage. I thought you had resolved never to marry. You startled me—greatly."

"It seemed as if you must know, father—as if every-body who has seen her would know that I could not help but love her. I never have talked of women and marriage as other men do, but—I am not different from other men."

"I have thought of your marriage. But I expected you to—I did not think you would go far afield to find a wife," his father said, under his breath.

But John was not listening. He was looking at the broken windows of the house, at the pigs asleep under the gallery.

"I am going to work now, sir, to make money, to repair the old house. It would be a beautiful home for her, if——"

"If? What has that to do with it?" cried the General vehemently. "We've been short of money since the war—yes. But we will soon set things to rights! You and I, down at Orleans! We'll go down to-morrow! You shall have her, boy! You shall have her!"

John put his hand on his father's knee. "Yes, if she is to be won, I'm going to win her," he said simply.

General Soudé sank back in his chair. He actually meant it? It was no passing whim. He never had thought of John as marrying a stranger. How could any woman but Therese come into this house and not guess its miserable secret?

Why had he hidden it from John?

If he had been told years ago he would have been used to it in his life by this time, as men grow used to inherited incurable disease. He would never have thought of bringing a stranger to pry and discover——

Ah! Perhaps it was not a stranger? Perhaps——

"John!" he called hoarsely, and when his son turned to him, he caught him by both hands, looking up eagerly into his face. "It is—it is Therese?"

"*Therese?*"

John drew back. His face looked colorless in the moonlight. "*I* marry Therese?"

"No, no! I beg your pardon, *mon cher*, I see it is folly. But I thought you were very fond of her."

"Yes. Not—not in that way," he stammered.

"No. Not in that way. I understand. Forgive me."

John walked up and down the veranda. "Therese?" he whispered, again and again.

The General meanwhile wriggled impatiently on his chair, muttering oaths at women in general and eying John furtively. There was good warm blood flowing through the mass of fat. His son was the one thing dear to him.

Why, he had lifted that big fellow, a baby, out of his dead mother's arms, and sworn to make every day of his life happy! And now he wanted to blast it, to rob him of all his birthrights of manhood!

But to bring a stranger into this house! What would Farro say?

He would keep the secret no longer. He would tell John all, now. Perhaps the boy would help him to bear the burden. "God knows, I'm tired of it!" the old man muttered, looking at John, at the prairie, with a groan.

He would tell him—now.

When John sat down near him again he leaned forward, and touched him.

"My son," he said. But the fumes of the turtle-stew came from the room inside. Garoche was lighting the lamps. The old man's courage balked at the effort and sank down. John was looking at the dim savannas with quiet, happy eyes.

"He is thinking of his sweetheart," thought the General, laughing. "I used to lie around thinking of Madeleine that way. John?" He coughed diffidently. "Is she—a fine woman? As to figure, now? Your mother had the finest arms and ankles in St. Mary's. I hope she——"

"Supper, sah," said Garoche.

John helped his father to rise. He only nodded

and smiled for answer. He had been used to discuss the fine points of all the beauties of New Orleans. But to talk of Mildred as if she were a horse!

The General did not press the question. He never talked when eating. You lost the flavor of a dish by such folly, he said. Wit and wisdom should come in with the cigars, but the meal itself was too important to be damaged by them. He munched away in silence, growling orders to Garoche, who anxiously watched his every mouthful.

John was the son of his father. The turtle and the famous Soudé sherry cleared the landscape of his whole future. Major Paramba joined them, and he and John gossiped of the Dutry dinner and the ball to-morrow, in an under-tone, until the General had finished his supper.

"Where have you been, Paramba?" he asked at last. "You were gone for a week."

"I thought you would miss me," the major said, with an important nod. "I have been at Orleans, looking after some business. What kind of bird is this? I believe Viny creates birds to suit her sauces! Yes, gentlemen. I have had important business to look into. And it concerns you, John. I said nothing about it before, for I was waiting to hear from Pomeroy this afternoon. Charles Pomeroy, of Lafourche. You know him, General?"

",Certainly. Grandson of Louis Paulet. Very good stock. The Paulets and Soudés inter-married in France."

"So I have been told, sir," said the major deferentially. "Well, Charles Pomeroy has a project in which I am greatly interested. John, too, if he looks at it as I do. I heard from Pomeroy to-day that matters were in train, and that I was to break the subject to you. There is not a day to lose in carrying it out."

"Not a day to lose!" puffed the old man contemptuously. "Eat your supper, Henri, in peace. The business will fare better if it waits a month or a year. You take my breath. Young men are so full of work nowadays! Making fortunes, rebuilding houses, marrying—all in a day! I thank God that I belong to the last generation!"

"We thank God for you, sir, wherever you belong," said M. Paramba, bowing gravely. "But really, this matter demands haste. It is a new paper, a review, to be published by Pomeroy, fortnightly. It is to be the literary organ of the South, and we wish to put her best men to work on it. I am Adviser-General as you might say. The first man on Pomeroy's list of contributors was John Soudé. The first name on my list was John Soudé. Yes, sir. The lad's letters in the *Picayune* yet ring through the South. Their glow and fervor, sir, have been equalled in our time only by passages in St. Elmo or Gayarré's finest efforts!"

"Oh, come now, Paramba!" John laughed, a sudden delicious triumph rising to his head like wine. "Those letters were poor things. Though," he added reflectively, "I did take a good deal of pains with the descriptive passages, and they have been approved by—a person of high critical taste."

"It may suit you to call them poor things, sir," said his father hotly, "but I recognized their merit. At once, Paramba, at once! I said, if the South does not appreciate such writing as that, it does not deserve to have a literature! What do I care that that penny-grinder Le Duc can make millions in Kansas lots! John here, by a few scratches of his pen, can bring tears to my eyes and lift my miserable old soul up to God!"

The younger men listened respectfully until the General, with many snorts and oaths and thumps on his knee, had ended this speech.

Then the major, leaning back with a business-like air, continued, "Pomeroy wishes you, John, to send him an article for each number."

John, with kindling eyes, reflected a moment, and deciding that he could take Farro's place in the management of the plantation, and have abundant leisure for authorship, nodded gayly.

"He wishes to consult with you. The very name of the review has yet be chosen. Pomeroy inclines to *The Casket*. But that is not absolutely new, and, I think, suggests death."

"Name, eh? Name?" interrupted the General anxiously. "A vital point, sir! Stop! *The Southern Constellation!* How does that strike you?"

"Admirable! I will send that to Pomeroy. Thank you, General."

"*Doucement!* I can do better than that. Oh, we must all put our shoulders to the wheel! A

Southern organ, at last? I am proud that my son," waving his hand toward John, his thick voice growing thicker under the influence of emotion and sherry, "that *my* son will help in this great movement."

"If the pen in his hand, General," said the major, with profound deference, "be as mighty in the service of the South as was the sword in yours——"

"Stop!" interrupted the old man sharply. "No more of that, Henri. We all tried to do our duty. It was our lot to fail. We will not beslaver ourselves with praise. Pass the bottle!"

M. Paramba hastily entered into details concerning the new paper. The General was lavish with advice.

"This is a tremendous undertaking, gentlemen," he said. "Had it been the will of God," bowing reverently, "that the South should succeed, she would have shown her resources to the world. It was His will that she should fail. This publication will take up that work; you will show the South as she is. The eyes of the civilized world will be upon you. Those nations of Europe who sympathized with us will demand to know what we are doing now. You will tell them."

Paramba's eyes twinkled as he stood up to light his cigar, but he said gravely: "What we most need is a man as editor whose power and brilliancy have a national reputation. We lost him, sir, when your brother Victor died."

The General looked at him quickly, but made no answer.

"The other day," continued M. Paramba,

"when the partners in the enterprise dined together, Pomeroy observed—I think I can recall his precise words,—' The South once boasted a man whose name would have ensured success to our undertaking. I allude to that gifted son of Louisiana—Victor Soudé.' We drank to his memory standing and in silence."

The old man's head was sunk upon his breast; he drew his breath heavily for a moment. Then he rose with an effort and said, speaking in French, as he always did when moved: " The young man was right. The Soudé family—my family. They have borne an honorable name in Louisiana—in this nation. The highest name in their record is —Victor's, my brother's."

His red eyes turned defiantly from one man to the other, as if expecting a contradiction. When neither spoke, he tugged at his cravat. "How hot it is! I am burning up! D——nation, Garoche!" he shouted. "Open these windows!" He walked heavily out to the gallery.

"Sit down, major," whispered John, as he threw open the casement. "There is always such an outbreak when my uncle is mentioned. It has been so ever since he was killed. He will be himself presently."

The men began to talk of the paper again, and after a brief space, General Soudé, with a flushed, apologetic face, shuffled back to his seat, and essayed to take part in the discussion. A little later Garoche came with bedroom candles. John, after he had escorted the major to his chamber, hurried back to his father.

"Now, General!"—standing beside him with a glowing face. "This is a turn of the wheel! A chance for real fame, sir! I wonder what she will think?"

"She? Oh, yes! You still—still think of her?" he stammered, looking up with bleared, confused eyes.

"Think of her?"

The words choked in his throat. The old man put out his hand and touched his arm apologetically.

"I think of her—yes!" John was silent a moment, and then, laughing hoarsely, said: "There never was a day in my life like this. Do you remember our old ostler Lippy? He was a pious soul. He used to take me on his knee and tell me that the Virgin and—and her Son—looked after me, that it was they who kept me from breaking my neck and brought me good luck. I don't know. I never was sure of it; but to-day, when Paramba brought me that chance to be famous, and to win her, I believed it. Somebody's caring for me."

"I've no doubt of it, my boy," said the General, sopping the sweat from his face. "God's been mighty good to me, on the whole," he added reverently. "He planned well for me. But the plans got infernally mixed up down here, John. Now, get to bed. Send Garoche. I'm tired out."

John patted his father affectionately on his huge back and went out, his eyes shining, whistling to himself.

CHAPTER XXI

GENERAL SOUDÉ dozed for a few minutes in the deserted room, and awoke with a start, conscious that some one was near. Farro was standing at the other side of the table, watching him. The lamp smoked in front of him, a swarm of moths buzzed about it or drowned themselves in the dregs of brandy in the glasses.

"Hah! Is that you, Farro? What is wrong now? What keeps you up?"

"I have come to tell you, sir. It would not wait till morning."

"No, I suppose not. This is a night of disclosures," the General said dryly. He moved the bottles before him, with a vain effort to appear at ease. He was never at ease before the little gray man who stood before him, insignificant and rigid, but watchful as a bird of prey. The General was a man who, in spite of the big brute within him, always held himself well in hand. The hotter the battle, the cooler he had been. He had once cowed a furious mob in the Place de St. Louis, as he would a dog, with his calm pluck.

But before this mulatto he was timid and unsure of himself. Whatever might be the secret relation between them, it unnerved him: he had never been able, during the years in which Farro had been overseer of the plantation, to speak to him naturally, as he would to any other man.

"Sit down, Farro," he said, nodding to a chair.

"No, I thank you, M's Gaspard. I'd liefer stand."

"You have come to talk business, I suppose? Cut it short, then. It is late. And once and for all, Farro, don't trouble me by these frequent consultations. The semi-yearly reports show me what our income is. I hear of the yield of other plantations, and I see that you are bringing a double profit from ours. I am satisfied with that. I don't ask for details."

"But M's John is not satisfied," said the overseer, coming a step closer. "He came to the office this evening, to say that he meant to take charge of the accounts next week."

"Take charge? John? What does he know of accounts? Tell him it is impossible!" shouted the General.

"It is not for me to tell him," said the overseer quietly. "I have often wondered he did not call me to reckoning. He knew that the crops were large, even when he was most stinted for money."

The General stared at him. "Why, Farro! If he overlooks the accounts he will ask where the money has gone!"

"Yes."

Both men were silent. General Soudé's eyes were fixed on the thin, immovable face before him. He rapped sharply on the table.

"What is to be done? Don't stand there, dumb! How can it be kept from him?"

"Why should it be kept from him any longer?" said the mulatto, in his usual submissive tone. "Why not be candid with him? Let him bear his share of the trouble. He will be more willing to economize."

"Economize? Why, the lad wants to marry! Must he live like a pauper then? His share of the trouble? God knows I've borne my share of it!" He rose and lumbered up and down the room, striking his hands fiercely together. He stopped before Farro. "Why should I be tormented this way all my life? A mistake was made. Godamercy! What of that? Look at Pierre Coteau. He shot his brother in a duel. That does not keep him awake at night! Or Jean Fernan? He kicked a negro wench and her unborn child to death. She does not haunt him. They are fat and happy. Why am I and my boy to be hounded to death for the mistake of an hour?"

Farro kept his eyes respectfully on the ground, but said nothing. The General dropped exhausted into a chair, the cold sweat oozed out upon his forehead. He leaned back, his eyes closed. Farro came nearer, keenly scanning the countenance before him. It was a patrician face, capable of noble meanings, yet, mean as were his own features, there was a subtle likeness between the two.

Farro's mother, however, had been a good housekeeper; a shrewd, practical woman as any white New Englander. There are many such departures in her race. Her cool common-sense was usually uppermost in her son. It was that which now managed the plantation.

He briskly closed the windows to shut out the ghostly night sounds from the marshes, built up the fire until it blazed, and said cheerfully:

"Just look at the facts a minute, M's Gaspard. That will make it plain to you what is best to do. The money must go as it has done. But M's John ought to know how it goes. He is your heir. He is not a minor. In one sense it is his property. It is only fair to him to tell him."

"Haven't I been fair to him?" groaned the old man. "Haven't I tried to hide from him what was worse than death? I've kept him like a beggar to hide it. Lord! The hunters I had at his age, and the hounds! All my clothes from Paris, too. I've hid it from him because—— But how could *you* understand why I hid it?"

Farro looked at him steadily. "I think I understand," he said calmly. "I couldn't have given my life to this work for ten years without understanding. But M's John ought to know why he cannot have hunters and Paris coats," he persisted.

"I'll not have him worried, I tell you! I have made up my mind. He has had all the life crushed out of him as it is."

The little gray man came up to the table before he spoke. For the first time in his life there was no hint of submission in his low tones.

"You are mistaken, General Soudé. M's John has not been crushed. He has had plenty to eat and drink ; he has played away his life comfortably for thirty years, and "—his voice changed meaningly—"he has always ranked as a high-toned gentleman in Louisiana. I took care of that. I don't want to speak of myself. I'll never do it again. But I'm driven to it now. The work of hiding this thing ten years ago belonged as much to him as to me. He didn't do it. *I* did it."

"Yes, you did, and well, Farro. Very well."

"I did not do it for praise, and I want none now. But I will not be called a thief. M's John calls me a thief to all the planters in Attakapas. It is natural. He does not know where the money goes. Farro steals it. Farro is an f. m. c. It is a thing of course. But I mean to keep a clean name. I will not be called a thief. I have little children."

"Why, of course, boy!" The old planter looked at the quondam slave curiously, as he might at a monkey who bore himself in some absurd whim like a man. "You want to keep an honest name for your children—certainly! I will explain it to my son. Why, if you had not thrown yourself into the breach that day—I know what you have done for me, Farro, and for John."

"I did not do it for you or your son. There was a reason——"

The General, regarding the mulatto steadfastly, held out his hand toward him and let it fall. It was the look that moved him. That same old look, so familiar when he and Victor were boys. It came out of the grave now to wrench his heart.

"You shall not be called a thief," he said quietly. "I will tell John. You can go now."

But Farro met John Soudé at the door, coming in hurriedly.

"I heard your voice, father. Why are you up so late? Where is Garoche? Come, let me take you to your room," putting his arm affectionately about his shoulder. "This man has been worrying you with business?" glancing angrily at Farro. "I will relieve you of that kind of annoyance in future. I mean to have a reckoning very soon with this fellow."

"Hush, John. We were discussing a certain matter—whether—I think I will tell him now, Farro?"

The overseer stepped eagerly forward. "Yes, now," he said.

"No. Why should you worry with business to-night?" urged John. "You have so many pleasant things to think of to-night. I could not sleep. Pomeroy's scheme, and—and the matter I spoke to you of—It seems as if every thing good was coming to us at once."

"Oh, you don't know what is coming to you! Good? When I heard it, it seemed as if every thing on earth was tainted and rotten. And now you must know it! I've kept it from you all these years——"

"What do you mean? Sit down. Don't be afraid to tell me. I'm not a child. Unless"— looking at him sharply. "Is it some secret disease? Are you ill?"

"No, no! I'm as sound as a dollar, thank God! The Soudés die of old age or rum—you know the saying. No. It's a thing that——"

He pulled himself up, took John by the arm, opening his mouth as if to speak, and then turned away. " I'll tell you to-morrow."

" No, father; to-night."

" I can't put it into words, Farro! "

" What has this man to do with it ? " said John sternly.

" I understand the matter, M's John. I can explain it to you."

" Be quick about it, then. My father is greatly shaken." He watched the old man anxiously while Farro spoke.

" It was a business transaction, M's John. Your Uncle Victor. He came home in '62. He wanted to equip a regiment, and he had no money."

" His heart was in the cause, John," interrupted the General, looking up piteously to him. " His poverty maddened him. He was not sane—not sane! "

" Go on! What is it ? "

" He found the money," Farro said, in a whisper. " He took the regiment into the field, and was killed, as you know."

" Found the money ? "

" It was a great sum. I have it all set down— you can see the papers—it belonged to Stohl et fils, bankers in New Orleans and Paris. He was their counsel and had access to their safes. He——"

John walked across the floor with a strange guttural noise in his throat. His father watched him in silence, gray pallor creeping over his huge features.

Farro hesitated, and then went on. He had done his duty in this matter better than the white men, yet perhaps he did not quite. understand what it meant to them.

"Stohl et fils have acted very considerately to M's Gaspard. He pledged himself to repay every dollar, and asked that the secret might be kept. They have kept it. Mr. Stohl himself receives the yearly payments. His receipts are all ready for you to examine."

John made no answer. His back was toward them.

"I wish you to go over the books, to-morrow, sir. They are accurate to a penny—the receipts from the crops and——"

John turned and came quickly to the General. He had forced a smile into his face. "And you've had this load all these years? Alone, while I—you should have told me—why, *I* don't mind it, father. It won't break me down. But we must make haste to pay it off! Every dollar! I've been wasting money frightfully. We can save in clothes—on the table, every way."

"I have saved, dear boy!" exclaimed the General miserably. "I am sure the table——"

"Great Heavens—Therese!" broke out John. "If she hears that her father—— How can I hide it from her?"

"You forget, M's John," interrupted Farro calmly, "this is not a new thing. It happened ten years ago. It has been hid."

John caught sight of his father's quivering lips, and suddenly braced himself. "Come, father," he said heartily, "you have done with this load now. I take it on my shoulders. It is an old dead matter, after all. We will soon set it right. Now you must go to bed."

As he led him from the room Farro hurried to hold the door open for them. John stopped short. "I did you an injustice," he said. "I am sorry for it," and held out his hand.

The General nodded kindly, and when they were out of hearing, said: "That is a faithful fellow, John. I am glad that you recognized his services. They have feelings very much like ours, after all."

Farro just then was creeping softly into his cabin, that he might not waken his wife and children. He knew that he had given ten years of hard work to protect the name of Victor Soudé, yet the consciousness of the *great sacrifice did not give him as keen a pang of pleasure as this shake of the hand from a man that he disliked.

It was a recognition of the white blood in him. It flamed in his veins. He stopped to look at the babies as he passed their trundle-bed, and kissed them both, but he patted one fondly. It was the whiter of the two and had reddish hair.

John left his father in his room and hurried out of the house. He had a queer shivering fit such as women have, and was ashamed of it. He had been thrown headlong into filth and never could be clean again! The Soudés, thieves! He plunged into the marsh and walked in the night for hours.

The morning rose at last on his wretched-

"'I DID YOU AN INJUSTICE,' HE SAID"

ness. Red lights struck across the vast slope toward the Gulf, with its population of spectral trees and moving mists. The fresh air blew; thousands of birds began to sing. Soudé ran to the bay and, undressing, threw himself into the water. He fought with the waves a while, shouting to himself, and came out all in a glow and laughing. He was so young! There was so much to do! The day was so bright and cold! Now for work. Every dollar must be saved to pay off that debt, and he must plunge into Pomeroy's scheme and earn a support for his wife. Milly and he would· take care of Therese, he thought, with a tender smile on his lips.

He hurried to the house. There was so much to do, and he was so strong and able for it, that the old disaster faded, dim and far off as the unclean fogs yonder upon the swamps.

CHAPTER XXII

MAJOR PARAMBA that morning found General Soudé at the breakfast table, inspecting critically the dishes which were to be set before his guests. His old neighbor perceived a change in him. He held his head erect; his color was ruddy, his voice hearty, as they had not been for years.

"You look as if you had heard good news, General?"

"No, sir. No. But I talked over my affairs with John last night. Some old troubles. He threw a new light on them, sir! You have no idea of the strength and intelligence of that boy. He is going to grapple with my—my difficulty. March alongside of me, as you might say. I feel twenty years younger this morning. Try that fish, Paramba."

"You are up early," the major said, as he sat down.

"I could not sleep. I have been down here for an hour, planning articles which John must write for the review."

"Pomeroy," said the major, "suggested a series of papers from him on our Southern cities; their condition, commercial, literary, and social——"

"Admirable! Nothing could be better! John must not neglect one of them. The least of our towns is liable any day now to become a metrop-

olis. I am particularly pleased that John has
this work to do," he said, lowering his voice.
"The lad has an attachment——" He ended the
sentence with significant nods. "Our Northern
friends leave us this evening, and I shall go with
them to New Orleans to look out a house for
the young couple."

"Ah, is it so near as that? I congratulate you
with all my heart," wringing his hand. "You
are just the man to fall in love with a daughter-
in-law and to make her happy. They will live in
Orleans then?"

"In Orleans in winter: here in summer, sir. I
planned it out this morning."

"I know of two fine mansions there for sale."

"I will look at them to-morrow, Henri. I will
look at them. I must have large galleries, where
the boy and I can smoke and she can work at
her embroidery. And a garden. She is, I believe, fond of flowers. She has, I imagine, all the
gentlest tastes of a gentlewoman."

"Of course. You will live with them then,
General?"

"Undoubtedly. Why, sir!" turning with sudden alarm. "Where should I live but with John?
Do you think she would object to the old man?"

"General! Do you mean to insult John's wife?
Object to *you*?"

"Well, well! You startled me!" He put his
hand on Paramba's arm, saying, with laughing
eyes, "I am full of plans for them this morning! I mean them to be rich, sir, rich! I am
going to join the money-making hordes to-mor-

row. There is no doubt in my mind that I shall succeed in speculation, Henri. It takes an old, shrewd head to go into that sort of thing. I shall not be surprised if I clear a hundred thousand the first season."

"No doubt, General." The major looked at him wistfully over his coffee-cup.

Therese and her guests came in at that moment. The group of girls in their airy gowns gathered gayly about the table. It was strewed with roses; a cool, bracing air blew in through the open windows. John hurried in, immaculate in white flannels, his olive skin glowing from his sea bath. Every-body was hungry and merry. The Soudés, father and son, joined in the laughter with as light hearts as if they had begun life afresh that morning.

Presently the major leaned across the table, and said in a low voice to John:

"You broached that matter to your father?"

"Yes. But we were grossly unjust to Farro. I have looked into the affairs of the plantation and am content to leave them entirely in his hands." He spoke with decision. "There is an old lien on the estate, which absorbs the income."

Miss Warrick sat next to John and, as he spoke, M. Paramba was watching the pearly tints in her chin and throat. They turned blood red suddenly. He stared at her. But how could the lien on the Soudé estate concern her? Besides, a woman in his opinion understood business no more than would a rose or a doll.

When breakfast was over, Milly went out to the

veranda. Old Tertius on his mule was jogging across the prairie toward Ste. Barbe.

"I tried to start him three hours ago," said Therese, laughing.

"I should think," said Mrs. Dane, "you would have your mail brought regularly, daily."

"We are content if it reaches us somehow once a week. Our world is all here, you know."

"And I would ask no bigger nor better world," said Doctor Warrick energetically, shouldering his tin cases and hooks for a start. "If I had my laboratory here, with these marshes I could finish my work in a year."

"He does not care what Tertius brings!" thought Milly, looking after him. "Yet it will secure his whole future, dear soul!" She had already planned to build him a little laboratory in this elysium for biologists, when her fortune was secure.

When? It would be sure to-day!

As she crossed the veranda she passed Ned Calhoun, who was painting a grinning negro boy. "I'll buy one of his pictures and make him the fashion, so that he can pay poor old Brooke back," she said to herself. "Mother was fond of Brooke."

Anne and one of the Fontaine girls were standing on the steps. As Miss Fontaine raised her hand, the flash of a great green stone struck Milly's sight.

"Ah-h!" Her eyes shone. She loved jewels. "That is the famous Fontaine emerald, I suppose. Poor little Nancy!" She glanced at her sister's ringless hands. "She shall have her trinkets, too. Mother would like her to have as much as I, though I have done the work." She frowned,

15

but in a moment the tender, sweet smile came back. Milly was affectionate and generous to-day as never before. She sauntered down to the lake, listening to eager steps which followed her. It was something in the steps which made her heart burn and long to give. The sunshine was warm, the birds cooed overhead. She was so happy that the tears actually came to her eyes. She sat down by the water, to wait, and began to pull idly at a vine near her. It was a monster passion flower. How her mother used to work, the year round, to win out some feeble blooms from that vine!

Milly looked around impatiently. Her mother's memory fairly hunted her to-day! The stout, commonplace woman was out of place in this enchanted country. Mildred did not like to remember how wholly she had been controlled by her—by a person who, so her advanced ideas taught her, had been narrow and ignorant even for her bigoted, ignorant times.

When John came to her, she was depressed and anxious. "It is nothing!" she persisted, in answer to his breathless enquiries. "Only I am not like myself here. I am beset by all kinds of queer fancies. Now at home I am a practical little manager."

"You, practical!" John roared with delight and then murmured, tenderly stroking her palm:

> " ' Have you felt swan's down, ever?
>   Or smelt the bud o' the brier?
>   Or tasted the bag o' the bee?
>   Oh, so white! Oh, so soft! Oh, so sweet is she!' "

"You are foolish!" she said. "I am very matter of fact. Did you ever know my mother?" she interrupted herself hastily.

"Your mother? How could I, Mildred?"

"No, of course not. But do you know, whenever I am with you, I think of her? She seems to be with us. On your side. Taking your part."

"Taking my part? Against whom? Who is against me?" Soudé asked, bewildered.

Mildred turned on him cold, questioning blue eyes, out of which a strange woman looked whom he had never known. The next minute she burst into tears.

"Oh, John, take care of me!" she cried. "Nobody but you ever understood me! I have had such a lonely life!"

"It shall never be lonely again, poor little girl!" said honest John, with a choke in his voice, taking her into his arms.

She was quieted at last and smiled through her tears, meaning to begin to talk business now rationally. And then her mind was suddenly filled with delight at his flannel clothes. How the creamy white brought out his rich coloring, and how the damp curls showed the noble shape of his head! And then she saw that the clothes were cut in a fashion of years ago. How people would laugh at them in Luxborough! "Oh, you dear stupid John!" she cried, patting the old coat fondly, and laying her cheek against it.

She lay there with soft, suffused eyes while John told his great news, of Paramba's offer.

"I shall go to work next week," he said. "I think there is something in me"—reddening like a school-boy. "You taught me to think that. And if I ever should become famous, it is to you——"

He stopped, stroking her hair tenderly. John had made up his mind that they should be married in the summer, and told her so with decision. "My salary on the review will be small at first, and it is all that I shall have, but——"

"The dear old plantation?" suggested Milly gently. "I heard you say something about a lien."

"Yes. I have given up all claim to any income from that. My father has use for it—An old lien—yes. No, darling, you are going to marry a very poor man! But there is a little cottage on Camp Street which I can lease and we will put a few traps in it—Why, Milly! What does it matter how we live? We shall have each other!"

Milly laughed. Her blue eyes were full of a mischievous ecstasy. "Oh, you poor John! With your funny dear old coat! And you are going to lease a little cabin in Camp Street! And I will make my own calico gowns, and sometimes, as a great treat, you will bring home some chops in a piece of brown paper! Oh, I see it all!" And she laughed until the tears came.

John, bewildered, said nothing, but broke a piece of wild vine with starry white flowers and twisted it around her head. "My queen!" he said.

Milly's swift fancy suggested that the wreath could easily be copied in a real crown. "The leaves in gold filigree and the blossoms in pearls. Tiffany shall do it for me. I shall indulge myself in jewels," she thought, lifting her radiant face to John. Ah! When he knew! Would Tertius never bring that letter!

"Mildred!" Mrs. Dane was crossing the field. She waved a yellow telegram in her hand excitedly.

"It has come!" Milly rose. "Wait here for me, John. I will bring you—I have something for you." She tried to run, but walked slowly to meet her cousin.

Mrs. Dane anxiously watched her whitening face. "She suspects it; I need not break it to her," she thought. Yet Milly stood waiting beside her a moment before she could say, "Perhaps you have heard too? One of the neighbors brought this. It is from Paul Franciscus. Mrs. Joyce is dead."

"Yes. I knew that she—Is that all?"

"No. He says"—the paper shook in Mrs. Dane's fingers, as she opened it—"he says, 'Will was read to-day. Legacy of five hundred dollars for Mildred Warrick. The entire remainder of estate goes to charitable and religious objects.'"

She folded the slip carefully, not raising her eyes. She never had loved Mildred, but she could not look at her now. Her old heart was sick for her.

Milly at last held out her hand for the paper. "Oh, yes! look at it, poor child!" Mrs. Dane broke out. "There's no mistake. The woman

always was a fraud. Your dear sainted mother
never could abide her! I warned Samuel against
her, goodness knows! To hang on you like a
vampire all the best years of your life—— And
now—five hundred dollars!"

Mildred stood looking at the yellow paper.
She did not speak nor hear. At last she handed it
back. "It does not matter to me," she said, with
a strained, polite voice. "Goes to charity—to
religion. She had to buy her way to—— It
does not matter to *me*."

"No, of course not," cried cousin Julia
eagerly. "That's the tone to take to stop
remark. That's what I shall say in Luxborough—
'Mildred always was aware of her cousin's generous intentions to the church and hospitals.'
Unless"—pausing anxiously—"the will could be
broken? I might wire Paul at once."

"No. She was perfectly competent to make a
will. Quite sane. If I broke it, I am not the
next heir."

"Something might be gained by contesting.
Let me wire Paul, Mildred."

"No!" Milly's voice rose in a shrill squeak.
"You will make me the town's talk. For nothing! It is of no use, I tell you!"   .

"Just as you choose! *I* should contest,"
grumbled cousin Julia, as she turned to go back
to the house. Milly crept down the hill. Her
legs moved like logs. Was she going to be ill?
She must hurry to him. *He* was left. There
was nothing now left her in the world but
John.

"And I meant to do so much good with it!"
she suddenly cried out.

When she reached Soudé, she threw herself
down on the ground with her head on his knees.
" I have you still!" she sobbed.

When John, amazed and terrified, tried to
soothe her, she clung to him fiercely, crying
again, "You! *You* are left to me!" Presently,
looking up at him, she laughed wildly. "I have
you—and the calico gowns and the chops!" she
said, holding up her quivering lips to be kissed.

CHAPTER XXIII

IT was a rainy afternoon in June. Anne and Mildred were comfortably seated at work in their parlor at The Oaks, but through the low windows they could see the gray mists driven through the valley below, and the sheets of blinding rain, with flashes of wet brilliance coming between. Anne incessantly dropped her pencil and note-books to run to the window, or to stir the smouldering wood-fire: but Milly never lifted her eyes from the seam which she was sewing.

She was to be married in a month. She had expended her five hundred dollars upon her wedding outfit, and she was at work upon it now.

The vista of poverty opening before her was so appalling to her that she hid it as a disgrace. No one but her father and Anne knew of her approaching marriage.

"I have something more serious to think of than rain or rainbows," she said now irritably. "You never will be more than ten years old, Anne. I should think that report would require all of your attention."

Her tone was a little acrid. For it was Anne, and not herself, who, so suddenly after their return, had been elected Secretary in one Woman's Charitable Board and Director in another.

They had found a charitable mania rampant in Luxborough. Nobody had expressed the sympathy for Milly's disappointment which she had so feared to face. Nobody apparently remembered that she ever had had any claim upon the Joyce millions. Mrs. Joyce's munificence had revived a dozen languishing asylums, hospitals, and libraries. Luxborough, especially the female part of it, was suddenly agog with philanthropic zeal.

At that time, the fever of Reform was not epidemic among the women of this country as it is now. Many of them had been reluctantly forced by the war into work, and a few old Quaker ladies were demanding suffrage. Here and there were sporadic cases of disgust with man's rule, but even the most discontented of the insurgents would have laughed at the claims of the Advanced Woman of to-day. Victory had not as yet tainted the rebelling sex with conceit: its discontent as yet found vent only in family or church squabbles.

So, in Luxborough. Mrs. Hayes, who now lectures by turn on Biology and Street-cleaning, and boldly declares all men since Adam to have been unamiable and vicious, then only found relief in nagging the rector of the High church until life was a burden to him. All of the prominent Luxborough women were in committees for the management of the Joyce money. But none of them dared to chirp a protest when Mr. Mears, who, as a charitable expert, was chairman of most of the Boards, placed the younger Miss Warrick in the most responsible positions. They might gibe and sneer at her behind her back, but the Tyrant Man was still king. They could do nothing.

Anne, who two months ago had been tortured by a soul which panted for love, for immortality, for self-sacrifice by turns, found herself suddenly bound down to note-books, committee meetings, and reports. She showed a keen insight and swift common-sense in dealing with these matters which enraptured Mr. Mears.

A dozen voluble committee-women had filled the parlor all morning. Milly in one corner bent over her sewing and listened in silence.

It was *her* government bonds which were to build the ward for incurables. It was her Pennsylvania Railroad stock which was to buy chimes for the church.

"I should think they would feel like thieves!" she said vehemently, as the hall door closed behind them.

Anne looked up bewildered, then, with an angry flash of intelligence, she said: "Do you suppose they can think *you* wanted Mrs. Joyce's money, dear? I thought it was such good taste in her to leave you so small a sum. If she had given you much, people might have said you had been kind to her with a purpose."

Mildred's blue eyes rested on her for a moment. "Anne is so stupid as to be imbecile!" she said to herself.

Mr. Mears came in at that moment, and he and Anne were soon busied with the reports. Milly glanced over her sewing at the dark and fair heads bent closely together. "A well-matched couple," she thought. "He has birth, position, money, every thing! Anne has won the race without making the running. And I——"

She gathered up her work and carried it to her own room, with defeat gnawing at her heart. But she had John, thank God! She took out of a drawer a package of crossed, badly spelled letters: a huge package, for they rained on her by every mail. She turned them over for a minute, and then put her sewing away. She would take a holiday of an hour to read them. There was no fire in the room. Every cent that she could screw out of the family expenses was going into her wedding outfit. She wrapped herself in her mackintosh, shivering, and sat by the window, the rain pelting outside, to pour over the blotted scrawls, laughing sometimes, with the tears in her eyes, or smoothing them out with tender fingers.

How hard the dear boy was working! And how he hated work! Then at some sudden word, her face would flame with passion, and she would take out Soudé's photograph and look at it with half-closed, dim eyes.

Presently, she unfolded a photograph which he had sent her of the house on Camp Street. A cheap wooden box, with a ten-foot side-yard in which grew a gigantic Gloire de Dijon rose. John had written a poem about the rose: "Its perfume breathed his soul to hers." "Let the rose speak for me." Surely no love was ever so high and fine! He had sent her a mass of rose-leaves: their pungent aroma filled the air as she played with them.

"Breathing his soul to mine——"

Ah-h! She buried her hot face in them.

As she raised it her eyes happened to fall on the table linen which she had bought yesterday. It certainly was coarser than she thought. And how yellow! She rubbed it critically between her thumb and forefinger. Milly dearly loved fine, delicate napery.

Her face slowly filled with disgust and misery. A bride to buy half-bleached table-linen! And cotton underwear! But when household plenishing, gowns, clothes, all, had to come out of a poor five hundred dollars, what could you do?

Go clothed like a pauper for the rest of your life!

The photograph of the house still lay on her knees. It was a cabin for a pauper. Couldn't John see that? John saw nothing but a trumpery rose!

She threw the leaves and the letters and John's picture into the box and shut down the lid with a snap.

CHAPTER XXIV

MILLY found Mr. Mears at the luncheon table, talking of the Ward for Incurables; then he diverged to the home missionary field in Luxborough, and presently meandered to his Colonies in the South. There was an intentness in his fluent voice and hazy eyes which made each work, as he talked of it, seem to bulge until it filled the horizon, and become the only thing worth living for. Even Milly's brain began to swim. Anne replied intelligently, but her face grew jaded and pinched.

The doctor shuffled uneasily, and at last broke into the steady monotone.

" Have a bit of beef, Mears ? Three hundred juvenile criminals! I don't know how you carry them all on your mind, I'm sure! I used to find three or four croupy children load enough for me. I can't shoulder my fellow-creatures in a mass. Heard the last news from Philadelphia ? Enormous rise in oil stock to-day. Franciscus told me. Our friend Plunkett played a bold game."

" I did hear some talk of it," Mr. Mears said, blinking as he dragged his mind down to Plunkett and oil.

" Did he win ? " cried Anne. " I hope he won. Poor David! "

"Yes. Franciscus said there had been no such successful coup in the market in his remembrance," said the doctor importantly. "David Plunkett is now one of the four richest men in the United States."

Mr. Mears listened civilly, and then in an undertone began to explain the prospects of a State Insane Asylum to Anne, and talked until luncheon was over, when he hastily bade them good-by, as he had to make a train to Harrisburg to push a reform bill through.

"Whew-w!" The doctor gave a sigh of relief as the door closed behind him. "Give me a cup of tea. My mind is too little to be spread over such big ideas. I beg your pardon, Anne!" with a gasp of dismay, "I forgot! Mears is a noble fellow."

"Yes, he is," Anne said quietly.

"And his work is noble. There's a good deal of it, to be sure."

"There could be none more unselfish or Christ-like," she said, with a little heat.

"Of course! Didn't I say so? You always had aspirations for that sort of thing, dear, and it seems providential that—— You are bringing so much practical ability to it, too. That does surprise me. Well," he broke out, rising suddenly and pushing his cup back, "it's a fine destiny for a woman to be chosen by such a great man as his comrade and helper."

"Yes, I think so, father," she said gravely.

"I—I suppose there is no doubt that Mears wishes you to be his wife, Nancy?"

"No. There is no doubt."

She was standing by the window, looking out at the rain-swept hills. There was no blush or hesitation in her face.

The doctor trotted up and down the room uncertainly, glancing at Milly for help; but she stitched on in silence. He stopped at last.

"I hope you may be very—My little girl—Nancy?" laying his trembling hand on her arm.

She stooped and kissed it. "I know all you want to say, daddy," she said. But she did not smile, and her face was still strained and pinched. She gathered up her accounts calmly and went out. The doctor looked after her. Anne never had seemed so horribly superior to him before.

"I suppose it is all decided," he said ruefully.

"It looks like it. A very good thing for Anne too. A queer couple!" Milly added, with a harsh laugh. "Two allied benevolences! I wish Nancy could have married a human being, for love. Poor child! She will have no dear mean little house to make ready for any body!" Milly looked at the silk pillow cover which she was embroidering. It was for John. When he came home tired he would lie down and rest his picturesque old head just there. She stroked the place tenderly.

"Where are you going, father? No. Let your spores alone. I want to ask you—What was it we were talking of? Oh, oil stock! What did you say about David?"

"Why, you heard. The news has been cabled all over the world by this time. It's an awful thing for one man to shoulder that mass of money."

"And such a man!" cried Milly shrilly. "He looks like a huge tobacco-worm set on end, with his leering, pasty face!"

"Mildred!"

"I can't help it!" She stood up, with a nervous shiver.

"David has many good traits," said the doctor gravely. "He is underbred, of course. But he means well. I intend to give him some hints. The other day he bought a thousand acres on Delaware bay, and bragged that he would build the finest house in America—copy of Warwick Castle. What does he know of architecture? I must give him some hints. He ought to help Luxborough charities."

"The Joyce estate has gone to them."

"Pah! The Joyce estate is a bagatelle compared to David's fortune."

"Do you mean that?"

"Certainly. David could buy out half the petty potentates in Europe. By the way," fumbling in his pockets, "I forgot. Here is a telegram from him. 'Shall be in Luxborough to-day. Will drop in to dinner, if I may.'"

"To-night?"

"Yes. What's the matter? He is here every week. He is no rarity, Heaven knows."

"He must have sent that despatch as soon as he found that he had won the game."

"Probably. What of it? There is the train now. Be civil to him, Mildred," he said severely, as he went out. The reticent, gentle Mildred had grown shrewish and vulgar lately; he could not blind himself to that. "A tobacco-worm!" Mrs. Joyce's death had unnerved the poor child, he thought.

She stood now, hesitating, looking down at her black gown. David hated black on a woman. He noticed women's clothes and talked much of them. Like a man milliner! she said with a sneer. There was a pale blue frock which he liked to see her wear, with her hair curly and loose.

She folded the cover of John's cushion with shaking fingers. "I must wear the blue!" she said loudly. "I must wear the blue."

But when she reached the door she turned and came quickly back, twisting up her hair in a tight knot, and taking up John's cushion sat down in her shabby black gown to wait for him.

CHAPTER XXV

DAVID, as he sat alone in his special car that afternoon, was filled with a strange exaltation, new in his life. The whole world was talking now of him and his great trick and the millions he had won. He did not care for the millions.

" I had enough before," he muttered carelessly. "But I was the only man with the wit to see that chance! It was my trick. *Me, Me*—Dave Plunkett, who can't spell, and never reads a book. There's a big brain here, after all," knocking his fist on his forehead.

One of the evening papers had called him the "Napoleon of finance." He had cut out the line and put it in his pocket book. He took it out and looked at it from time to time, his huge face glowing.

To-day for the first time he knew that he had a great mind. He was simple and happy as a boy with his first prize at school. He was going to tell his triumph to Milly, of course. She was the only human being he loved in the world. He had always loved her.

"She'll marry me now," he repeated a thousand times. "She'll see what I am. The whole country sees it now. I'm the master of my trade!" He laughed and shouted out songs, so loudly that the thunder of the train scarcely drowned his noise. When they stopped at a station he poured out his oaths on the brakemen and drank huge drams of whiskey. It was flat as water to him, so hot was the fire of exultation and passion within.

The rain had ceased before he reached the Luxborough station: the sunset shone on the wet meadows and dripping trees. Plunkett, his head thrust forward, pushed past old Jem and his cab and climbed the hill toward The Oaks, panting for breath.

She must marry him now. He would not wait a day! All his old doubts and suspicions of Milly vanished in the fury of his triumph, like gnats in a flame. She was the one living woman on earth, and he was worthy of her. The Napoleon of finance!

As he climbed the hill, his huge mass of flesh weighed on him. He "damned the fat" more than once. Within, he was young and alert and handsome—a king among men. Oddly enough, David never had recognized his own hideous ugliness. He invariably thought of himself as a gallant, brilliant young fellow; and always saw the vapid clown's face in the glass as a stranger's, with a vague surprise.

Milly would know him now. He had taken his place among the great intellectual forces of the day. His soul looked through his dull eyes over the world, with full consciousness of power.

Some men passing stared curiously at him. "A hundred millions," he heard them say, and scowled savagely at them.

Money! Was there nothing of him but money!

The doctor hurried across the lawn to meet him, smiling. "I congratulate you, my boy," he said. "Franciscus tells me you are to-day one of the richest men in the United States."

"Damn Franciscus! How can he understand *me?* They all talk of me as if I were nothing but a rich man. When you stick a knife into me, gold don't run out. It's blood, like any other man's!" They plodded on in silence. David suddenly halted and pointed to the grave among the crocuses. "*She* didn't talk of me like that!" he said, in a low voice. "She saw what I was."

"She thought you a poet, I've been told, David," the doctor said soothingly.

"Poet? I don't know. I can't tell what I may do in the future," he answered gravely. "We'll see. When I was a boy, I thought I wrote pretty fair poetry. If I get what I want to-day, I'll make a man of myself. If I get it——"

The doctor watched him askance as they went into the house. Plunkett was strangely excited to-day. But was it any wonder? A hundred millions——

"Milly," he said, hurrying in, "here is David. Come to take pot-luck with us. Come in, Plunkett. Why do you stand out there? Ring the bell, Mildred, for Peter."

David stood just inside the door, immovable. "You do not say that you are glad to see me, Milly?" he said, in his hoarse voice.

"Why, of course I'm glad, David," she piped

"SOME MEN PASSING STARED CURIOUSLY AT HIM"

feebly, without looking up, being busy with her embroidery. She felt his eyes on her; and, presently, peeped up through her curly lashes.

How she loathed the huge creature standing there, with his great, obese body and round, unmeaning face! She stitched on. Just here, on these roses, John would rest his dear old head, when he came home tired, to the mean cabin— she in her calico gown! She peeped up again.

A hundred millions!

Some mighty power outside of herself dragged her to her feet. Her hands dropped. The embroidery fell to the ground.

" Doctor," said Plunkett, " I want to see Milly alone for a few minutes. We'll walk down the hill."

" It's very wet, David. And dinner is almost ready," protested the doctor, uneasily.

Milly hesitated. Plunkett waited, looking at her, without a word. Why should she stand there apart from him, her head on one side, like a cooing, coquettish bird ? Had he not wanted her all of his life ? Every drop of his hot blood claimed her. This palaver about the damp and dinner maddened him. Why should he not rush forward and take her now ? No doubt the blood of some of his ancestors—cave men who clutched the women they chose and carried them off to pick the wolves' bones with them—was hot in his veins to-day.

Yet he only said quietly, " Will you come with me ? I want to talk to you a little."

He opened the door again. Milly looked

steadily, not at him, but at the embroidery on the ground. Then she followed him, leaving it there. But she beat with her finger incessantly on her smiling mouth, like a machine, as she went down the hill, saying to herself, "John—John."

David did not stop until he came to her mother's grave.

"You know what I want to say to you," he said abruptly. "You have always known it. You pretended you didn't, with your pretty little tricks. Don't be tricky to-day, Milly, for God's sake!"

"What did you bring me here for?" she cried, pointing to the grave.

"I don't know. I couldn't help it. She was about the only friend I ever had, and I want her to hear. When you were a little thing, tagging after her, I wanted you for my wife."

"Your wife? I——"

"I feel as if I had a right to ask you now," said David, lifting his head proudly. "I've proved to-day that I am—not a fool——"

The sun shone in his face, the birds were chirping, the grass was blue with flowers. He felt as if he suddenly were crowned a man of men, and spoke resolutely and with force.

"There's only one woman in the world, and that is you, Milly—for me. Why, I love you so that night after night I've gone on my knees and prayed God to give you to me. And to-day, when I saw what the paper called me, and knew there was something in me after all, I thought, 'He has done it! She'll come now!'"

"You want *me* to marry *you?*" she said

slowly, looking up at him through her half-closed eyes. Something in the look silenced David. He watched her, drawing his breath heavily once or twice.

"No," he said at last. "Not unless you love me. If there's any body else, say it. That Soudé fellow is somewhere. If you love him, go to him. I'm a man. I'll bear it. Don't let the money come in. Don't let the money damn my whole life. For God's sake, Milly, tell me the truth, to-day. If you can't love me, say so. Don't sell yourself to me."

"Come away from here!" she cried, looking at the grave with whitening lips. "This is no place for your love-making."

"I am not afraid of the dear soul down there." He took her by the wrists. "Tell me. It is only a word. You won't lie to me when she can hear. Do you love me?"

He drew her near to him. She stared up into the round pasty face. Behind her innocent eyes was a soul in extremity, but David saw nothing of that.

In the silence the grasshoppers chirped shrilly.

"One of the four richest men in America," her father had said.

It would be higher than a throne. And the dusty cabin in Camp Street, and the beggarly gowns, as long as she lived! As long as she lived!

She smiled up into his face.

"I love you, David," she said, steadily.

His whole huge body panted. He gathered her up into his arms and kissed her lips.

"Oh, my God!" she gasped, as he set her down. A cold, clammy sweat broke over her body.

But she still smiled up at him.

David did not smile. He was too deeply moved and excited. He said, "I can't go back and talk about dinner and folly. This is the day of my life. I want you. I have waited a great many years. Put on your hat and come down to the station. In an hour we can cross the line into Jersey and you will be my wife to-night. Will you come?"

She stood bending before him, overpowered, he thought, by his love. Poor little thing! He watched her fondly, reverently, as he would an innocent child.

In those swift minutes Milly's busy brain scanned all the difficulties which would be surmounted by this hasty marriage.

"And I will have no chance to repent," she thought, beating her white lips again with her finger.

"It shall be as you choose," she said aloud. She came directly, decisively to him. She stepped upon the grave to do it.

But there was nothing down in that grave, for her, but clay and sodden grass.

CHAPTER XXVI

OLD Luxborough shuddered to its depths with honest disgust at the news of Mildred's runaway marriage. The women were most vehement. David was a monster, Milly a mercenary little minx. She never had been content with the footing in society which her birth gave her, but made vulgar pretences of fashion. All of the poor little woman's secret devices to make a show—her cheap suppers, her paste pearls, her home-made Worth gowns—had, it appeared, been known to them for years, and were now dragged to remembrance amid shrill peals of laughter. The men, according to the wont of men, said little, but felt themselves to be quite judicial in their remarks. Plunkett, they declared, was a lout, a mere bag of money. No doubt the poor little girl had been forced into the thing. Nobody could look into that innocent face and suspect her of any worldly wisdom. Most probably the old doctor had contrived the bargain and sale. A lazy crank, who had given up work to prowl about picture-shops! They had an idea, too, that Anne had some share in the ugly job. What could you expect of an eccentric, strong-minded female? A very likely person to drive that soft, feminine little thing into it. They were amused at their wives' censure of Milly. But when, they said, were women ever just to a pretty woman?

Meanwhile Anne, more than any body else, bore the brunt of the blow. The catastrophe in the household tore away all that was false and factitious in the girl as a sudden death would have done. She said nothing. Whatever was her opinion of Mildred's marriage, nobody has ever heard it to this day.

When David's despatch, announcing the wedding, came that night, the doctor raged through the house, sobbing and trembling like a child.

"She has disgraced us! I will never hear her name again!" he cried.

It was Anne who thought of John Soudé.

"Yes, write to him, Nancy. I cannot. Tell him I have cast her off. She is no child of mine!"

"I will telegraph him. He must not be left to see it in a chance newspaper," she said.

"I will write to him to-morrow, then. I will wash my hands of the whole foul business. I will tell him that I disown her. Never speak her name to me again!"

Two days later, a letter came from Mildred, dated in New York, quite calm and affectionate, but with a slight tone of authority. They were about to sail for Havre, and would not return until the fall. She enclosed a check for five thousand dollars. "David gave it to me to-day to throw away, if I chose. But I choose to give it to you, dear papa. Deposit it *at once*. The interest will lighten your current expenses. When I return I will see to investing it, and any other sum which I can give you, in a permanent way. I hope now to make your life and Anne's more comfortable, my dear father."

"We will deposit it for her," said Anne. "But we will not draw the interest. We will pay our own way. We are partners now, daddy. Just you and I."

"Yes. We won't use the money, of course. It is blood money in *my* opinion. But, it was sweet in Milly to send it, Anne? Very! I'm sure I hope that we can pay our way. But you must put your shoulder to the wheel. This grind is telling on me. I haven't long to stay in the world, Nancy, and I must give myself now wholly to pure science. I can't be bothered with butcher's bills."

Anne put her shoulder to the wheel with a will. The bills were paid more promptly now that there was no pretence of fashion to keep up. If she had lost faith in her father's consecration to pure science, she did not hint it. When he sat down to write about his microbes, she always left a new novel near him, and went out of the room. She contrived excursions to New York or to the theatre, which they enjoyed as keenly as mice do their play when the cat is gone.

But when Mr. Mears shared his thoughts with Anne, she rose into an ecstatic fervor very different from this jog-trot happiness. He gave her work twice a week in Blockley Almshouse in Philadelphia, and she would walk through the wards rapt in pious ecstasy. The paupers were so wretched and vile, and she—"Sent of God!" she would say to herself. "Sent of God to them! I! Stupid Nancy Warrick!" Mears's purity and unworldliness impressed her more and more as the months passed. When her father joked about him, it hurt her as if he had jeered at her religion. She began to have queer thrills of awe when the man spoke to her.

Mrs. Dane and Mr. Franciscus came out one day in September to luncheon, and left the table in high good humor.

"A delicious meal, my dear!" Paul said gallantly, when they were out on the porch. "Who would have thought our little de Staël would turn out a good cook?" He sauntered out to the stable. Cousin Julia laughed.

"How like a man!" she said. "As if a clever woman would not be clever in a kitchen! I think we can venture to sit down here," dropping into a hickory rocking-chair. Anne sat down on the steps at her feet, and Mrs. Dane talked on. "There was frost this morning, but the sun is warm. You ought to have some fancy-work. In my generation, girls did not sit with their hands crossed like that. But you'll do, Anne, you'll do!" nodding affectionately down at the dark, sparkling face upturned to hers. "I said to Paul this morning, 'Anne is wholly satisfactory.' As for Mildred, the thing is monstrous! A girl should be duly prudent, of course, and that Soudé engagement was pure madness. Those people were only well-bred paupers. A due prudence, of course—but—David Plunkett! Why, my dear, he is brutal. Did you ever see him gorge terrapin? Not all of his hundred millions can make me forget that sight. Oh! I didn't mean to worry you, Anne," with a quick glance at the girl's face. "But, as I told you, I said to Paul, 'Anne will vindicate the family honor.' You're such a good daughter, so loyal and tender, and a careful little housekeeper, and taking a prominent part in public charitable work too. Oh, these things tell, child, in the world's eye! 'Let your light *so* shine,' we are commanded. And Luxborough is watching you, Anne."

Anne laughed. "It usually is occupied with some trifle," she said.

"Don't say snappish things like that. Nothing kills a girl socially so fast as a sarcastic habit. There is no dearth of intelligence in old Luxborough, and it is watching *you*," she repeated significantly. There was no answer. "You will have a warm welcome when you take your rightful place in society there," she added tentatively. Still Anne made no reply.

Cousin Julia put her arm around her shoulder. "I ask no questions, Nancy," she said tenderly. "Still—You seem like a daughter to us—Paul and me. It will make us very happy to see you Mr. Mears's wife." She felt the girl's body start and shrink beneath her arm, and smiled to herself. "He is a great and a good man. You will have a commanding position, where you can help many people. And much more—much! Mr. Mears belongs to the oldest family in Luxborough. His income——"

"Oh, he is more than all that!" said Anne vehemently. "He is like St. Augustine. He lives away up there above other people——"

"Then why in Heaven's name don't you decide to live with him?" Mrs. Dane broke in sharply.

"For one thing, I'm not fit. Oh, cousin Julia, you don't understand. If I fasted and prayed for years I should not be fit to be that man's wife, nor to help him in his work."

"Fasted and prayed! Fiddlestick! If you made some new gowns and baked cake for your wedding, you would be much more in the line of your duty," cried Mrs. Dane angrily. Then controlling herself, she took Anne's hand gently. "You wish to help him, dear?" she said. "You have been groping all of your life for some great work. Here it is. God gives it to you. You see that you ought to do it?"

There was a long silence.

"Well," dropping her hand with an impatient sigh, "we will not talk of it any more to-day. Here comes Paul with the buggy. I must go. Will you bring out my cloak, dear? Oh, look, Anne! Who is that coming up from the station with your father? It looks like that man, Calhoun."

"Yes. It is Brooke," said Mr. Franciscus. "We must wait to welcome him home."

"I am not anxious to do it, Heaven knows! A coarse-grained, loutish fellow! I thought we were rid of him!" Mrs. Dane said irritably, with a furtive glance at Anne. "They told me he had found work somewhere?"

"Yes. So he had," said Mr. Franciscus leisurely, stroking his horse. "But Brodie, to whom he mortgaged the farm, had an opening in California, and he offered to lease the place to

Calhoun. He was telling me about it yesterday. He expected Brooke to-day. They think it will pay as a dairy farm."

"Ah, cows?" sniffed Cousin Julia contemptuously. "Well, I should think Mr. Calhoun had found the right niche for himself—tending cattle and selling milk."

"Julia!" said Mr. Franciscus sternly, "you women are always blind in your judgment of a man who does not belong to your set! You know, as well as I do, why Calhoun is penniless and homeless at his time of life."

"I know that his brother is said to have ruined him. Well, Paul, I may be weak-minded and a woman, but one faculty I have. I am a judge of character: and Edward has always seemed to me the finer man of the two. Eccentric, I grant. But he has soul—genius! The other is a clod."

Paul laughed. "Ned's eccentricity has turned into a new channel now, Brodie told me. He has taken to opium this summer. Brooke took him away from the Soudés, and has had the doctors at work to cure him. But—Ned has found one thing at last in which he can persevere."

"Opium? Oh!" said Mrs. Dane, with a shudder. "And Brooke has taken him in hands? It's a job for life. Well, he *is* a good fellow," she said frankly, finding that Anne was not in hearing. She had gone in for the cloak, and coming back, she stood waiting, watching the short, stout man as he climbed the slope to the house.

"As indifferently, thank Heaven!" thought Mrs. Dane, "as if he were a cart horse!"

Mr. Franciscus, too, scanned Calhoun with a critical eye. He could appreciate his sweet moral nature, but he could not forgive his kneed trousers and slovenly necktie. A man, he held, should look to his hat and gloves if he were going to the stake.

"Poor devil!" he said to Anne, "he is going down-hill, fast! There are some men born to ill luck. There's a God over all, too. It's queer! That fellow started as a boy with high ambitions, and he has done the best he could, yet for the rest of his life he will sell quarts of milk and be the keeper of a drunkard."

"Nothing more than that?" said Anne slowly. She was looking intently at Brooke, who took off his hat and waved it to her in the old boyish way. But his beard she saw was grizzled: his look that of a middle-aged man who had fought hard and been worsted. There was a history in his face which never had been there before. She leaned over the railings; the blood rushed to her head. She could not breathe, so eager was her—curiosity. What was this story hinted in his face? It never had been there before!

"No, I do not see any chance for him," said Mr. Franciscus judicially. "Men do not win fame or fortune peddling milk, especially when loaded with a weight like Edward. And opium eaters live long. How are you, Mr. Calhoun? You are welcome home!" going down to him gayly, with outstretched hand. Mrs. Dane, too, was polite and friendly. There was a little flurry of welcomes and questions and good-bys, and then Mr. Franciscus and Mrs. Dane drove away.

CHAPTER XXVII

CALHOUN found himself seated beside Anne on the old settee on the porch, while the doctor fussed up and down, giving orders to Peter and Jane.

Brooke looked after him, the old sweet affectionate smile lightening his heavy face. " He has not altered one bit ! " he said.

" No."

" Nor you," his keen blue eyes on her face.

" You have only been gone one summer," she said, moving uneasily.

His eyes still rested on hers; he averted them with a sudden consciousness. He reminded himself that there was nothing to say between them now. That was all over long ago—on the day in New Orleans when he decided to shoulder Ned for life.

He began to tell her of his journey yesterday, and its funny incidents. Queer adventures were always happening to Brooke.

" Now, I suppose, Calhoun," said the doctor, bustling up, " that in taking the farm your idea is to pay off the mortgage some day."

" I certainly shall try for it," he said cheerfully. "If I could call the old place mine again, it would be one solid good in my life."

" Why didn't you try ranching in the West ?

Enormous profits out there for a man of skill and energy."

"That big farming does not interest me," Brooke said indifferently. "I know every foot of my old place. Every tree and stone means something to me. But a ranche would be only so much soil and crops. I'm afraid," he said, with a deprecatory glance at Anne, "I hardly belong to this ambitious generation. I never shall fight hard for money or position. I don't want to keep up with the procession."

"You think," said the doctor, knitting his brows anxiously, "that a higher life can be reached through indifference to luxury, simple routine—repose? You are right, boy! Now *I* find pure science most elevating—But, good gracious, Brooke, what can you do in any direction? You can neither make money nor reputation as long as poor Ned is with you."

Calhoun's face contracted as if he had been struck. He did not speak for a moment, and then it was with effort.

"My first duty is to Edward," he said. "I have not told you." He rose and walked up and down the porch. "Nobody knows the truth except the physicians, but you are so near to me——"

His back was toward Anne and he spoke to her father; but she answered him, in a whisper:

"Yes, we are the nearest to you."

He heard her.

"You mean the opium?" said the doctor. "I have heard that; poor boy!"

"ON THE OLD SETTEE ON THE PORCH"

"It is no new thing. We find that he has been addicted to it for years. There is no hope of a cure, the doctors tell me."

"Not in an asylum?" said the doctor. "They have a system now——"

"No. That I will never do!" exclaimed Brooke. "I don't care what the doctors say. I will cure him, and at home, too. Think of shutting up that fellow in captivity! I'll watch him day and night. I'll try and bring what chance of happiness I can into his poor spoiled life. They tell me he may long outlive me. His physical health is perfect."

He stretched out his arms with a long breath and sat down. The doctor hopped around him sparrow-like, with little pitying clucks.

"Tut, tut! And to think what a brilliant career was before Ned! Why didn't he restrain himself?"

"He couldn't!" Calhoun said angrily. "He is not responsible! It is hereditary, no doubt, in his mother's family. He is no more to blame for it than if it were tubercular consumption. I will have no injustice to Ned."

"No, no!" chirped the doctor feebly. His face suddenly lightened. "Anne, dear, go and find—find Mildred's last letter. It may amuse your cousin." He waited impatiently until she was gone. "Brooke, I have an idea! You shall not drudge like a day laborer, with that boy to carry! Let Plunkett buy the farm for you. He is a gold mine. Milly has but to ask and have. I'll write to them to-night. It is a bagatelle—nothing to him."

Calhoun reddened. "Nonsense! Beg from Plunkett! What do you take me for? But it is just your kind heart," laughing. "If you were a gold mine, I'd dig fast enough."

"Well, just as you choose," said the doctor. "Anne has the same feeling. She will not accept a penny from her sister. I think it an over-strained delicacy, for my part."

The men sat silent a while. The house dog came up to Brooke, who stroked its head. Presently he said, in a forced tone: "Anne will never need kindness from her sister, if the rumor that I hear is true. They say that——"

"That she is to marry Mr. Mears? Yes, I suppose that it is so. They have not told me of their engagement yet. But he is most persistent, and Anne—it is very suitable, eh? He is one of the saints of the earth, and he can give her every thing—wealth, position, opportunity for a full life. Nancy always has craved a great career."

"Yes. It is suitable." Brooke said slowly, and then sat silent again, pulling the dog's ears and looking down the slope.

Anne brought the letter and gave it to her father, who put on his eyeglasses and read it with many delighted important chuckles. "Berlin, eh? Yes, this is the one about the Empress. Milly was presented, you see? Ah—here it is." While he read Anne walked with long, noiseless steps up and down the porch, and Calhoun sat silent. He did not once look toward her.

"Yes. That's all she says about the Empress,"

the doctor said, when he had finished. "I must look up Peter now. But after dinner I will read you all the others, Brooke." He hurried away.

The sun was going down. The porch was already in shadow and the wind chilly. But yonder the spires of the city rose airily against the red sky, a cross glittered high, and the chimes rang out softly.

Calhoun was not a morbid or imaginative man; but his life seemed to stand still just then and face him. The regular, soft footfall passing—that was his little comrade. He had always hoped—— But she belonged down there where the sun was shining. "Wealth and position and a great career——" A man, too, who was noble, doing Christ's work.

"God knows, there's no soul of a saint in me!" Brooke thought, glancing down at his stout body and coarse hands. He had nothing to say to her. He had chosen, that day in New Orleans. He would bid her good-by now, and never come to The Oaks again.

The farm and the milk, and Ned—there was his place for the rest of his life.

He got up when Anne turned to him, and began to button his coat. He would only say good-by, as usual; there was no need that she should know that it was for the last time. He wanted no questions, no kindness——

Then, when she came up, without looking at her, he said, "Will you sit down here beside me? Just a minute. I have something to say to you."

She sat down, but did not speak. He fancied that she looked down to the city where the light was, and the cross, and the man—to whom she belonged.

"I have something to say," he went on hurriedly, standing before her. "I began to tell you once, but did not finish. I am a fool and a brute to talk to you of it now—only to pain you." He stopped a moment. She did not speak nor look at him. "I think I ought to tell you. So much, at least, is due to me. It cannot hurt you to know that you always were more than life to me. You always will be. It can't do *you* harm. It may make you think kindly of me now and then, and that will be—something for me to have."

She spoke, after a time, with an effort, still looking down at the far-off light. "That is not much to have. Have you nothing else to hope for?"

"No, Anne. You know what my life has been as well as I do. Even when you were a child, you were the biggest part of it. You were the end of all my plans. You were to be my wife and we would live on the old farm, and dear old Ned would come and go, winning fame and glory for us. You must have known?"

"Yes, I knew," she said quietly. She looked directly at him now. He had never seemed so ugly or heavy to her before. His very eyes were sodden. Something—courage, hope, his God only knew what, had died out of the man.

"Things have gone against me," he said, with a dreary laugh. "I ought to have won my wife

and my place like other men, but I did not. I
lacked push—ability, I suppose. I did what seemed
right every day, and—here's the end of it! You
are going to your place with a better man.
That's right. It is where you belong, I see that.
It could not be too high or too bright for you."

"And you——?"

"Oh, I shall work the farm and watch Ned. I
shall make out!" with a sudden effort at hearty
cheerfulness. "Don't worry about us. We shall
be comfortable enough. But I wanted to tell
you the truth about it—what you've been to me?
And to say that you mustn't be hurt, Nancy, if I
do not come here. I don't want ever to see you
again! When you are another man's wife——
Oh, my God! I can't stand it!"

He caught the fringe of her shawl and twisted
it in his fingers, holding it to his mouth as he
crouched before her.

"Why, Brooke!" She took his face in both of
her hands. "Oh, your cheeks are wet! Why,
there is nobody else! It is you—*you!* I never
meant to be any body's wife but yours! But I
thought you never would ask me!"

CHAPTER XXVIII

CALHOUN went home early that night, putting his horse to the gallop as soon as he was out of the gate. Ned had not heard this thing that had happened to him. He was impatient, even when he was with Anne, to know what the dear fellow would say when he heard of this great joy coming into their lives.

Ned was asleep, but he routed him up and told the news. Edward laughed and yawned. "Anne, eh? You'll be a queer husband for *une belle Précieuse!*"

"Don't talk French, Ned. I don't understand it. This is so much to me! I thought you'd be glad. You might as well talk French when I was dead as now."

Ned sat up in the bed. "Forgive me, dear old man. Here, give me your hand. I'm a selfish brute. But you were as triumphant as if you'd won the Grand Prix, and it was only Nancy Warrick! I'm very pleased, really. She certainly has points of remarkable beauty—eyes like the Ferronière's—though her hands and feet are atrocious. But that needn't worry you. We all have some faults. Well, we'll talk it over to-morrow. I'm horribly sleepy. God bless you and your wife!"

He was not sleepy. His bright eyes watched

the lamp for hours while he pondered the situation. "It will never do," was his decision at
last. " There can't be two rulers in one house.
She or I will have to knuckle under. Well, we'll
see!" and then he fell calmly sleep.

When Anne went to her father with her story
he expressed great concern. " But really, what
have you to live on ? If there were nothing to
consider but feelings, I should give you my
blessing, and be very glad——"

"You *are* glad, and you know it!" laughed
Nancy, with her arms about his neck. He kissed
her.

"I don't deny that it is a relief. Brooke is
like a boy of my own, and Mr. Mears—I'm so tired
standing on tip-toe to catch his ideas! But taking a business view of it, child, the outlook is
alarming! Naturally, you, being a woman, don't
take that view. But I am a business man."

There could be no doubt, however, of the
doctor's happiness during the months that
passed before the wedding. He thought that
his anxiety at this time justified a temporary
neglect of science. His microbes dried up while
he trotted from The Oaks to the farm, carrying over every trifle which could make Anne feel
at home in her new life. In the evening, when
Brooke and Anne were together, he would come
in quite accidentally, book in hand, and, "being
there, might he read a passage which pleased
him just now ? " The passage was invariably on
love, whether the book were Shakspeare or one of
the new young writer, Bret Harte's; and the old

man's cheek would redden and his voice choke as he read, and the lovers would sit with averted eyes, and not look at each other until they were alone. For they had the sweet, old-fashioned shyness about their secret, and hid it from the world. It was so holy a thing that even to think of it took away their breath.

During these months Mrs. Dane often visited The Oaks.

"I have been quite frank with Anne," she told Mr. Franciscus the day before the wedding, when they were walking out together. "I told her candidly once for all that she had made a fatal mistake; that she might have married a man of intellect and position instead of a penniless drudge. But it had no effect. She always was obstinate, so—let it go!" shaking her fingers into space. "Anne Warrick is my dear daughter even with a boor for a husband."

"I am pleased to see how old Luxborough has acted in the matter," said Mr. Franciscus. "There was a good deal of jealousy when Mears made Anne chief cook in his charities. But now that she is to marry a poor man, she is 'dear Nancy' to them all. They talk of making her a Patroness of the next annual Club Minuet."

Cousin Julia nodded, smiling. "People are pleased with her choosing the poor man instead of the rich," she said. "Even old Luxborough 'loves a lover.'"

Paul pulled at his Vandyke beard thoughtfully. "Yes," he said, "it is my experience that decent, well-bred people always stand by the dog that is

"'I'VE BEEN QUITE FRANK WITH ANNE'"

going under in the fight. Lose your money or be paralyzed or die, and all that is good in your friends comes out. But be successful, and they'll crowd into corners and sneer at you behind your back. See how they tore poor Milly into rags as soon as she had her millions."

But if these worldly folk felt any disapproval of Anne's fatal mistake, they forgot it when they reached the house. Cousin Julia threw off her bonnet and anxiously inspected the rooms, made gay with flowers, and the bill of fare for the breakfast. "Very good taste. Simple and dainty. Now, my dear, for the presents, and your gowns."

Anne brought out her treasures with ecstatic little laughs and blushes. "No girl ever had such lovely things!" she cried, "and you gave me the best of them all. You have been a real fairy godmother to me."

"Nonsense. Aren't you my daughter?" She hugged the girl, choking a little, and turned it off with a gay, "Now, for Milly's gift! Something regal, no doubt."

"Milly's?" Anne turned away to close the closet. "It has not come yet. She will bring it, I suppose, when she comes next month."

"Oh?" Mrs. Dane's lips shut meaningly, but she said nothing. She watched with an amused smile as Anne folded her basques and skirts. "When you were so busy in the club for municipal reform you did not care so much for foulards and muslins?" she said slyly.

"I always liked pretty things," said Anne, patting the flounce affectionately.

"Are you going to give up your public work?"

"For the present—yes. Oh, we have so much to do!" She threw herself on the ground, leaning on Mrs. Dane's knees. The motherless girl had longed for some woman to be glad with her.

"We are saving every dollar! I would not go upon a wedding journey. I made Brooke put away the money for the first payment on the mortgage! And when the farm is released we will add more land, and more—and I will manage that land as never has been done in Pennsylvania. I am going to study farming, thoroughly."

"You? And your husband?"

"Oh!" Anne's eyes sparkled. "He shall go back to the law. That is where his heart always has been. So you see, with the farm and the house to manage, I shall not have much time for public virtues."

"No," said Mrs. Dane, dryly. "And Edward?"

"Poor boy!" said Anne, with a motherly shake of the head. "I hope I can make him happy. He has a miserable life."

Ned flung the door open that moment with a face which belied her words. It was radiant with kindness and pleasure. Brooke hurried after him, smiling and excited.

"This reckless fellow," he said to Anne, "has bought you a gift fit for a princess."

"I ran down to Philadelphia," said Ned, with affected carelessness, "to make myself fit for the wedding. I was literally in rags; and I bought you a trifle—all that my poor purse could afford." He put a little box in her hand.

When it was opened Mrs. Dane gave a startled cry, and looked up at him in amazement. It was a single emerald, pure and large, hung by an invisible wire to a tiny gold chain.

"Yes," said Ned, nodding, "Caldwell had nothing better."

Anne thanked him gravely, and turned it over uneasily.

"How could he do it?" she asked Brooke bluntly, when they were alone.

"Oh, he probably had an order for a picture. Don't fret him about economy. He had the money, or he would not have bought it. He has the generosity of a prince."

Brooke felt his own economy bear hardly upon him that night, when the brothers smoked their pipes together for the last time in the old farmhouse. "No wedding journey!" cried Ned indignantly, "nothing but a week on the Jersey coast! I never heard of such niggardliness! When I marry, I shall take my wife to Arcadia. The world will not have breadth nor beauty enough to satisfy me for her."

"Why, you see, Ned," said Brooke earnestly, "Anne is as anxious as I that we should own our farm again." He unlocked his desk and took out an old Bible. "Mother's book, you know? I have been saving these notes for months, for our little holiday—eight hundred. But Anne insisted they should go for the first payment. It was her fancy to put them in this book, as they are to buy our freedom." He touched the notes softly, shut the book, and closed the desk.

Ned nodded. He watched his brother furtively as he went about the room, his eyes shining. "I'm rather glad we are to come back home so soon," Brooke said at last. "You see I have thought of it—of bringing her home here, since I was a boy. Now it really is to be, I can hardly believe it." He put his hands on Ned's shoulders. "You are a little glad too, boy? She is so anxious to make your life happy, Ned!"

"Oh, that's all right!" Ned said loudly, throwing up his head. "I appreciate her at her full value. And you too, Brooke. I see what our home will be, quite clearly. I'll do my part."

"I know it, Ned." Brooke wrenched his hand, and then with a beaming face went up the stairs.

Ned smoked in silence a while, and then knocked the ashes out of his pipe on the andiron. "So, so!" he said half aloud. "Economy is to be the rule? I don't think the change of weather in this house will suit Edward Calhoun! And good Lord! To see her pour tea with those big hands, every day—every day——"

The brief honeymoon was over. Brooke and his wife, coming home again, left the porter to follow with their luggage from the station and walked slowly through the woods toward the old farm-house. Calhoun held her arm tightly, as though she were a baby learning to walk.

"Take care. There are so many roots under the grass, dear. There comes your father, with all the dogs. I suppose Ned—he will have the house all lighted, and fires in every room. So many years I have looked forward to this coming home, Nancy."

They walked on in silence. The doctor, coming down the avenue, waved his cap jubilantly—being too far away to speak.

"I thought Ned would have been at the station," said Brooke uneasily. "The dear fellow is busy with his preparations, no doubt. Where is he, doctor?"

"Did you not know? He went to New York the day you left. He said he had told you——"

Brooke hurried through the lighted house to Ned's room. Upon the table was a letter directed to himself.

"Dear old man, I need a change. I shall run over to Paris for a few months of hard work. Here are some bills which I wish you would settle for me at your leisure. I have borrowed a little money from you, but will wipe the slate clean when I sell my first picture. My fondest love to my charming sister. "Yours,

"NED."

Beneath was a pile of bills, the upper one from Caldwell & Co.

Calhoun went to his desk and opened it. The Bible was in its place, but there was no money in it. He beckoned to Anne and handed the letter to her.

"He must not be there alone," he said. "Poor Ned! He will be so miserable when he understands what he has done. I will bring him back at any cost."

CHAPTER XXIX

THE Plunketts did not come home in the fall. Milly fluttered from one capital of Europe to another until more than a year had passed. She cared nothing for their history or associations or social life: but she studied pictures and statuary and gems with breathless eagerness.

" I want to make a capable woman of myself," she said one day, when they were in the Louvre. " I want to know the value of things."

" Why don't you let me buy what's pretty?" said David. " I'll ship home an acre of these canvasses, if you like," waving his hand to the wall of the Salon Carré.

"Hush-h! No," she said gravely. "I have decided that pictures are a bad investment unless you buy the works of some unknown artist of merit. You are sure to make on them. But how to know them?"

"But you don't let me buy you any thing! Now, laces. That yellow veil they said belonged to Josephine? You look so pretty in fluffy things."

Milly's brows were knitted anxiously. "No. I only like the finest lace. And that does not gain in value. We can't let so much money lie idle in a bit of worked net."

"Money—idle!" David shrugged his huge

shoulders with lazy delight, as he trotted after her. He knew that it was only her silly fondness for him that made her wish to save for him ; that made her hunt out the value of things, or count up the hotel bills with her red lips pursed. She always seemed fond of him. He had no doubt of her now. He was steeped in happiness. It had altered him. A nobler man than the old David Plunkett looked out of his eyes. She was chary of caresses ; but to feel her cool little palms now and then stroking his flabby cheeks he would gladly trot after her like a dog for the rest of his life.

"Now, here is the Regent," she said, leaning over the cabinet with an excited laugh. "You can buy that for me."

"Pardon, madame," interrupted one of the guards. "It is the great diamond of the world. It is a crown jewel of France, worth twenty million francs."

Milly said nothing, but smiled calmly. To know that she could pay twenty million of francs for a little stone, if she chose—It was worth having lived for the silent triumph of that one moment.

"There is a man yonder, Milly," said Plunkett a minute later, "who has been watching you as if he knew you. That Spaniard by the pillar, with the red cravat."

Milly glanced at the carefully dressed, bearded little man. He came toward her, bowing, hat in hand.

"I do not know him. Oh !" with a shrill cry.

"It is—He is not a Spaniard. He is a—a mulatto. I saw him at Le Reve des Eaux."

David looked at her and turned away abruptly. Soudé or his home had never before been mentioned between them.

Milly did not look after him. She did not remember that he was in the world. Now! At last! Now she would hear of John—what he thought——

"This is—?" Her voice sounded shrill and high to her.

"They call me Monsieur Farro here," the little man said, with a set smile. "I hope madame will pardon my intrusion? I saw her on the Soudé plantation two years ago. I was manager there then."

"Oh, I remember you very well. You do not manage the plantation now?"

"No. I live here. I never shall go back to the States." But poor Farro was more home-sick than he knew. The sight of this woman brought the old place back to him. He clasped his hands nervously and broke out into the uncontrollable chuckling ya! ya! of the negro.

"It's so surprising to see any body from home, ma'am," he said apologetically, putting his hand over his mouth. "I had got through my work there. Just after you left a Northern company bought the marshes from the General, to drain for rice-lands. The price they paid cleared off his debt—a debt that was on the plantation——"

"Yes, I know there was a lien," said Milly. "And then—— ?"

" Then my work was over. General Soudé
paid me a handsome sum as soon as he got the
money. I wanted to leave the Soudés. There
were reasons for that. And I wanted," he said,
throwing up his head, " to bring my children to a
free country where their black blood wouldn't tell
against them. And why should it tell against
them, ma'am ? " he cried fiercely. " There's some
of the best blood of Louisiana in their veins, I can
tell you that. Nobody minds their color here. I
take my boy—the black one—to the theatre, to
church. Nobody stares, nobody says ' Damned
nigger!' It's not that way anywhere in the States."

" Yes, yes," said Mrs. Plunkett, wiping her dry
lips with her tongue. "That's very pleasant!
I'm very glad, I'm sure." What was the wretched
negro or his race to her ?

Suddenly recollecting David, she glanced down
the corridor and saw him standing in one of the
great windows, watching her, blotting out the
light. He might come back at any moment and
then—she would never know!

" Mr. John Soudé. Is he—well? " she said.

A keen flash of intelligence lighted Farro's
insignificant features. He smiled, hesitating to
find words strong enough.

" Oh, very well! Never better. The lien's
cleared off. The General and M's John's as
happy as two boys. They have repaired the old
house. It's the gathering place for the whole
parish—full and plenty as in the old times—Lord!
if I was there now! "—shaking his head.

Then the lien, she calculated, must have been

paid off about the time she eloped with David. If she had but waited a few days John would have come to her with the good news. And that little cushion she was making for him—she could never force herself to touch a needle since—He was coming to her with the good news.

She put out her hands feebly.

"He—he lives at home now? Not in a little house on Camp Street?"

"Oh, of course he lives at home! Didn't you hear?" laughing significantly. "Mr. Louis Choteaud, you see, he was waitin' on Miss Soudé. M's John comes home an' hears it. He'd been used to thinking of Miss Therese all his life, but he'd never thought of Miss Therese's husband. That opened his senses to what he wanted, I suppose. So one morning they were married, quite suddenly. And a dear wife and lady she is to him!" Farro said, fixing his eyes mercilessly on the little bloodless face before him. "He watches over her as if she were a leetle, tender child——"

"Yes," said Milly, holding herself erect with a laugh. "She needs especial care. She is a cripple, if I remember rightly. Well, good-morning, Mr. Farro. So pleased to have seen you! I wish you success in Paris."

She stepped lightly to the window and laid her hand on David's arm, smiling up into his face. He looked at her sharply. She had been talking to that fellow of her old lover, and yet she never had looked at him so fondly! Soudé was nothing to her, thank God!

They left the Louvre and drove out to the
Bois. Milly slept most of the time. Her white,
exhausted face against the cushions made David's
heart ache. He bade the coachman drive slowly
down a lonely road, and watched her, shading
her closed eyes from the flickering lights, thinking that he was secure at last. She was his; she
never had cared for Soudé. But how ghastly
she looked! He knew the reason. God was
giving him every thing: first, the woman who had
always been dear to him, and now——

As they passed slowly down the forest aisle
David prayed with his whole soul to God to care
for her and the child that she was to bear to him.
In the midst of his prayers he would stop and
almost shout aloud.

To think that he—Dave Plunkett—should have
a son of his own!

He winked his eyes to get rid of the tears.
He must make a different man of himself—he
had begun already! The little fellow must learn
no harm from his own father! David had given
up his brandy smashes and had not sworn now
for weeks. He nodded over Rawlinson's "Ancient
Monarchies" every night. He would like the boy
to think his father was a scholar, and he had
so much to learn! He meant to begin at the
beginning.

When they reached their hotel he insisted on
carrying her up the stairs, and laid her on the
sofa. She was very quiet for a long time; he
thought she was asleep, but at last she cried out
sharply:

"For pity's sake don't go tip-toeing about in that ridiculous fashion, like an elephant on eggs! Can't you talk? What shall we buy? Let us settle on something." She sat up, throwing off the cloak with which he had covered her, her eyes burning, the blood flaming in her cheeks. "You've dallied long enough about investing for me."

"Dallied? Why, there's nothing I haven't wanted to buy for you!"

"Oh, yes! finery, bric-a-brac—just wasting money! But something real that I can hold and feel. Let me have some good of the money."

"Yes, yes, dear!" There was a little table in front of her and David sat down before it, watching her with an alarmed smile, as an anxious nurse might a sick baby. The doctors had prepared him for fretfulness and foolish whims.

"I have been thinking," she cried, "and I've decided that I'll have some money put into diamonds. A large sum. I am fond of jewels, but that is not the reason. Money is safe in diamonds. You lose the interest, but the principal is safe, which is an object this fall, when securities are so uncertain."

"Yes, certainly." Plunkett nodded, with an amused smile.

"I want them to-day!" She opened and shut her hands as they lay on the table. "I want to know that I actually have them here—I have lost so much! I must have something!"

"You have me, dear."

She stared into the big, smiling face before her without a word.

David looked at his watch. "You want them to-day, eh? It's late, Milly. The diamond brokers have closed. And I'm sorry, but—Don't you think it is risky to buy stones after dark?"

"Oh, I know just what I mean to buy. And they will open their shops fast enough for a man who comes with a hundred millions in his pocket!"

David laughed. "Don't repeat that foolishness, Milly. People might think you really believed it."

She half rose. "Foolishness? Do you mean that it—is not true?"

"That I am worth a hundred millions! Why, of course not. Nor the half of it. Nor the quarter."

She stood looking at him steadily, but all the meaning had gone from her shallow, light eyes. After a long time she said, "Will you tell me what you are worth?"

"I? I'm not one of the four richest men in the States; you surely never believed that nonsense, dear? I really don't know exactly. I have a shrewd partner, and my being on this side has enabled us to work together effectively. But we lost heavily lately. In western bonds, and oil is—— But surely you don't care to hear these things, child?"

"What are you worth?"

"Well, at a rough guess, eight or ten millions. The little lad won't be a pauper, Milly!" He laid his hand softly on her arm. She shook it off.

"The little lad?" she muttered, with a shiver. She dropped into her seat, her lips moved. "Eight or ten," she said mechanically to herself, under her breath. "Eight or ten."

She had had many hurts to-day. Her brain was dulled by them. She saw no difference between this sum and beggary. For a year she had believed that she held one of the two or three vast fortunes of the world in her hands. They were suddenly empty.

"What is it, Milly? Are you ill?"

She only stared at him. Her soul blazed into a fury of hate. He had tricked her. He had bought her with a hundred millions when he only had these petty sums. She would have shrieked out that he was a liar and a fraud, if she had been any other woman. But Milly's life-long habit of reticence stood her in good stead in this crisis.

She must use him—and the money he had—to make more.

"What can I do?" cried David, hanging over her. "Do you want to go into the fresh air? Shall we go for the diamonds?"

"No, no! No diamonds now. I must begin to work, to—to speculate. I'll go to bed now. I am not well."

She pushed him back and tottered into the chamber. David hurried away to see the doctor. He was alarmed; yet he smiled to himself tenderly. He had been warned that these foolish whims would come and go.

CHAPTER XXX

A FEW days, however, convinced Plunkett that his wife was influenced by no whim, but by a fixed purpose. She explained it to him one morning when a heap of newspapers, French, German, and English, were brought to her. "I am studying the markets. You have much less money than I thought, and I intend to help you in increasing that little. You will find that I can be of use to you."

"Yes, Milly," he said meekly. It was a pity that the morbid fancies which he had been told to expect had taken so troublesome a shape. But that was a small matter. His patience was untiring.

She no longer studied the value of pictures or stones, but of stocks; dragging him to Brussels, to Antwerp, to London—wherever she scented a good investment—plying him with a thousand silly questions which she thought profound and shrewd.

"He always was shallow," she told herself. "I have the brain of the partnership. But I must learn how to use it." She usually decided upon the most risky investment, which promised huge profits. "We must make haste," she would tell him, "even if we venture a little. We have so much to make up." She had set her limit at the hundred millions which she now believed she had once carried and had lost. "Let me get that, and I will stop and attend to other things," she said every day.

David humored her, when small sums were involved; but when the risk was too great he probably lied to her.

She thought of nothing but investments; even the little preparations for her baby which she had begun to make with a shy delight were all forgotten.

One day David stopped with her before a house where layettes were sold. The window was full of tiny snowy garments. "Milly," he said shyly, "won't you go in and buy something? We have nothing ready for him."

"Oh, nonsense! There is time enough. I have too much else to do to-day."

Plunkett was credited with a vast fortune wherever they went. The better class of Americans avoided him, and told each other anecdotes of the Man-mountain, his ignorance, his brutal ill temper, his enormous appetite. He was the typical vulgar *nouveau riche*, and they were heartily ashamed of him. Hence David found himself lonely in the days which dragged slowly on to Christmas. Milly refused to go home.

"Here is the place to watch the markets of the world. In Paris you are in the center, in New York in a suburb," she said so sharply that David dared not tell her his anxiety that their child should be an American.

"She forgets," he thought, with an aggrieved

frown, "that he never will have a chance at the White House if he is born over here."

Milly had gathered up some text-books on finance and studied them incessantly. Plunkett laughed to himself at them. He would have been glad to read them aloud as a pretext to be near her, but she drove him away. When the time which he regularly gave to his business every day was over he spent many solitary hours prowling in Old Paris, on the Bois, in the cafés, but everywhere there went with him the thought of this intangible holy thing, the mystery of this new life coming into the world.

The scholar that he might have been, the great poet, the gentle, well-bred man which he knew he never could be—that was the little lad!

One fear beset him day and night. Milly perhaps did not know that she could influence that child now in body and mind. She never had heard that, or she could not be so indifferent, so engrossed in trifles that counted for nothing.

David stood one day beside her, staring out of the window. His soul was torn within him. God was sending him this child, and nothing was being done for it. He clenched his hands helplessly.

" If *I* could make it a stronger or a better man. I'd be on my knees half the day ! " he thought, " Mildred," he said at last, "would you like to go this morning to look at some of those wonderful statues, or to hear some great music? If you would listen to fine music every day, and let me read to you in the Bible, they say—I've been told

—such things will have an effect upon *his* body and soul, for all of his life."

"What absurdity !" she said sharply. "Don't worry me with talk about 'him' any more ! it's not modest."

What he could do for her he did. He leased a house near Paris which he fancied was like The Oaks. He filled it with American furniture, he imported a trained nurse from New York, he called in English-speaking physicians. One of them, an old man with a shrewd, kindly face, took him aside one day, and told him that it was his duty to warn him that madame was in a peculiar state of high nervous tension.

"You think it will be prejudicial in the future? To the mother or the child ?"

"To both, monsieur. Humor her. Give her her way ! You cannot turn her out of it !"

"Oh, I do," said poor Plunkett. The physician talked with him for some time, and it was noticeable afterward that Doctor Jacot treated the loutish fellow, at whom every-body jeered, with marked respect.

By this time Mildred had found that there were many women in Paris, who, like herself, were stock gamblers—Russian princesses, American adventurers, British matrons, some of them wrinkled and senile, some young and pretty, most of them *declassée*. They and the brokers, their comrades, soon gathered about the ignorant wife of the great Yankee millionnaire, like buzzards around fat prey. Every day some secret was whispered to her, by which success was to be made

sure. Milly complacently sat in judgment upon
the schemes, hugging herself in delight at the
shrewdness with which she decided this one to
be a fraud and that honest.

At last, a certain Rhysfontein Syndicate for
gold mining in South Africa commended itself
to her. She was to be let in on the ground
floor; the operation would pay in a month two
hundred per cent., etc., etc. While she deliber-
ated the stock suddenly rose; then she threw herself into the speculation, overhead. She sold all
of her other securities to invest in it. M. Campan,
the agent, a finical *petit maître* of a Polish Jew,
was running incessantly in and out of the hotel or
whispering with her in corners. Milly's laugh rang
out gayly, her blue eyes sparkled with triumph.

David asked no questions. He scarcely seemed
to see the unsavory crowd that buzzed about his
wife. But there was something in his look now,
as he watched her, which affrighted her. What
did he know? What did he see which she could
not see?

But she asked no questions, and he dared not
speak. Day by day he knew that she was coming
closer to the frail bridge stretched across that
dark abyss; and she went capering and dancing
like a juggler, playing with toys!

Sometimes he made a feeble effort. "Milly,"
he said one day, "there were some things you
once had very much at heart which are yet un-
done. You told me you would like to settle a
certain sum on your father, to make his old age
secure. Why not do it now? To-day?"

Her face sharpened and grew hard. "I see no necessity of giving any money to papa. He lives very simply. Anne is married comfortably, and will see that he needs nothing. Besides, I did send him a large sum of money, just after we were married."

"Oh, that's all right, then!" said Plunkett, smiling tenderly down at her. She did not tell him that she had recalled the five thousand dollars a week ago to invest in Rhysfontein.

The next day was Sunday. He hung about the room awkwardly. "Milly," he said at last. "suppose we go to church? You never go now. What do you say?"

She looked up. "I never knew you to go to church in your life. Why this sudden attack of devotion?"

"No, I didn't." Plunkett stopped shuffling, and stood quite still. "I've been a godless fellow, I know. But I've thought of things lately—I'd like to go with you, Milly, so that we could kneel together once and pray for you, and—the child."

"Oh, certainly," Mildred said civilly. "I'll put on my things. You'll hear a very poor sermon, though, and the choir is wretched."

The chapel happened to be crowded that morning. Milly stepped alertly to a single seat, leaving David to find a place in the back pews.

"I wish I could have knelt by her, once," he thought as he sat down. The people near him noticed the huge man, who during the service neither stood nor knelt with the others, but sat motionless, his head bent forward on his cane.

But Milly did pray. While she joined in the Creed and Te Deum quite correctly, she was counting what her profits would be if the investment paid even a hundred per month? Why, in two years she could talk of her millions—her own millions. To-morrow Campan had promised a decisive cablegram from the diggings.

It flashed upon her.—What if there was a real Something to whom these prayers actually were going—who could control things as He chose? Even the market.

She was on her knees at the moment. She dropped her head, and her little frame shook with the frenzy of her entreaty.

"Lord, send me good luck!" she cried. "Give us a hundred per cent.!"

Then she suddenly remembered what David had said about the child, and a gush of warm womanly feeling sent the water to her eyes. "I wonder what mother would think if she knew I had a baby?" she thought, smiling softly. She did not move for a long time.

Every-body was going out. She got up. "I'll have time to think of these things after the cablegram comes," she said to herself.

M. Campan brought no cablegram on Monday nor on Tuesday. Milly neither slept nor tasted food. Sometimes, in the agony of suspense, she was tempted to tell David her secret. But no, her triumph would be the greater when it came.

On Wednesday, Doctor Jacot found her pacing

steadily up and down the salon. He laid his hand on hers, a grave alarm in his face.

"She will not stop, nor sit down. I can do nothing with her," said David.

A maid came in at that moment with the morning's paper. Mildred took it from her and tried to open it. Her hands shook, and her teeth chattered.

"But, madame!" said the doctor, gently drawing it from her; "let us not concern ourselves with affairs. Let us look to our health now."

"One moment, doctor," said Milly courteously, a smile on her bloodless face. "This is of interest to me."

She shook open the sheet. In bold head-lines were the words:

"*Rhysfontein.* A certain tricky fellow, passing under the name of M. Felix Campan, has, it appears, beguiled large sums from many ignorant dupes, as agent for the above-named stock, and has absconded with them. On inquiry, yesterday, the company proved to be a fiction, and Campan is suspected to be a professional swindler, well known to the police of Berlin."

Milly turned her bright eyes on the doctor. "He has taken my money," she said gently. "My money," and then, with a shrill scream, she sank down in a heap upon the floor.

They carried her to her room. The physicians came and went all day.

Late that evening David Plunkett sat alone in the unlighted salon. He had been waiting there alone many hours. The door of the chamber opened at last.

He stood up. Now he would know what the rest of his life was to be.

Doctor Jacot stood in the lighted space, beckoning to him. When David came up, he took his big hand in both of his and led him into the chamber.

"It is the worst, my friend," he said. "Be a man——"

Upon the bed lay a motionless little figure, scarce larger than a child's, covered with a white sheet.

The doctor turned away when David went to it.

Presently the nurse wiped the tears from her own eyes, and lifting a little bundle of flannel from her knee, looked enquiringly at the physician.

"Yes. Take it to him," he whispered.

She carried it to David. "It is your son, sir," she said, and put it in his arms.

David stood a long time holding it close. He stooped at last and kissed the child reverently, muttering something which ended with:

"So help me, God!"

CHAPTER XXXI

In the winter of 1890, the anniversary of Jackson's long-ago victory was made the excuse for a national caucus in Philadelphia of the Democratic party. All of its leaders and second and third-rate bosses hied to this informal *pour-parler*, and with them every possible and impossible candidate for the Presidency. Each man came prepared with a speech on the Hero of New Orleans, in which were carefully set forth his own opinions on the tariff, free silver, and pensions.

The convention met in the Academy of Music, and for that night the huge, dingy building glowed with color and patriotism. The floor was occupied by the delegates; the galleries were crowded with the curious public; but the tiers of boxes were reserved for the wives of the great party chiefs. They had been instructed as to the importance of the ponderous deliverances to which they listened, and knew that the platform for the party during the coming campaign was being published in them, and that as they were spoken they were flashed by wire across the whole continent, so that obedient Democrats in Maine or San Francisco should know by breakfast time to-morrow what they had to do.

So the women clapped their gloved hands softly as each speech was finished, and declared eagerly that it was "a masterly effort," and yawned behind their fans when another man got up, and whispered sharp little criticisms of him to each other.

Two hours of these weighty utterances had reduced even the bosses to the bored condition of the women when a tall, dark man, a Southern delegate, rose to speak. He had been a rebel soldier; it was the first time he had faced his party in the North. He had something to say to them, and he said it. His voice had a cordial, honest ring in it. Before he began his second sentence the eyes of every delegate were on him: as he went on the boys in the lofts called "Hush-h," to each other, and the women dropped their fans and leaned forward, motionless.

Anne Calhoun, who was one of them, was the most startled and moved among them. She had known John Soudé in his youth and thought him slow and dull. Was it out of such material that a great orator was made? Did eloquence only mean to have something to say and to say it, direct, to each man in hearing?

Soudé had once had a fight to the death with these people. Now was his one chance to justify his side in the fight and then to strike hands with his foes. His heart rushed to his lips in every word. Many men who listened to him had never seen a conquered rebel face to face before. When he ended, there was a thunder of applause. Nobody had remembered exactly what he had said in his homely, downright talk, but they all wanted to go over and shake hands with him and then turn in honestly to work to help the country.

Anne's eyes filled with tears as she listened. She leaned back, drawing a long breath when he sat down.

"I never heard any thing like that!" she said to his wife.

Therese smiled. "All the men of our family have been like Aaron; they could 'speak well,'" she said calmly.

"Mr. Soudé always had a curious power of clutching at one's heart," Anne went on excitedly. "I remember a little story of a child dying in a train——"

"Pathos would be of small use in a politician," said Mrs. Soudé coldly. "My husband is one of the closest logicians in the country."

"Oh?" ejaculated Anne. She scanned her old friend curiously. Therese had altered in the years during which she and her husband had been political and social powers in Washington. The little *grande dame* was used to the public eye and bore herself with an unconscious dignity and repose. It mattered nothing to her that a dozen reporters were sketching her face now for the morning papers. She had not looked once at John while he spoke, but Anne had noticed a small scarlet point grow hot and hotter in each cheek as he went on: her lips moved, too, repeating his sentences: often, as Anne saw with amusement, hurrying in advance of him.

"You have heard the speech before?" she said now.

"Certainly. I know it by heart. Mr. Soudé is a brilliant extemporaneous speaker, as I suppose you know. But this is a crisis, and he represents his section. It would not do to risk chance ideas." She asked presently, " Does not Mr. Calhoun speak to-night ?"

" No," said Anne. " Brooke is no orator. He does not even plead in court; he has altogether a chamber practice." She went on with a certain doggedness in her tone: " He is of some weight in the party, I believe, but only concerns himself in public affairs from duty. He has no ambitions—he is no politician."

"A statesman, rather," said the politician's wife gently. She sent for a messenger and scribbled a despatch, smiling to herself as she wrote. "It is to the General," she explained, when she had finished. " Nothing would induce him to leave the plantation or our little girl, so I wire him every night a full account of the day."

The convention had adjourned, but the two women sat tranquilly in the box, watching the enthusiastic delegates crowding about John Soudé on the stage. He stood erect, flushed and handsome, making hosts of friends with every hearty word.

" He is the king of the hour," Anne said cordially, laughing. But her eyes turned to the stout little man who quietly presented the others to him. " In the background always," she thought. "The man with the best brain and the biggest heart in the house! " and then, as she fastened her cloak, she told herself, as she had told herself a thousand times before, that he was right. No ambitions, a little farm well tilled, a chamber practice, and the background of an honest, true life, were the highest wisdom after all.

"Who is that immense, ungainly man by the pillar?" asked Therese. "I think he bowed to you."

"It is my brother-in-law, Mr. Plunkett." Anne beckoned to him to come up to the box.

The night had tried Plunkett sorely. He was an eager, intelligent Democrat. He did not approve of one plank of the platform just laid down. Even Mr. Cleveland, he thought, had made a mistake in his speech. He wanted to tell the convention that they were on the brink of a fatal error. His ideas were quite clear, and he knew that his position as a great capitalist would give them weight; but he could not speak two sentences of grammatical English. Twice he rose and dropped into his seat again, the cold sweat breaking over him.

"I'll not get up and talk like an ass, and shame Boy!" he thought. "If I'd chosen to take an education I might have been the equal of any man here."

He stood a while, scowling and glum. Suddenly his face lighted and he whistled softly to himself. Just then Anne beckoned to him, and he hurried to the box. After he had bowed to Mrs. Soudé, he drew Anne aside.

"Gosh, Anne! D'ye know I nearly made a doggoned fool of myself. I got up to make a speech! No, I didn't do it. I know my place.

When education's needed, I've got to take the back pew; but I was just thinking, what an orator Boy will be! He's got the voice for it, eh? And the presence, and the brain—we all know what Harry's brain is. He shall go at elocution right away." He stood silent, looking at the crowds below, whistling to himself.

"Lord, Nancy!" he said, with a chuckle, "you and I may sit in this box some day and hear Harry speaking on the floor yonder. Why not? He's sixteen. In ten years—the party needs just such a man to lead it. There! he's beckonin' for me in the foyer to go home. He's trainin', you see, an' he makes me eat an' drink an' be rubbed down an' go to bed an' get up along with him. He says I'll 'enjoy the sports more when they come off.' I've got to go—goodnight," and he lumbered away, laughing to himself.

The next morning a committee carried John Soudé away to speak at Harrisburg, and Therese went to Luxborough with the Calhouns. She was enchanted with the picturesque hill farm and the old house with its low ceilings and great fireplaces. Brooke drove them in the afternoon to the dairies, and Anne gave a little lecture on the different grades of milk.

Therese laughed merrily. "Are you inventing all that? Do you really know so much?" she cried.

"Certainly; it's my business. I am the farmer," said Anne.

As they stood in the door of one of the dairies,

Brooke pointed out several houses for tenants which he had lately built.

"But you have here a fine estate!" exclaimed Therese. "You have been most fortunate."

"I deserve no credit," Brooke said eagerly. "We owe the old farm and homestead to my brother."

There was a moment of painful silence.

"We heard of my cousin Edward's death in Paris when it occurred," Mrs. Soudé said, in a low tone.

"Yes," said Calhoun, "yes." He paused, frowning. He could not yet control his voice when he spoke of Ned. "He only lived two years after our marriage," he said presently, "and he chose to spend them abroad. I went over twice to persuade him to come back. But the life here was too narrow—too cramped for him. He had a great, generous nature! In those two years he painted a couple of pictures which he sold, just before his death, for a large price. I inherited the money, and with it I cleared off all claims on the old farm. I like to think of it as Ned's gift!" he said, looking down at the fields and house with dim eyes.

Therese glanced keenly at Anne's face, but it told her nothing.

"That woman has a great talent for silence," she told John long afterward. "But to think of her spending her days among cows when she might live in Washington! She could push her husband into office there, and place her sons as they grew up. I know no woman with more personal magnetism."

"Cows are better companions for every day than Congressmen. And I suppose her husband needs her at home—magnetism and all, as I do you, Totty," said honest John, who was foolishly fond of his clever wife.

Brooke that afternoon drove them over to The Oaks, where David Plunkett and his son lived with Doctor Warrick. The doctor walked feebly as he escorted Therese gallantly over the old house, opening at last his cases of rare prints with much pride.

"These are a foible of mine," he said, "in which my son David indulges me. He thinks I have a right to my idle play now after a life of hard work."

"I remember your devotion to science, sir," Therese said, with much deference.

"Yes, yes!" the doctor replied vaguely, but greatly pleased. "I was one of the pioneers, madam, one of the pioneers! These later fellows, Koch, and—I forget their names—have all the glory. We did the work, and they got the credit."

He and David took her to see the new gymnasium which had just been fitted up for Boy. Plunkett handled the clubs and rings gravely. "Owing to circumstances," he said, "I never myself was an athlete. Even as a boy, I was large of my age. But they tell me that my son has remarkable ability in all athletic sports. I wish you could see him run. He goes to Princeton next year, and I have no doubt will take a first rank in all their contests."

When they came back to the drawing-room

they found Mrs. Dane, who had come out to welcome Therese. She had altered much in the last decade. Mr. Franciscus, her nearest companion, was dead, and after he was gone, she had allowed herself to change with old Luxborough. For old Luxborough had changed. It had at last given up its leisurely pace and now kept brisk step with the times. The women marched in companies; in innumerable clubs, associations, and guilds. There was no science, however recondite, which some battalion of them did not attack; no evil, as old as the world, which the young girls did not drag out, to peer into and paw over, declaring that they were the first to discover it and the first to cure it.

Mrs. Dane was in the thick of the moving armies; her very nod was official; her voice was that of one who speaks for an organization.

Her especial errand now was to find from Mrs. Soudé what the women of New Orleans were doing in biology, and whether they had formed themselves into a Municipal Reform Club.

"It is so seldom," she said, "that we meet an influential Southern woman. We are most anxious that your women should fall into line. My own especial interest lies in Archæology and Drainage. But it is essential that women should combine now for all good purposes. It is a crisis. The world has been misgoverned by men long enough. For the most part they are brutes or fools. If the human experiment is to be run through to the end successfully, our sagacity and purity must take command."

Therese listened with her usual kind, calm smile. "But why not make a proselyte nearer home?" she said, when Mrs. Dane stopped to catch her breath. "Does not Anne neglect her public duties?"

"Oh, wholly! Her farm, Brooke, the children, two or three friends, and her work people—there is her one-acre lot in the world! It is women like Anne who block our wheels!"

Therese laughed, and skilfully brought the children up for discussion. She was curious about Mildred's son. "An honest, lovable looking lad!" she said. "But he does not resemble either father or mother?"

"No. He is very like Mildred's mother. Now, there is a strange thing!" said cousin Julia. "Sarah Warrick was a dull, commonplace woman! but she has left her mark, deep, on all of her descendants. When I look at Boy, or either of Anne's children, I feel that Sarah is living still."

Mrs. Dane left The Oaks early that evening, to go to a suffrage meeting, and in a little while Mr. Plunkett put Anne and Mrs. Soudé into their sleigh and saw them drive away with jingling bells, making a flash of color down the snowy road.

The sun was setting, and the red was fading out of the cold sky. David buttoned his coat and paced up and down the porch. The sight of John Soudé had wakened old uneasy doubts in his mind.

"Thank God!" he said to himself, "I've no fear as to Milly! It was me she loved and not that dingy mulatto!"

But it was natural that he should think it all over and measure himself against the dingy mulatto.

"I had more to say last night than he had. My brain is as good as any man's there," he repeated anxiously, again and again. If he could only have said something decently? Boy would have been so pleased!

As he walked up and down he could see Harry in the brightly lighted room, bending over his books. He halted.

"If I could even go in and help him with his lessons! It was in me to be a scholar, but nobody knows it. Boy will never know it!"

He walked on, whistling. Usually David was content with his business and his cares for Harry and the old doctor. But sometimes he felt the strength that was in him to do wider work in the world; strength that could never be used. Every man or woman over fifty has felt that struggle in the soul, that choking pant of unspent power.

The lad inside hastily closed his Virgil and came out. He loved his father passionately, and he had Sarah Warrick's fine tact. He knew as soon as he heard the whistle that David was in trouble: so he took his arm and marched up and down with him, whistling too.

Plunkett laughed. "I've been worrying, wishing you knew me better, Harry."

"Why, I know *you*, Dad."

"No—not altogether. No. But—it don't end here, you know, hey? For instance, I don't reckon on having this mass of fat to carry round—out yonder. There's other chances."

Harry naturally cared nothing for "out yonder." He began to talk of Swift, who would play half-back to-morrow.

But Plunkett gave vague answers. A workman, going home, passed just then down the road. David's eyes suddenly kindled. He leaned over the railing looking after the man.

"Now you see, Boy," he said earnestly, "that fellow has tools in his kit that he didn't use to-day. He doesn't care. He knows that he'll have them and use them to-morrow."

"I don't quite follow you, Dad."

"No. You'll understand some day. It's all right," said David.

THE END.

www.ingramcontent.com/pod-product-compliance
Lightning Source LLC
Chambersburg PA
CBHW031337070726
47496CB00017B/1186